HeroNet
Files
Book 1

Wayland Smith
Dara Hannon
Harry Heckel

Published by Blue Oranda Publishing
Mechanicsville, VA
USA

Dedicated to everyone who ever played City of Heroes.

Table of Contents

Argent and the Cobalt Rose

By Wayland Smith

Chapter 1

LAURA MCGILVEY CROUCHED behind a large shipping crate and rechecked her equipment – what there was of it. Some people could afford fancy devices and toys, and some had to make do with what they could. For a low-powered hero, costumes tended to have two options: heavy and armored, or light and easy to move in. She'd gone the light route, backing it up with speed, agility, a lot of martial arts training, some intensive training in parkour and the newest hero-inspired discipline to be sweeping the gyms – combat gymnastics. Not having to worry about armor had left her a lot of options when designing her costume. After extensive research on heroes, she'd gone for form fitting and skimpy, for the dual advantages of helping hide her secret ID (with this much cleavage showing, she might even have been able to skip the mask. She made sure once more that was in place at the thought) and general distraction value. Most villains tended to be guys, after all.

She'd been working the seedy bars and dives for over a week, looking for a hint of something that would work for her debut. Finally, she'd found it. She'd heard two dumb muscle types boasting about their new job, security for a big drug buy– weapons, thugs, cash, drugs, and the almost-required deserted warehouse. This had all the makings of a great first case. She'd followed the shorter one around for a few days, until she was sure this was the place, and then checked her equipment one final time. Her cell phone, a new special disposable she'd bought for this night, had the numbers of several different TV news stations programmed in. Laura would be happy with Channel Four or Seven news covering the debut of the Cobalt Rose, as she'd christened herself. Preferably not Nine – the guy who did most of their crime stories was really not that good looking.

She snapped her head around suddenly. Had she heard something behind her? Holding her breath, she slowly played her gaze over the various crates, barrels, boxes, and who-knew-whats scattered about the large open space. Laura had read that people were more likely to pick up movement with their peripheral vision than by happening to catch something dead ahead, so she worked at keeping her gaze slightly unfocused, which was a lot harder than she thought it would be. She took her time, and finally satisfied herself it was most likely her nerves playing tricks on her. Check the costume one more time, everything's fine. No one close by. First few points of cover to move to, all look good. OK, then, it's time to...

"Hey! Shoot the damn mask already!"

Laura hadn't fully come out of her crouch, and now she hit the floor. Who had seen her? How? What was going on? The fusillade of automatic weapons fire that erupted was staggeringly loud, making her wish she'd added earplugs to her rather limited pool of resources. Realizing that none of the shots were coming anywhere near her or her trusty crate she'd been hiding behind, she kept herself almost flat and eased her head around the corner. The Colombian drug runners and the Maracili family soldiers were all firing at... Oh, no. Oh, come on! This was HER case, damn it! Her big debut, and now the damned silvery stalker was getting all her bad guys!

Moving through their ranks as though they were nothing, fists and feet lashing out to drop foe after foe, the masked hero Argent closed in on the vans that held the drugs and the cash. Of course, it was Argent; he was in the news all the time, the hero of Southside, all that shit. Damn it! No way was he getting away with this. Tensing up her muscles and eyeing her next bit of cover, Laura (no, Cobalt Rose, damn it!) sprinted to the pile of empty drums and slid in behind them. No one noticed, all of their attention being focused on Argent.

She stole another glance at him and saw something she'd never heard about in the news reports. As he flipped over one thug to land on another with both feet in a powerful kick that flattened the man, he held his hand out, fingers spread, towards several of the gunmen. There was a barely noticeable ripple in the air around his hand, and a slight reddish glow, and the bullets that were racing towards him ricocheted, striking some not quite seen barrier.

Huh, Argent has powers. That's not fair, she thought, then shook her head. Game time. Stay in the game, bitch about glory hounds with hidden powers later. Quick peek, everything's clear. GO GO GO! Cobalt ran to a pyramid-shaped stack of crates, grabbed the edge of one and vaulted up, landing on the next level effortlessly, and swung her way up to the top. This part was working just like she'd practiced, and she loved the feeling of pushing herself. She got into the rhythm easily and in no time reached the last level, and then found out that the high ground wasn't hers alone. A guy in a cheap suit crouched there with a large rifle and scope, drawing a bead on Argent as he fought thugs down below. Letting her training take over, she turned her momentum into a low arc, pivoting on her hip, her legs scything out and catching the sniper high on his spine. He gave out a surprised "Fuck!" as he pitched forward, bouncing down the other side of the stack with far less grace than Cobalt had shown climbing it. She winced inwardly as he landed on the crate two up from the ones on the floor, rifle clattering to the ground.

"That's gonna leave a mark," she muttered, moving already to the left edge and leaping down. If there was one sniper, odds were good there might be another, and she was far from bulletproof. The Cobalt Rose was most of the way down when another thug noticed the downed sniper and looked up.

"Oh, the hell with it." She gathered herself and leapt, arcing cleanly though the air to land feet first on his chest, knocking him back against a large metal drum. The impact knocked him cold, which was good. It was also thunderously loud, which wasn't. Even over the gunfight, several heads turned towards her. "Oh, shit," she thought as she dodged to one side, bullets pockmarking the floor where she'd just been. She saw a man turning at her, almost in slow motion, with a shotgun in his hands. Between them was a small folding table where they had been testing the product before Argent upstaged her.

Cobalt Rose slid along the floor, hearing the shotgun roar and feeling pellets close enough that she thought she might have lost a few strands of her long blonde hair. She got under the table, and kicked up hard, sending it flying into the shotgun-wielding man. When he fell back, she jumped up and landed on the table with both feet, driving it down onto him. The air rushed out of his lungs and he wheezed faintly. Cobalt fanned the air in front of her, coughing slightly. Knocking over the table had set off a cloud of something or other, and it stuck to her.

She kicked the shotgun out of reach of the man she'd just dropped and glanced through the now murky air towards Argent. He had almost finished taking out the rest of the gangsters already. How'd he do that so damn quick? She ran behind a large crate and then stopped.

A shadow moved on the ground next to the crate. Careful... wait for him... as the thug edged around the corner, he carried his pistol held out before him, like you see on cop shows. It was a good shooting stance, but bad for moving when you can't see in all directions. Cobalt Rose darted her right hand out to grab his wrist, and drove the stiffened fingers of her left hand high up under his arm. She hit the nerve cluster just right, and his fingers flew open in reflex as he cursed from the sudden pain. She lashed out with her left leg, kicking him once, twice, three times in the stomach in rapid succession. He doubled over in pain as she moved in, spinning away from him but still holding his wrist. She drew him close to her back, bent, and tossed him through the air to land hard on the concrete a few feet away with a loud thud. He curled up on his side and didn't do much more than twitch.

Cobalt Rose stole another glance at Argent. She had to give him credit. He moved with a certain kind of grace as he fought. The silver (or was it grey? It seemed to shift) body suit, with the matching gloves, boots, belt, and wristbands should have been boring, but somehow it worked for him. The mask covered his whole head, giving no hint of his features. He filled out the silver costume nicely though. She watched as he caught one man with a high kick to his chin, dropping him, as a second man swung a knife, only to be parried with a sharp metallic sound as it slammed into one of Argent's wristbands.

Cobalt Rose shook her head. No time to be staring at guys, even hot ones. Time to work. She looked around for a new target, and saw a man in a suit picking up a briefcase. She grinned fiercely and sprinted after him. He saw her, and scuttled for the door. Realizing he wouldn't make it, he stopped and swung the case at her.

Cobalt Rose brought both her arms up, catching the clumsy blow on her forearms, and the leather-like wrappings that covered them. The material caught the impact as it was supposed to. She flexed her muscles like she'd practiced... and the metallic "thorns" embedded in the arm guards failed to pop out. Son of a bitch! She cursed to herself as she drove her right elbow into the man's face to send him reeling. They'd worked last night, damn it! She followed up with a low punch to the gut and then a rising knee to his descending chin and let him fall to the floor. Dusting her hands off, she looked around, satisfied. Between her and that case-stealing upstaging Argent, everyone seemed to be down for the count.

The Cobalt Rose turned on one practical boot heel (she'd experimented with high heels, which did great things for her legs but were a bitch to fight in) and stalked towards her rival. Time to settle the matter of credit here and now. A high powered rifle bullet slammed into the floor right next to her foot, missing by the barest margin. Rose dove for cover, as Argent did the same.

"Well, it looks like the mighty Argent has a sidekick now," came a taunting voice from above.

"Sidekick?" both heroes echoed, Argent sounding puzzled, Rose furious.

There was muted sound of hurried footsteps above. Apparently, the sniper was trying to get away. Rose sprinted for one of the walkway ladders, wishing again she'd managed to lay hands on one of those grapple guns most heroes seemed to have. Was there a catalogue she was missing somewhere? There was a rush of air, and Argent sailed over her, easily landing on the catwalk. Did he have one, too? She hadn't seen what he'd done to get up there. Cobalt heard two heavy blows, something hitting the ground, and then Argent himself landed lightly in front of her. Even with his eyes hidden behind grey lenses, she was sure he was checking out the tight blue body suit and low cut top. She smirked to herself. At least that part of her equipment was working.

She let her eyes narrow behind her mask. "Let's get this straight, big guy; I am <u>not</u> your sidekick." She said, pointing her finger at him accusingly. Which is, of course, when the thorns suddenly decided to pop out of the wrappings in her arm. There was a moment of uneasy silence as they regarded each other, Cobalt Rose embarrassed, Argent amused.

"Nice... spikes?" Argent said, glancing at her forearm. His gaze moved from her arm to the stylized flower at the low point of her neckline and to her face. "No, thorns. I get it. Blue Rose?"

"Cobalt. Cobalt Rose." A warmth was suffusing her, filling her. She wasn't sure why, but it was starting to feel really good. "And I'm still not your sidekick." She paused, breathing in deeply. "But maybe we could talk about that." What? What was she saying? She was mad at him for stealing her gig. Wasn't she? That silver costume clung to him really well.

"Not really looking for a sidekick. I don't do those. I'm sure you could find someone else if you need a teacher, or mentor, or whatever the hell." Argent looked around the room, surveying their work. "Nice job, though. For a beginner, I mean."

She should've been furious, but somehow wasn't. "Why do you say I'm a beginner?"

He shrugged, ticking off points on his fingers. "Your gear isn't working right yet, and that aggravates you but doesn't surprise you. You snuck in and then started fighting. You sneak in for recon, not fights, because then you leave armed men behind you, between you and out. Not good. Just something in the way you move, you're new. Not bad, just new."

"And it's such a rush, isn't it? I mean, my God, it's just... wow."

Argent laughed. "Yeah, it's like that for some of us. Some supers are all noble and righteous about what they do, but yeah, some of us just like a good fight and get a charge out of it."

"Yeah, and it's a hell of a charge." She leaned in closer, looking up at him. He was a good bit taller than she was. She liked that in a guy. "That mask of yours come off, even a little?" Her pulse was speeding up, too. What the hell was going on? She was like a kid who'd been making out for the first time.

Argent's head tilted. "Are you ok? You look like you're not feeling right."

"I'm fine, but we could be a lot better." She practically purred the words, and a small piece of her wanted to shout out that this wasn't her, but that piece was fading.

"Hey, the rush hits you like that sometimes, but I don't think it'd be... Wait, what's this crap?" He ran a gloved finger along her collar bone, taking a smudge of the dust she'd fought through earlier, working it between his finger and thumb.

"You sure you don't want to touch lower?" Cobalt thrust her chest out at him.

Argent looked at her, suddenly more intense. "Oh, crap, this is Venus. No wonder you're acting that way."

"Don't like what you see?" Rose was almost taunting him now, even as she shouted at herself inside her own head, "What are you doing?"

"You look great." Argent moved closer. "The costume's sexy as hell. But here's how it is, kid," he said, even as his gloved hand caressed her cheek. "You're fucked up right now, and I'm not a total asshole. Talk to me after we get this shit outta your system." His hand moved to her neck, his fingers pressed in suddenly, and she collapsed. Argent caught her easily, and jumped upward. Again, the faint distortions appeared, this time around his feet, and he soared up to the skylight, and through the open section. Landing on the roof, he bounded again, using his com-link in his mask.

Chapter 2

"DOC, THIS IS ARGENT. I got a medical emergency coming in. We need a decon."

A British accented voice answered. "What did you do this time?"

"Wasn't me, new kid got coated in Venus during a drug deal."

"Oh, my. Well then, come along, and we'll do what we can."

Argent leapt easily from roof to roof, carrying the unconscious girl in his arms. He had to admit, she was kinda cute, and that was a hell of a costume. Maybe he'd see how she felt about him when she wasn't out of her mind on designer drugs. And maybe he needed filters in his mask. This really wasn't the time to be checking her out.

After a rapid dash over the rooftops, he landed on the roof of the lab. He walked over to the door and leaned into the speaker grille. "I'm here."

"Please state your password." The automated voice was inflectionless, emotionless.

"It's Argent, I have a medical emergency, the Doc should be expecting me," he said, a bit louder now.

"Please state your password," it repeated.

"Doc! You down there? Tell this damn Xbox with delusions of grandeur to let me in!"

"Please state your password," came the voice again.

"God damn it, I don't fucking remember my password!" he yelled at it, frustration combining with worry for the girl who was starting to get a bit heavy.

"Password accepted. Voiceprint matched. Welcome, Argent." The door hissed open.

"Oh, that's fucking hilarious," he muttered as he moved inside, walking rapidly toward the medical bay.

A short, red headed woman stood beside one of the high tech looking beds, her white lab coat over jeans and a sweater. "Put her here and let's see what we shall see," she directed.

Doc Lydia (Argent never had learned her last name) was one of those rare individuals with an array of useful skills who were happy to aid heroes and stay out of the public eye. Argent knew she had made extensive studies of superhuman physiology and all the complications that could create. He wasn't entirely clear on how she paid for her building here, with home, lab, and tons of gadgets, but she was always willing to help, and some others he knew spoke well of her.

The woman took a blood sample with a device of her own creation and design, and fed it into the diagnostic imager above the bed. She frowned at the results. "Yes, it's Venus, with a few nasty little twists as well. Where did you get this?"

"Hey, it wasn't me. The Rose here took a dust bath in the stuff when she kicked over a table. Some nice moves, though." He saw the doctor's look and went back to the story. "It was a drug deal, the Southside Kings were buying. I think the sellers were out of town-Chinese, maybe."

"Well, we need to get her decontaminated and let the diagnosis analyzer run. Can you help me with her?" The doctor was surprised, and amused, to see Argent shift uncomfortably.

"Don't you have some kind of 'bot for that or something?" his voice had lost his usual street-tough sound, and almost taken on a note of pleading.

"Is there a problem I should be aware of?" The doctor asked him, awaiting an explanation.

"No, just... she was dosed pretty good, and she was hitting on me kinda hard."

"And you did what, precisely?" The amusement was gone now, and Argent held up his hands defensively.

"Hey, no, nothing like that. I nerve pinched her and brought her to you. I just... it'd be weird helping you get her costume off after that. And I doubt she'd love the idea when she snaps out of it. Can't you just...?" he waved his hand vaguely at the machinery.

Doc Lydia stifled a laugh. "Yes, we'll be fine. Should I contact you when I know more?"

"Umm... Yeah. That'd be good. She's new, this a kinda tough first shot, ya know? Poor kid." He looked down at her again and then left.

Lydia shook her head. This was a first for Argent, usually one of the more abrasive characters she dealt with. She brought out a remote control device, and specially designed mechanical arms gently picked the young woman up and deposited her in a variation of a chemical shower. Lydia went on with her work, devising a counteragent to the drugs and placing the unconscious hero back on the sick bed, all the while chuckling to herself. If she didn't know better, she'd think Argent smitten.

Chapter 3

LAURA WOKE UP SLOWLY. Awareness came in fits and starts. She was lying down in a bed. Her skin tingled all over. She was sore, like after a major workout. And, most disturbingly, while she was wearing her mask, she didn't seem to be wearing anything else. "Musta been one hell of a party," she muttered, looking around. Nothing looked familiar. At least the sheet was covering her well enough. Just as she was trying to figure out what to do next, the door to the small room opened, and a woman in a long, white lab coat came in.

"Oh, good, you're awake. How are you feeling?" The woman had an English accent, which left Laura even more lost.

"Confused. Where am I, and how'd I get here?" She paused for a moment. "And where the hell are my clothes?"

"You're in my medical laboratory, still in Southside, never fear. Argent brought you here after you managed to get yourself coated in Venus, and your costume is being decontaminated."

Laura reached a hand up to her face, touching her mask. "Shouldn't this have gotten covered, too? Wait, Venus? And Argent? Oh... crap." Bits of memory surfaced, and she fought the urge to pull the sheet up over her head.

"Well, yes, the mask had to be treated, too. Sorry, dear, I've seen you without it. But don't worry," the woman patted Laura's hand gently twice. "You're not famous, and I have no idea who you are."

"So... who are you, and can I go?" Laura felt restless and embarrassed, and really wanted to be somewhere else.

"I'm certainly not holding you prisoner, but you might want to wait until your costume has been cleaned. As for who I am, most people call me Doctor Lydia. I help people like you when you have certain problems, like tonight."

Laura paused for a moment, thinking about this, then suddenly bolted upright, nearly losing the sheet covering her. "Wait, you mean HeroWeb is real? You guys are really out there? I thought that was an urban myth or something."

"Oh, yes, we're quite real. We just prefer to keep things a bit quiet. It wouldn't do to have some group of villains come bursting in while we were treating an injured hero, now would it? Let me go see if your costume is ready, since we seem to have flushed the rest of the drug out of your system."

Laura shook her head in disbelief. She'd heard whispers of HeroWeb, a group of people who provided special support services to heroes that weren't independently wealthy or members of large, well-supplied teams. Running across any of those people made her feel a lot more like she'd taken a bigger step towards becoming a real hero, and she smiled in spite of herself.

Lydia came back in a moment later, holding the Cobalt Rose costume on a hanger, with her accessories in a small bag. "Here we are, cleaned and processed. Are the 'thorns' in your arm bands working right? They seemed a bit dodgy when I looked at them."

Laura remembered her last exchange with Argent (about the last thing she did remember, now that she thought about it), and flushed a bit again. "No, they aren't. Can you fix them?" She reached for her costume, and Lydia turned her back to allow some privacy.

"I can certainly look at them sometime, but I didn't want to presume to mess about with your equipment without asking you." Laura hurriedly pulled on her costume and equipment, becoming Cobalt Rose once again.

She looked around, adjusting her equipment belt. "So... where is Argent, anyway?"

Lydia gave an amused chuckle. "He ran off after delivering you to me. I think you made him a bit uncomfortable."

A hazy memory of their confrontation at the end of the fight surfaced, and Cobalt Rose's face took on a color that was decidedly in keeping with the plant part of her codename. "Oh my God... yeah... I, uh... I should talk to him, or something. Explain that. Do you have a way to get hold of him?"

"I can arrange a meeting if you like. I'm sure you understand that I won't give you his contact information, just as I wouldn't give him yours."

"That's fair, I guess. Can you do that?" Cobalt Rose was almost hoping for a no. She wasn't quite sure what she'd say to him.

"Of course I can. Just you give me a few moments." Lydia left the room, and returned a short time later, saying "The roof of City Hall at midnight tomorrow. Is that all right?"

Rose blew out a breath. So much for that hope. "Yeah, I can do that. Can I go now?" she said almost petulantly.

"Of course you can. Let me know if you start having any sort of new symptoms, and maybe sometime I can help you get the bugs out of your thorns." Lydia handed her a simple business card, with just an e-mail on it. One very confusing trip through a series of underground tunnels and passages later, the Cobalt Rose found herself exiting an unremarkable looking door in a small alley. She began making her way home, rehearsing things to say to Argent at their next meeting.

"Okay, first off, that was my case the other night!" she found herself saying that next evening, her finger pointing at Argent. "That wasn't the plan," she thought to herself, but somehow he made her feel very defensive about that night, even though he hadn't really said anything in the few moments since she'd arrived.

"Oh?" his voice was neutral, but she was fairly certain she heard some irritation in it.

She took a deep breath and tried to get control of herself. "I mean, I followed up on everything to get there, dealt with that creepy Louie Verch to find out where it was all happening, and you're famous already, you've been in the papers, on TV, on the Internet, all that, and I'm just starting here, I mean... c'mon, give me a break?" The last few words sounded a lot more like pleading than she had wanted.

He stood with his arms folded, looking at her, impossible for her to read behind his full face mask. "Is that what this is about? The reporters?" At the look on her face, he shrugged and waved his hand in dismissal. "Like I give a crap what they say. Tell 'em anything you want. Is that seriously why you're doing this?" Rose heard the note of contempt in his voice and winced a bit.

"No, I just... I don't know... how do you get anyone to take you seriously if you don't deal with reporters?" Frustration colored her words.

Argent stared at her for what seemed forever. She could practically hear the smirk in his voice when he finally said, "Well depending on what you're going for, maybe not look like you're about to fall out of your costume?" She felt his gaze on her chest and flushed. "Not that it's not a good look for you and all."

"It's a distraction! It keeps them from looking at my face, and makes them act even stupider," she went on defensively.

"Hmmhmm. So why are you getting into this? You don't seem pissed off enough to be one of the revenge types, and you're not a government agent. What's your story?" He leaned on a nearby exhaust vent, folding his arms again.

Several responses raced through her mind, and she almost spit out several of the more biting ones, then sighed and sat on the edge of the roof. "I like helping people. I like pushing myself. And, hell, I guess I like the rush. It's stupid, I guess. I broke up a mugging once, and the look on the girl's face, the feeling after I dropped the guy," her voice trailed off, and she shrugged, then raised her arms, stretching, encompassing the city and half whispered, "There's nothing else like it."

She was surprised to hear a faint laugh from Argent. "That's for damn sure. Look, kid–" he started.

"Cobalt Rose! My name is Cobalt Rose!"

"Right. Rose. Look, seriously, I don't care what you tell the reporters or any of them. Idiots like that ain't why I do this. Makes you feel better, go for it. But if you really want this, really want to help people, then train harder, figure out what's important to you, and call Doc Lydia and get help with your gear. You do that, you'll be ok. Meanwhile," he adjusted the ear piece under his mask, "sounds like the Fangs and the Blades are about to go at it over by Centennial Park. Wanna go have some fun?"

The next day the news was full of reports of a major gang fight, the police being almost overwhelmed while trying to respond, and the sudden intervention of the city's newest crime fighting duo, Argent and a new hero, the Cobalt Rose, who was also credited with interrupting a major drug buy two nights before.

Chapter 4

IN A FLUID MOVE, the Cobalt Rose leapt over Argent, who was crouched low, sweeping the legs of a thug in gang colors. She sailed over him and landed a perfect side kick into the chest of the man who'd been stalking up on Argent with a large knife. He staggered backwards as she landed easily, springing forwards to drive a fist into another gang-banger. They'd been working together off and on for a few months now, and she had to admit they made a good team. While his powers did give him an unfair edge in her view, she'd also noticed he didn't always use them. His fighting skills were amazing without the powers, and she'd learned a bit from him. Argent punched another man hard in the face, sending him backwards in a spray of blood as his nose broke. Looking around, Argent said "Good job, kid." He'd continued to call her that off and on, probably because he knew it bugged her. She shook her head, knowing better by now than to rise to the bait. "Now, let's see what all this was about."

He moved over to a large shipping crate that the gang had been delivering. "Wait, you don't know?" Rose asked, disbelief in her voice.

"No clue. These guys were up to no good, and most of them have rap sheets long as your arm. Hell, I bet some of 'em have outstanding warrants right now. But what this is? Only one way to find out." Rose watched him move up to the box and saw the now familiar ripple around his hands. She turned to survey the downed thugs quickly, making sure no one was trying to take advantage of the heroes' attention being elsewhere to either sneak off or attack.

"What are you doing, anyway?" She asked. She still wasn't sure how his powers worked, or exactly what they were, for that matter.

"I got two ways I can use my power. I can do an attraction thing, which is how I stick to walls and shit sometimes. I can also use 'em to repel things, like bullets, or make it seem like I'm hitting with superstrength. The combo is how I sometimes send attacks back where they came from." She nodded. She'd seen it a few times and it was damn impressive, but she wasn't telling him that. "But when I send out attraction and repelling at the same time, into the same thing..." his voice trailed off as he concentrated a bit. The lid glowed once, twice, a third time, each pulse of light showing more and more cracks, thicker and more pronounced. Finally, the top flew apart, sending a spray of wood arcing out.

"Hey! Warn a girl!" She yelled, although none of the pieces came anywhere near her.

"Yeah, sorry 'bout that," he said, not sounding it in the slightest. He produced a strong mini-light from his belt and looked inside, then made a low whistling noise.

"What?" Rose came closer, peering over his shoulder. Inside was lots of foam padding, and in the foam rested some kind of small vials with strange looking liquids. Each was marked with a large design that looked like some kind of stylized eye, with an elaborate "TB" in the center. "What's a 'TB'? Tuberculosis?" She asked, leaning in for a better look, her hand resting on his shoulder.

"Not what, who. I've seen that before, this shit belongs to El Tigre Blanco." The Cobalt Rose was trying to remember everything she'd ever heard about El Tigre, and felt a sort of flutter of excitement. This could be her first supervillain! Argent was pursuing quite a different set of ideas, wondering why her hand on his shoulder had surprised him so much, and a bit startled about how natural and how good it felt. Argent had never really been a relationship kind of guy; he'd had various brief flings that ended usually as dramatically as they began. But he'd caught himself thinking about her at odd times lately. He shook his head. Back to business. "All right, kid, what do you know about him?" Argent turned on his com-gear and began reporting to the police where they could come pick up the gang members they'd just fought, but Rose had learned early that while he might not seem to be paying attention, he'd catch every word she said and call her on whatever she got wrong.

She began ticking points off on her fingers. "No one knows much about him, he runs a high end crew dealing in designer drugs, some folks are saying he's getting into things like genetic modifications, he's really hard to find, he allegedly killed two rivals already that didn't accept him as their new boss when he took their territory, and he's supposed to be some kinda ladies man, or thinks he is."

Argent nodded in approval. "Good. Ok, now the big question. Do you think you're ready to step up to the next level here? Take on a villain with a name, not just some thugs?"

Rose stopped for a moment and thought. She had a hunch this was going to be an important answer, and she wanted to be as honest and accurate as she could. Then she nodded. "Yeah. I can do this. I don't think I'm up for someone big like one of the high powered guys or teams, but I can do this."

"OK. We'll give you a shot. Now, let's get outta here before we're helping the cops do paperwork all night." Sirens were getting closer, so there wasn't much chance any of these guys were going to get away. Rose took out her new line thrower (there wasn't so much a catalogue like she had wondered about, but the HeroWeb guys had some cool toys after you proved yourself to their satisfaction) and used it to get up to the nearest rooftop, while Argent simply leapt upwards, using his powers.

On the roof, they leaned over the edge, looking down to make sure no one scurried off as the police arrived. "Ok, here's all I'm going to ask you. Don't do this alone, and tell me if you think you're getting in over your head. Deal?"

"Deal," she even stuck her hand out, and Argent shook it. Even under his mask, she could tell when they made sudden eye contact, feeling the weight of his gaze. They stood like that until a roving searchlight from the police below startled them out of it. They both hurriedly let go and almost jumped backwards from each other.

"Right, ok, I'm gonna go do some research," Rose said.

At almost the same instant, Argent said, "I got something to go take care of, catch you later."

Cobalt Rose returned to her apartment, using various techniques Argent had taught her to make sure she wasn't being followed. Inside, she changed out of her costume and pulled on some comfortable ratty sweat pants and a faded t-shirt. Sitting at her computer, she used the passwords she'd been given to access secure data-sites. The online side of HeroWeb was called HeroNet, and it was an amazing collection of information about various villains and criminals. She began pulling together everything she could find on El Tigre Blanco, his associates, hangouts, and anything she thought might be even marginally useful. She caught herself daydreaming about Argent a few times and shook her head, annoyed. She made some coffee to try and keep herself focused as she did what she had come to think of as homework for Heroing 101. Laura softly hummed to herself as she sipped her coffee and clicked away on the keys.

Argent arrived at the small building he had eventually managed to buy. The bottom floor was a theme bar, called the Dark Knight, which drew all the renaissance nuts, although an occasional confused comic fan showed up. He'd heard it described once as "Medieval Times for grown ups" and it worked, more or less. Sure, the belly dancers and the like that performed there on occasion were out of place in something supposedly set in medieval Europe, but no one complained. The second floor was offices for the bar, storage, and some clutter he really needed to clean out sometime.

The top floor was a very simple apartment, and a large dojo. Argent had carefully designed this, and built much of it himself. He rarely took on students, but he kept it well maintained. Mats, punching bags, various practice weaponry, and a lot of open space made up the bulk of it. There were two changing rooms, each with a very nice shower, which is where he headed now. He pulled off the costume and stored it in the hidden vault all his gear went into. He caught sight of his reflection and paused a moment. He'd never really cared much how he looked, but women seemed to like him alright. "The rough side of handsome," one date had described him. When his powers had developed, they had made one more bit of disguise necessary to pass as normal. He looked at his face in the mirror, and his golden eyes almost shone in the dim light. His short dark hair was a mess, but it usually was, especially after any time at all under the mask. He showered off, put in his contact lenses, and went downstairs to check on the bar for the night. Walking through the dojo, he wondered why he'd never brought the Rose here. He was certainly teaching her, why not more formalized lessons? He felt a bit on edge about the idea of bringing her to his home, and pushed the thought aside again. Downstairs, the Dark Knight was doing its usual brisk trade, and Juliette, the head bartender when he wasn't around, nodded as he came in, her hands not stopping from making drinks. "Hey, JT. Good night tonight, we're getting low on vodka, and that new tequila is doing great." Jonathan Thomas Leir, JT to some and Argent to others, began taking notes on what he'd need to restock before pitching in himself behind the bar and trying to not think about a young woman with long blonde hair and a very revealing costume.

Chapter 5

A FEW DAYS LATER, Rose went over her notes once more, and then went into the small conference room. The room was simply furnished, with a large table and a few chairs around it. A small computer sat at the head of the table. Midway down the side furthest from the door, Argent lounged in a chair, tilted far back with his silver boots on the table, legs crossed at the ankle, hands behind his head. "Lydia must like you, letting you borrow her conference room and all," he observed. "What, I don't get a drink, too?"

Rose shrugged and sipped her coffee. "I'd offer you some, but you have that full mask and all," she taunted back. The verbal banter seemed to be on its way to becoming a hallmark of their partnership, or whatever this was. Rose allowed herself a moment of amusement at scoring a point on her more experienced partner and pushed a button on a small remote.

A projector that was built seamlessly into the tabletop glowed to life, projecting a floating holographic image above it. The image resolved into a picture rendered into 3D by Lydia's computers- a shot of a man who was believed to be El Tigre. A very smartly dressed but tough-looking young Latino man glared out from the hologram. Argent commented "Hey, you didn't say there'd be a movie. Where's the popcorn?"

Cobalt Rose allowed herself a small grin but kept going. "I've checked a few sources, and Lydia helped me out with some computer searches, and I think I know where El Tigre is. Lydia managed to run down some questionable supplies that would be real useful for the genetic stuff he's supposedly doing." She hoped she wasn't blushing as she recalled trying to find an informant in a bar she hadn't checked out thoroughly enough and found she was mistaken for a dancer there. Embarrassing, but a nice boost for the ego in some ways. "According to everything we could run down, this looked like the best bet."

The image now became a blocky building with a garish sign announcing it was the "Noche Encanto" club. The building turned transparent, and hallways and rooms became visible. "This is our best info on what the inside is like from blueprints we got from the city. He might have made changes that won't show here, but it's what we have." The view zoomed in a bit and sank. "Looks to me like there's a lot more room down in the basement than they need, and the power that part of the building draws is really high, so I'm betting that's where his lab, or workroom, or whatever you want to call it is." The image changed again, showing several nighttime shots of the building, with large crowds moving in and out and several men in suits and shades. "Also seems to have more security than a nightclub needs to me. If this doesn't pan out, I think there's something a bit fishy about another place called the Dark Knight, but none of the rest of the stuff lines up for that place."

Argent was grateful that the mask covering his face prevented her from seeing how surprised he looked. "You did your homework. How sure are you?"

Rose wanted to look certain, but she gave a regretful shrug and decided honesty was more important. "Probably about seventy five percent. It looks good to me, but there could be something else going on down there."

Argent ran a gloved hand over his masked chin. "But if there is, it's probably something else we oughta look at." He stood up. "Let me make a few calls to check something, and I'll get back with you." He started to leave, then stopped and looked at her. "Good job, kid."

Rose felt a flash of pleasure at the praise and said, "We'll see if it holds up."

The following evening, the Cobalt Rose and Argent perched on the roof of an office building, long since closed for the day. Across the way lay the Noche Encanto, which Argent was examining with a small pair of binoculars he'd pulled from a section on his belt. "I need to get one of those," Rose thought as he surveyed the club.

"That's just way too much security for a club, unless they got a tip about a freakin' gang war about to jump off in there tonight." Argent passed the glasses to Rose, who looked at the building for a few moments and then agreed.

"So, what, we go in the back and look for a loading dock or a storeroom or something?" She asked, handing the binoculars back.

"Nope, they usually put more guys on those when they're up to something. I figure, it's a club, they have to let people in, right?" She nodded, looking a tiny bit confused. "So, we just walk in."

"Like this?" She waved a hand in front of her, indicating her costume.

"Well, you might get away with that, but I wouldn't. No, follow me, kid." He leapt over the side of the building, down into an alley. Cobalt Rose followed a bit more slowly but more gracefully as she used her parkour skills to swing, jump, and slide down the fire escape that ran down the side of their former vantage point. She found Argent unlocking the back of a nondescript van. Opening the door, he tossed a duffle bag at her. "Let me get mine out of here, then you can get in and change." Argent picked up another bag and then leapt back up, alighting halfway up the building on one of the metal landings of the escape.

Raising an eyebrow, Rose climbed inside the van, pulling the doors closed behind her, and opened the bag. "Oh, you have to be kidding..." she muttered as she saw the contents. A few moments later, Argent stood beside the van again, knocking on the door.

"C'mon already, we got places to go..." his voice trailed off into something that might have been "Wow," as he looked at her when she came out. Black leather boots rose to just under her knees. The silver dress shimmered, catching even the faint lights of the alley in its metallic fabric, the skirt barely long enough to keep her from being arrested, and the top cut lower and wider than her Cobalt Rose costume, if that were possible. A black belt with small red studs sat at her waist, riding low on her hips. From a coppery necklace, a small blue stone hung between her breasts.

She glared at Argent, snarling, "What?" in a challenging tone.

He held up his hands defensively. "Nothing, you just... you look great." She was pleased at the look on his face, and then suddenly realized she *could* see his face. Turned out Argent had light brown hair, a bit longer than she would have thought (she'd half expected a buzz cut, this was almost curly), brown eyes, and a rather handsome face. She already knew he was in great shape from working with him, and the light, almost white, shirt fit him very closely, the cuffs buttoned neatly and the front open to part way down his sternum (no gold chains, thank God). The tight black pants hugged his legs, but clearly let him move easily, and the cuffs brushed some black shoes.

"Not bad yourself," Rose said, smiling at him. She stifled a laugh when she saw his embarrassed expression. "Not cocky all the time, huh?" she thought to herself. Instead of saying anything, she put her hand on his arm and they walked down the alley towards the club. "You have a way to get us in?" she asked in a low voice.

"Yeah, pulled a few favors," he answered. They moved past the small line awaiting entrance, and Argent took a business card from his back pocket and gave it to the doorman. The large man's face took a slightly more welcoming look (or at least a less menacing one) and he unhooked the red velvet rope, motioning them inside. The two moved in through the door, ignoring the various protests behind them. They were in a short hallway that was dimly lit.

She leaned in close to him, looking like she was nibbling his ear (ever mindful of the possibility of security cameras) and breathed out the words, "So what do I call you in here?"

"JT," he whispered back. "Rose?" he asked.

"That'll work for now." They pushed the doors at the far end of the corridor, and the music that had been slightly muted broke over them like a violent downpour, lights everywhere. The dance floor was packed, people stood three deep at the bar, and the wait staff were hard pressed to keep up with orders.

JT frowned, wondering to himself if he needed to make some changes back at his own bar. Business was jumping here, that was for damn sure.

"Guessing we should blend in before we do anything sneaky, so come dance with me," Rose tugged JT's arm as she pulled him towards the floor. She managed to not laugh out loud at what, on the face of a lesser man than the "Hero of Southside," might have been described as a flash of fear.

Chapter 6

ARGENT, NO, JT RIGHT NOW, she corrected herself, wasn't a bad dancer. Although it amused her that someone who fought as well as he did, and flowed so easily in combat, kept stiffening up on the dance floor. "If he'd just relax..." she thought to herself for the fifth time in as many minutes. Laura draped her arms over his shoulders and pulled him in close, speaking into his ear above the music, but still at a level that would be hard for anyone else to hear, "Any ideas on where we need to go?"

JT almost seemed relieved to have something else to focus on. "Back of the room, seems to be a door with a guard on it all the time. It's not the office, it's not storage, I figured out where those are already. If it's worth guarding, it's probably worth checking out." Laura nodded, turning as part of her dance and eyeing the door JT had been talking about.

After looking at the rather large guard for a moment, she moved in very close to JT and whispered, "Any ideas?"

JT leaned in close, and Laura was distracted for a moment by his warm breath on her neck as he moved his lips to her ear. "How are you at 'bimbo'?"

***

Jacque Martine was bored. He'd come to America and managed to get a good job through some contacts, but it was nothing like he'd seen back in Buenos Aires. Here, mostly, he stood around in a suit and told drunk people to go away. On the one hand, the pay was good, but on the other, nothing ever happened. He'd grown accustomed to using violence, and was good at it, but rarely had the chance now. He kept thinking he would try for another job, but the boss was not known for simply smiling and wishing someone "Buena suerte" when they announced they were leaving. In fact, their luck tended to be very bad indeed, often fatally so. Still, a man of action, as he fancied himself, couldn't stand around doing nothing every night, especially in one of these damn suits. But maybe things were looking up, he thought as a stunning blonde stumbled towards him. She smiled drunkenly and said "Hey, I gotta go... lemme use the bathroom?"

He answered her with his accented English. "There is no bathroom back here. Try over there." He pointed at the restroom sign on the far wall.

"Ewww... those are always so gross. Can't I just use the one back there?" She pointed at the door again.

Irritation was overcoming attraction for Jacque. "I told you, there is no..." he was suddenly interrupted by a new voice.

"Andrea! What are you doing? I told you to wait at the table!" Jacque turned to look at the new arrival, a good sized man who seemed to be weaving a bit to stay upright. "Do I have to tell you again?" The man's voice had taken on an unpleasant edge, and Jacque moved to square off with him, relishing the chance of some recreational mayhem.

"You need to calm down, man." Jacque said, knowing that telling a drunk such things would usually incite them. "If you have a problem, I can," Jacque broke off his comment with a muffled grunt as something slammed into the side of his neck. Staggering, he saw the woman, no longer seeming quite the worse for wear, smiling sweetly at him.

"That's one," She said, raising her index finger. Jacque tried to clear his head; the blow had jangled him badly. Suddenly there was a hand on his shoulder and a fist caught him dead on the point of his chin, nearly lifting him off his feet and forcing the blonde to dart forward to catch him, muttering, "That's... ooof... two." Before his sagging weight made her fall, the man was back with a chair, into which they dumped the no longer cognizant Jacque.

"'I told you to wait at the table'?" Laura said, looking at JT.

He shrugged as he placed a pair of dark sunglasses on Jacque's nose, hiding the fact that he was out cold. "What, you want script approval next time? It worked, didn't it?" JT looked at the man again, then back at Laura. "What'd you hit him with, anyway?"

Laura looked around a final time to make certain they hadn't attracted attention, but the club's dark atmosphere, punctuated by random blasts of light, thunderously loud music, and the great trade the bar was doing had all helped cover their actions. "I went for that nerve cluster on the side of the neck," she said, rubbing the side of her hand.

JT shuddered slightly, involuntarily. He'd been hit there before, as well as using the technique himself, and knew how painful, and effective, it was. "You probably would've had him without me, then. Good job, kid. Keep an eye out, would ya?" He rolled back his shirt sleeve and Laura saw one of the metal wristlets he wore as Argent. He tapped a catch she couldn't see, and it opened, showing a very complicated looking array of electronic equipment.

"What's that?" She asked, then caught his look and his circling finger motion and turned to make certain no one was creeping up on them.

"Doc calls it the 'Exterminator.'" He pushed a button and a small antenna extended from the side of the metal band. "It was for picking up listening bugs at first, but she kept tinkering with it and now it does alarm systems, too." He looked at the flashing lights and hit another button. "Which there is one of... and now it's disarmed." JT pulled a few slender tools from a section of his belt, and in a few moments opened the door and gestured grandly to Laura. "After you."

She moved through the door quickly, looking around. Laura wasn't sure what she had expected, but she was surprised to see a short, dark, near featureless hallway that led to an elevator. She relayed this to JT, and saw him nod once before moving away from the door they'd just opened towards a smaller, unmarked door further down the other wall. After a few moments, he opened this one, as well, disappeared through it into the alley beyond, and came back quickly with two duffle bags. Seeing Laura's look, he said, "I figured we might end up doing something tonight, so before we met up, I stashed a few things." He tossed one bag to her. "Merry Christmas."

Laura unzipped the bag and found the costume and equipment of her Cobalt Rose identity, but newer looking. She got more excited when she found a belt with small compartments. "You got me some toys?"

JT smiled in spite of himself; she sounded like a kid on Christmas morning. "Doc Lydia put together some stuff she thought you might need. There's not a lot of great places to change in here..."

Laura shrugged. "This is fine; just get it over with before someone comes along." She took her bag back, walked a few steps away from Argent down the hallway, and pulled the dress up and off. He caught himself looking at her bare back before he shook himself and hurriedly changed, trying not to be distracted by the sounds of cloth sliding over skin. Her simpler outfit vs. his much longer experience meant they finished at about the same time.

Argent re-cached the duffels outside the fire exit and they moved to the end of the small hallway, studying the elevator. Rose searched for a hidden button to open it when a thought struck her, and she turned to Argent. "Hey, if you could get that side door open for the costumes, why did we need to come in the front at all? Couldn't you have just gotten us in that way?"

Argent shrugged slightly, fiddling with his high tech wristband. "No. It works better from inside for some reason. I think Doc is just screwing with me sometimes or something, but it does a better job on alarm systems from inside. No idea why… don't ask me. I tried to get her to fix that, but she said something about me asking for a sonic screwdriver next, whatever the hell that is, and then wouldn't talk about it anymore." He hit a few more buttons and finally got the elevator doors to open. They entered, and looked at where a panel would normally be beside the door. Here, there was just one button. He pressed it and the elevator moved downward so smoothly and quietly they almost weren't sure they were moving at first. When the car stopped, Argent looked at her and said, "Basement: supervillains, mad schemes, hidden labs and house wares."

They crept out of the doors, into yet another short, bland, hallway, with all the surfaces colored white. They exchanged mutual puzzled shrugs and moved toward the door at the far end. Rose held up a hand to her silvery partner and produced a pair of lock picks from her new belt. "Right where I designed them. Doc's been hacking my files or something," she thought as she went to work, and seconds later felt the click of the heavy lock disengaging. Stowing the picks, she smiled at Argent. He gave her a quick thumbs up and then cracked the door slightly ajar. He saw a man in a grey suit facing away from them. To Argent's experienced eye, his body language read both "guard" and "bored." Argent slipped the door slightly further open and reached through. With a sudden darting move of his hand, he grabbed the surprised man by the tie and pulled. Stumbling, the man ran headfirst into the door, stunning himself. Argent quickly yanked him through and swung him against the wall as he closed the door. Rose used a nerve strike Argent had taught her a few weeks ago to the man's neck, and the guard collapsed. They moved past where he'd been standing, finding another short hall.

"God damn maze down here," Argent muttered, then motioned Rose back. She saw the slight ripple effect she'd gotten used to watching for when he kicked his powers on, and he climbed up the wall, peering around the corner at considerably above head height. He hung there, staring at something, then dropped down lightly next to her and said "Another damn door. This is getting old fast. Didn't see any alarm systems." They rounded the corner, and Rose got a look at two large, ornately carved wooden doors. The designs seemed Asian to her, which didn't seem right in a Latino club, but Argent, with some of the impatience she'd noticed in him at times, simply moved forward and opened one.

Half a pace behind him, Rose looked past his shoulder into the cavernous space in front of them, and had time to think "Oh, shit," before the night got very interesting. The door had revealed a room full of men in black clothing and hoods. Various weapons hung in sheaths, from belts, or were in hand already. Behind them, men in fatigues raised assault rifles.

Chapter 7

ROSE LEANED AGAINST THE WALL. Her costume, revealing by design, was now much more so, with various tears and slashes in it. As her adrenaline faded, she was increasingly aware of more and more bruises, cuts, and aches. Sweat and a few other substances she resolutely refused to think about plastered her blonde hair to her head. Her breath still came in gasps and pants. She looked over at Argent, whose costume looked a bit better than hers, but very much the worse for wear. "Damn power-using cheater," she thought, but even that lacked heat. She was too tired to be pissed off. "Those were ninjas? Like, real ninjas?" she asked out loud.

"Yeah. Bright Fang Clan. Seen them before, but not that many at once." He sounded out of breath too, she was pleased to hear.

"Did some of them turn into werewolves?" She was half hoping to get a different answer than the one she knew was coming.

"Yeah, that was... new." Argent looked back out at the room they had burst in on what seemed like a few days ago. The floor was strewn with beaten ninjas, a few werewolves in the process of shifting back to human since they were unconscious, and some men in suits, as well as others in more normal combat gear. It was an impressive collection of unconscious opponents.

"So who were the guys in suits with the assault rifles?" Rose was starting to get her breath back, and, despite her many aches and pains, was trying to figure out what had happened here.

"Russian Mafiya. Bad news." He paused, looking at the nearest formerly rifle-welding thug. "Not sure why they're here, though. Japanese and Russians don't usually work together."

"So we've got ninja, werewolves, organized crime, but no Tigre Blanco?" Rose looked around again.

"Yeah, we got set up pretty good. Damn Tigre is smarter than I thought." Argent shook his head. "So, we go back to working the streets and contacts and anything else we can think of to get a line on him." He stood up and winced a bit. "Maybe not today." The elevator dinged, and then began disgorging the first of many policemen with lots of questions to be answered. Both heroes ended up thinking that fighting for their lives against vastly overwhelming odds and not being sure they'd see the morning was the easier part of their night.

Several hours later, after a long, hot shower, pain killers, sleep, and more painkillers, Laura was using her recently-granted higher level of access to HeroNet to search for any more of anything about Tigre Blanco. Her eyes were starting to cross as she read report after report, occasionally with a few fuzzy pictures that didn't really help identify him. She heard a faint buzzing, which took her a few minutes to figure out was her communicator. Laura pawed through the heap of equipment she'd dropped on the way to her shower when she'd gotten home, and finally found it, somehow or other in her left boot. She pulled it open and slipped on the ear piece. "Cobalt Rose," she said.

"Find anything?" Argent's voice filled her ear, and she hastily turned the volume down (when had she ever needed it THAT loud?).

"What makes you think I'm looking?" she answered, putting her feet up on the desk and crossing her legs at the ankles. She moved her keyboard to her lap, grateful for a reason to not stare at the screen any more.

"Because you're new, and you're driven, and you were pissed off that he got over on us and almost got us killed." Argent sounded a little more relaxed, and she wondered if "JT" were his actual initials and what he did when he wasn't all dressed up in silver spandex.

"Ok, you got me, I'm trying to find something new on HeroNet, but nothing looks too promising. What about you?" She leaned back and then winced a bit as she found yet another new bruise.

"Kid, I'm sore all over. I'm giving myself a break. I feel like I got beat by someone with a baseball bat."

"You did. Two or three of 'em had bats, and one got you at least once. I would've done something, but I was trying not to get sliced and diced by a were-ninja, or whatever you call those things."

"Were-ninja works." His thoughts drifted back to the end of the fight, and just how much of her costume had been cut away. "Mostly, I just thought I'd make sure you were ok."

"Sore and stiff and in need of a hot tub, but ok." She shifted again. "Do you get used to this kind of thing?"

"Well, the idea is to not get hit that much. Consider this motivation to get better." She heard something she couldn't quite make out in the background, until his next comment. "When that fails, though, the hot tub is a good investment."

"Oh, you suck. I'm making do with Advil and white wine, and you actually have a hot tub? What is that, some perk if you get enough take downs on HeroNet?" She half closed her eyes, and got a startlingly clear image of him in the spa and was glad no one was around to see her cheeks tinge a bit red.

"No, that's something I got from a lot of hard work on my own business when I'm not out running around on rooftops. And you can keep the wine, I'll stick with beer."

"Oooohhh, famous hero by night and rich business man by day?" she teased, wondering why she'd never really thought about him out of costume before. Then she embarrassed herself all over again by realizing what that would have sounded like if she'd said it out loud.

He chuckled softly. "Long way from rich. I just work my ass off at it, and sometimes it goes ok." She could hear the bubbling water now and a faint splash as he moved. "But yeah, hot tub is a good way to go."

"Not in my apartment. Damn it, that sounds good right now," she sighed.

JT found himself opening his mouth to make some smart ass comment about their being plenty of room and then stopped himself. Somehow, it didn't sound right to him all of a sudden. Unusually at a loss for words, he heard himself babbling slightly. "Yeah, so... if you're doing ok, I can let you get back to Tigre hunting, or something."

"Well, we've talked work, it's not an obscene phone call, and you're not asking what I'm wearing, so I guess we're done." There was a very long moment of silence as he wondered if he'd heard that right and she tried to imagine what the hell she was thinking to actually say that. Desperate to break the unbearably awkward silence, she finally said "Ummm.... that sounded a lot funnier in my head."

"Yeah... uh... keep looking for Tigre, and I'll poke around tomorrow and see what I can find. Catch ya later." JT disconnected, and both of them sat there wondering what the hell they'd said and how much of an idiot the other thought they were.

Chapter 8

BY UNSPOKEN AGREEMENT, the two worked on their own for the next few days, each running down leads as they could find them. They worked well, even if they were each distracted. For his part, Argent kept finding himself bemused by daydreams (he refused to go so far as calling them fantasies), of what might have happened during their conversation about the hot tub. Cobalt Rose found herself wondering at odd moments exactly what Argent, or JT she guessed, was like "off duty." Distractions to one side, they were still quite effective.

Argent stood in an alley. One booted foot was on the pavement, the other resting on a thug's chest. Argent's attention was more immediately engaged by the other man that he held against the wall with one hand, his other hand taking something from his belt. "I'm really running out patience with you boneheads. So here's the deal. Give me something about El Tigre, and I let you go. Don't..." his voice trailed off and he held up a small dart which began sparking, very bright in the dark alley. "Tazer dart. Useful toy. Usually I just throw 'em at people to drop 'em. But, keep pissing me off, and I get creative." He moved the dart closer to the man's groin. The man's eyes practically popped out of his head as he began speaking, his voice rushed as the words almost tripped over each other.

***

"See, here's the thing. I kinda have a bet going... well, more a competition, I guess, really, and I really hate losing. So, help a girl out, huh? Tell me where El Tigre is." The Cobalt Rose gazed intently at the man she was speaking to. He had a slight reputation for occasionally providing information, and she was doing her best to encourage him. Aside from her looks and costume, the persuasion took the shape of her standing easily on one leg, the other foot pressing against his throat, lightly at the moment so he could breathe, and, hopefully, talk. "I can do this all night, for me, this is just a workout stretch. For you?" She shifted her weight slightly and he made a gagging sound. He gestured frantically, she eased back, and listened to his raspy tale.

***

Argent leaned on the wall of the doctor's lab. "I don't know why it's doing it, but your little toy there is screwing with my coms. Last time I used it, I lost my signal completely."

Doc Lydia examined Argent's wristband. "No, it shouldn't be doing that. But you are awfully hard on your equipment." She pulled a tool off the rack on the wall and started poking at the wristband.

"Kinda comes with the job."

"You seem to be spending a lot of time with this new hero, Cobalt Rose," Lydia observed.

He shrugged. "Yeah. She's a good one. She's really impressive for both a non-powered and a newbie."

"And that's why you're spending so much time training her? Argent, the loner?" she teased him as she started replacing a loose connection in the band.

"No, I just... I like her, ok? She's got some fire in her, she's smart, and she's not out for revenge. She's actually trying to help people because she can. A little bit of a thrill-seeker, maybe, and kinda hung up on the reporters, but I think that part's wearing off."

"I'm sure her costume doesn't hurt, either."

He laughed. "It's a great view, but no, it's not that. Or just that, I guess," he added. "She's fun. She's a good fighter, and getting better. And she understands the life, since she's in it, too."

Lydia finished her repairs and handed the device back to him. "That should take care of it. And I agree, she's very talented. Have you told her that?" An uncomfortable silence stretched out for a few minutes, and she shook her head. "Men." Argent muttered something she couldn't quite hear, snapped on his wristband, and took off after a hurried thanks.

***

Argent crouched on a fire escape, using a small electronic scope to survey the building across the street. It appeared to be an average apartment building, but everything he'd been able to dig up said different. He tapped his fingers on the rail, wondering what the best way was to go. He heard a slight sound from above him and glanced up, then went back to looking at the building. "You too, huh?"

"Were you gonna tell me about this?" the Rose asked as she dropped down lightly next to him.

"Before I went in or anything, yeah. I just figured I'd check it out first, wait till I had something to actually say. Besides I didn't wanna just call ya..." he let the words trail off and they both felt awkward silence fall around them. He cleared his throat. "If you got here the same way I did, sounds even more like we're in the right place, right? I mean, if we'd been hitting the same guys, one of them would've said something."

"Yeah, probably." Rose looked across the street. "So, what's up over there?"

Argent shrugged. "Looks like a damn apartment building at first, doesn't it?"

"'At first,' huh? What am I missing?" She looked again, frowning behind her mask.

"You tell me, grasshopper." He pointed across the way, and she rolled her eyes. He was pretty good at teaching her things without making a big deal of it, but every once in a while he got to be pretty damn irritating, and this was one of those times. She leaned on the rail and drummed her fingers, unknowingly echoing Argent's earlier motion. It was a quiet night, there weren't many businesses here, it was a residential block. So what was he seeing? Looking around again, she added, or not seeing.

"The parking lot. It's the middle of the night, most people should be home, watching tv, eating dinner, whatever. But the parking lot's half empty."

He nodded approvingly. "Right. So, either this place has a really crappy landlord, only one on the block that does," he swept his hand up and down the street, where all the other buildings looked much more occupied, "or there aren't as many apartments. Like, someone really clever converted some of the interior space to something else."

"And got a lot of hostages in the bargain. Slick." She slid her hand down the railing, lost in thought, and brushed his. They both pulled back, and she rubbed her hand without realizing it. "So, what's the plan?"

"I've been watching a while. I don't see anything looks like security patrols, at least not out here. Last time, we tried to get tricky, and it didn't work." He resolutely pushed the image of her bare back while she changed out of his mind. "So, this time, I say we just go snoop around and see what we can find."

"What, you wanna just kick in the front door or something?" Rose didn't like the idea, not with so many potential innocent bystanders in the building.

"Not exactly. C'mon." Argent moved past her, brushing against her as he got to the steps and climbed quickly to the roof.

"Head in the game, girl," she muttered to herself, her fingers almost tingling from the feel of him, hard muscle under the silver costume, from where he'd moved against her. She was going to have to do something about this before she drove herself crazy, but after that last phone call, wasn't sure what to say to him.

"Ok, we're here. Now what?" Rose didn't think her line thrower, another gift from Lydia, would reach all the way across the street, and even if it did, there wasn't enough height to swing, and she wasn't sure she could tightrope walk that far, and didn't want to find out this far above pavement.

"I don't think you're gonna like this part, but I don't see another way, so.... sorry, I guess?" Argent suddenly reached out and grabbed her, picking her up in his arms. She let out a startled sputter of protest as he moved back to the far edge of the roof, and then sprinted forward. She hung on tighter, arms around his neck, realizing what he was about to do. As he reached the edge of the parapet, the Rose saw the distortion that indicated his power was in use, and he sprang outward. After what seemed like a very long time in mid-air (which she would never admit to Argent she spent with her eyes closed and holding her breath) they finally landed on the far side of the street. Argent stood there a few moments, very relieved he'd made the jump (he'd been almost positive he would, and a line ready if not, held in the hand under her knees), breathing a bit hard.

Rose looked around, not seeing any sign of cameras, or security devices. She was impressed, that had been a hell of a leap, even allowing for his powers. Finally, she said, "I think you can put me down now."

Argent seemed startled, then almost embarrassed. "Yeah, right, sorry." He dropped her, and she landed lightly on her feet. The two of them moved toward the doorway that no doubt led down and inside, to begin their newest assault on El Tigre Blanco, hopefully in the right place this time.

Chapter 9

ARGENT BROUGHT HIS ARM UP and opened his wristband once again, sweeping back and forth. "Ok... no surveillance systems up here," he walked around the edges of the roof and then moved back towards the doorway again, "but there's a hell of a security system here. This is gonna take a while." He pressed a few buttons and the device made a few chirping sounds, and the lights settled into a regular, rhythmic pattern.

He looked around and then shook his head. "I don't like this; there could be way too many people in here." Argent raised his other hand to activate his communicator. "Hey, Doc? We got a good line on El Tigre, but this place looks like it's an apartment building. Run... hell, I don't know, everything you can on 384 Hartwell. And uh... anyone around might be free for backup?" He paused, listening. "Yeah, I know I don't, but this isn't feeling right. Ok, just get back to me when you can, I've got your Exterminator thing running on the door." He clicked it off.

Rose stood, arms folded, looking at him. "Back up?"

Argent shrugged, looking at his wrist band again. "It's not about how good you are, how good you think you are, or how good you want me to think you are. We don't know how many people are in here, and we don't know if any of them work for El Tigre or just really crapped out on the landlord front. They come first, they have to."

Rose flushed a bit, but found herself nodding. "Yeah, ok. I guess that's fair." She looked over the edge and down the street, and then turned back to him. "Didn't I hear something about you being on a team or something?"

Argent made a low sound in his throat. "The Mayor wanted me in on this Freedom Squad thing he's setting up. But he's slimy. I don't trust him at all. Plus, I don't work and play well with others. Or so I keep hearing."

"Yeah, I could see that." Cobalt Rose muttered.

Argent tapped a few more buttons on his wristband, impatience clear. "Must be why we get along. We have stuff in common."

"What are you talking about?" Rose snapped, clearly irritated.

"I doubt you're sloppy enough with your secret identity that your name is actually 'Rose.'"

"And yours is JT?" she asked, irritation deepening.

"Not my name, obviously, but yeah, it's what I go by when I don't have the mask on." She actually looked embarrassed at that, but he waved his hand at her. "Don't sweat it, you don't trust me a lot, that's smart, makes sense. I get it. But don't make yourself sound like you're some great team player like the Protector or Spira or someone. I don't think either of us is likely to end up on one of those big league teams. Or even a smaller one. We might be all the team each other can stand."

"Well, it's not like you're telling me everything, either." Rose started, and then stopped when he brought one hand up to his ear.

"Yeah, ok Doc. No, I don't think we can wait. We'll... think of something." He turned to his partner. "No backup. Everyone's busy or out of the country or off planet or something." He dropped his voice to a low mutter. "Damn cosmic heroes. No good for anything useful."

"So just us, then?" Rose asked. She'd been fine with the idea before, but now suddenly it was making her uneasy. She blamed Argent for that; this was the first time she'd seen him this– what was the right word? Cautious? Whatever word you used, it was making her nervous now.

"Yeah, looks like. So, we get in, we see what it's like, and we try and figure out if the apartments have guns for hire and whatever other lackeys Tigre needs, or if they're just wrong place, wrong time. If they are, we get 'em out somehow. Then we figure out what's going on in here, and stop it." Argent pressed another button and shook his head in irritation. "C'mon already."

"Oh, is that all? Piece of cake." Sarcasm dripped from Rose's words.

"You thought this would be easy? Wrong line of work." He paused. "What DO you do, anyway? You're out here a lot, you had some decent first versions of your gear when we met, you can't have a nine to five gig or the hours would be getting to you, and your co-workers would be wondering about all the bruises and shit if you had a normal job."

"I have a little bit of money. I'm not rich, but I can keep my bills paid, and do what I need to from home between being out here and sleeping." She looked away, clearly uncomfortable.

Argent went back to studying his wristband's display, and muttered, "Great, wanna invest in a bar?" Before she could respond to that, the band beeped twice, and the door popped open.

He closed his wristband, gave a very elaborate shrug and said, "Let's go see what we got." He pulled the door open wider and they crept down the stairs. She pointed at the door at the bottom of the flight of steps, and he checked his wristband once more, then shook his head and opened that as well, very slowly and cautiously. They looked out at what appeared to be an average- looking hallway in any apartment building. Slightly worn carpeting, fluorescent lights in the ceiling, and lots of doors along the corridor. Argent moved to the closest door, pulled something from his belt, and held it to the peephole, looking through it. He pulled it down, and moved back to her, his practiced step making no noise. Putting his masked mouth to her ear, he barely breathed out the words "Looks like a normal apartment to me." He checked several more doors at random, and then held out the device to her. It looked almost like a miniature telescope

Rose moved to a door and put it over the hole as she'd seen him do. Peering through it, she saw a view of a small, average looking apartment, dimly lit as occupants were likely asleep at this hour. "What is this, another toy from Lydia?" she asked as she handed it back to him.

"Nah, cop toy, just not a lot of folks know about 'em," he answered as he took it from her. "This floor looks pretty standard. One down?" She nodded, and moved toward the elevator, but he shook his head and opened the stairwell door. They moved down the stairs, and found the door to the next floor locked. Argent pulled a set of lock picks from his belt and went to work.

"Isn't it weird that this is locked?" Rose asked as she watched him.

"No, most emergency stairs you get into from any floor, but only out of at the bottom, it's a standard security thing. No alarms that I see, so that's pretty normal. I don't see anything off here. Not yet." He worked the lock easily, and then opened the door. Once again, a corridor only remarkable for its ordinariness confronted them. Shrugging again, Argent pointed to the left and they moved along, checking doors with his scope. After several doors, he stopped, head cocked to one side. "Wait a sec..." he muttered, and went back to the last door, looking again.

"You have something?" she asked, curious.

He rubbed his chin, and then handed her the lenses. "Check the doors here and tell me if you see something," he said, his voice thoughtful.

The Cobalt Rose took the device and began her own examinations. At first she was puzzled and irritated, wondering why he was bothering to throw tests at her in the middle of this mission. Gradually, she began noticing an oddity, and checked a few more doors at random to be certain, then turned back to him. "All the ones on this side," she pointed to the right, "are fine, but all the ones here," she indicated the left, "look the same. Like exactly the same."

"Yeah, that's what I thought. And since I doubt these come some furnished, and some not, or that they all got the same decorator..." he let his voice trail off.

"They're fake." she finished, getting that much but not putting it all together completely.

"Right. And that," he pointed to the wall of what seemed genuine apartments, "is the outside wall. All the fakes are on the inside."

Light dawned on Rose. "So the whole building is a fake?"

"It's a shell. The outside, top floor, bottom one, maybe bottom two, are all legit. But all the inside look to be fake, which means there's a hell of a lot of space unaccounted for. So, I think we know where. Now let's find out what." He moved back to the corner counterfeit door closest to the elevator and began studying it, eagerness in his voice.

Chapter 10

ARGENT EYED THE DOOR, scratching his cheek through the mask. "No, this isn't the way in."

The Cobalt Rose looked from him to the door. "Some other gadget of Lydia's tell you that?"

"No. Trained observer." He tapped his temple. "Look at the other doors, the ones we worked out were real ones."

Rose practically growled at him, but began looking from door to door. After a few minutes, she shook her head. "Ok, I'm missing it. What?"

"You go in and out your door all the time, you bump into it eventually. You hit it with your umbrella, miss the lock occasionally with your key, whatever. Plus, going in and out, you wear out the rug, the threshold. All these fake ones, there's no wear and tear. They're not being used."

Rose looked closer and swore under her breath. He was right. "What do you mean, 'trained observer'? Is there a class somewhere I should be taking in picking things up like that?"

He looked almost embarrassed as he led them back to the stairwell. "No, I used to be a cop."

"What? Really?" Rose wasn't sure what she'd expected him to say, but what wasn't it.

"Yeah, a long time before all this stuff." He waved his hand, encompassing the costume, belt, and all of it. "I figured I could do more, and started doing the hero thing. More direct action, less paperwork, ya know?"

She shook her head, still surprised. "Yeah, ok, I could see that, I guess. So where are we going?"

"Playing a hunch. Just like being a cop, sometimes it's eliminating possibilities to get to the right one." Several flights of stairs and picked locks later, they were on the second floor. Argent nodded in satisfaction. "Human nature beats security almost every time."

"What do you mean?" She saw him staring at the doorway.

"I bet they had orders to change up which door they use, all that. But people are lazy and they start doing whatever's easiest. So, lowest floor, closest to the elevator, that's the door they use. And wear out the carpet. So we can see which one it is." They walked down the hall and he pointed. One door showed the kind of wear he'd been talking about, and he nodded in satisfaction. "There we go."

Argent walked over to the door and once more flipped open his "Exterminator" as he had called the wristband earlier. Rose followed and watched him punching buttons for what seemed like a longer time than usual. "Problem?" she asked.

"Lot more security on this one. Take the surveillance first, then the alarms, then the lock..." he muttered to himself and the now familiar sounds began coming from it.

"So when do I get one of those?" Rose asked, half teasing.

"Ask the Doc. I didn't really ask for this, we were just talking out ideas one night when I was on a really long stakeout and she was on com." He shrugged. "She had it for me in about two weeks, and she's been playing with it ever since. I dunno, ask her, or come up with your own toys. She likes making this stuff work, putting it together, all that crap. Good thing, too, since I don't get much more complicated than replacing fuses."

"What's her name, anyway?" Argent looked over at her. "Doc Lydia. I'm guessing she has a last name?"

Argent shrugged and went back to his work. "I would guess so."

"You've worked with her for a long time, from what I can tell, and you don't even know her last name?" Cobalt Rose sounded surprised.

"Hey, I respect her privacy. If she wanted me to know, she'd tell me. All those HeroWeb folks take a pretty big risk helping us out. What I don't know, I can't tell someone if I get captured, hit with telepathy, or that kind of stuff." He paused. "Besides, I don't know your name, either. And I haven't pushed you on it." The Rose looked a bit defensive at that, so Argent turned his attention back to his gadget. "C'mon, already." He looked at his wristband again. "It never takes this long. Either we're in the right place or we're tripping over some government black-ops crap. Again."

"What do you mean, again? I've never had a problem with the feds." She looked at him more closely. "Does that happen a lot?"

"Eh, depends. Sometimes I run across some spook types who are good guys. Sometimes some sub-division of some damn three letter agency gets a really bad idea and does something really dangerous and stupid. Most of 'em are just like everyone else, doing their jobs and not really thinking about it." The wristband beeped and he looked at it. "Never heard that one before."

"What's going on?" Rose looked up and down the hallway. It felt like they'd been standing there forever.

"Got everything else, can't get the lock. Someone paid for some really fancy toys here. OK, plan B."

"What's plan–" she broke off as he backed up and kicked the door "– oh."

He shrugged. "Hey, the alarm's down, the cameras are down. We should be fine." They moved in through the doorway and saw two figures walking towards them. "Or not."

The pair approaching were a man and a woman. The man was a huge behemoth, well over seven feet tall, with a costume of mostly black, bared arms, and wristbands that went almost to the elbow with metal spikes all over them. The woman was average height in a costume of skin tight leather, also black, with a long whip trailing from each hand. She displayed a generous amount of cleavage, a spill of blonde hair, and a black headband which matched the knee high black boots.

Argent shook his head. "Great, Brute and Lash, the bondage twins."

"We're not twins!" they both yelled.

"See, that might be more convincing if you didn't say it together like that. What is that, the twin telepathy thing I keep hearing about?" Argent mocked them.

"I'll kill you, you asshole!" Brute roared as he charged forward. "I'm stronger than you are, than anyone is!"

"Stronger than me? Sure." Argent grabbed one of Brute's outstretched arms by the wrist. "Than anyone? Not likely." He pivoted so his back was against Brute's chest, shot his leg back to kick one of Brute's legs out, and then bent forward, throwing the larger man to the floor. The force of Argent's throw added to the momentum of Brute's rush, hurling him to the floor with a crash. "Of course, I fight better than you do, I'm smarter, and I'm much better looking."

Brute shook his head, groggy, struggling to his feet. "Kill you." he panted.

"Get some better dialogue at least. I'm sure someone could write something down for you. You can read, right?" Argent kicked Brute's chest, driving him back a bit.

With a wordless roar of rage, Brute staggered forward, swinging wildly. Argent blocked the blow, caught his arm again and spun, sending his foe face first into the wall. The tell-tale shimmer of his powers in play surrounded his right hand as he drove it into Brute's kidney, eliciting a howl of pain. Brute clapped his left hand to his kidney and swung wildly behind him with his other hand. Argent dropped to a low crouch, then dropped back on his hands and pistoned his feet, also surrounded by the faint shimmering of power, into the back of Brute's left knee. Brute fell backward as Argent rolled to the side and up to his knees. As the giant smashed to the floor again, Argent cocked his fist back and slammed it downward into Brute's face. The villain twitched and lay still.

As Brute charged Argent, Lash shook her head. "Typical. The guys go hide in the corner and hope to watch some girl on girl action." She swung her arm and her whip cracked through the space that Cobalt Rose has been standing in, but Rose was moving, jumping forward diagonally, landing on the wall and pushing off, launching a strike at Lash's head.

"You're so not my type," Rose shot back, as Lash managed to barely evade the blow. Her whip cracked again, and sparks crackled from the wall where she struck. "Great, electric whips," Rose thought, dodging another whip strike. The narrowness of the corridor cut two ways, limiting her ability to dodge, but making it hard for Lash to use her weapons to their full potential.

Lash struck again and again, her whips snapping and crackling just behind where Rose was as the heroine dodged and spun. Finally slowing, Rose felt one of the whips graze her left arm, and it went almost completely numb.

There was a crash from behind Rose, and Lash shifted her gaze for a moment, saying "Brute?" Rose stepped forward quickly, her insulated boot pinning one whip to the ground as she raised her other leg in an arc and kicked Lash solidly in the chin. Lash reeled backwards, and Rose landed two more kicks, finishing with a strike down onto the edge of Lash's neck. Lash stumbled, managed to get out, "Bitch," and fell to the floor. Rose heard clapping behind her, and spun in a fighting stance, to see Argent applauding.

"Nice job, kid. She's not the easiest to take down, especially with no powers." He passed Rose to pull the whips from their wrist mountings in Lash's costume, using the first to tie her securely. He paused for a moment to take in his handiwork and nodded approvingly. "Bondage twins, like I said." He took the other whip and began similarly securing Brute.

"Is that going to hold him?" Rose asked.

"Well, I hit him pretty good, and these are pretty tough, reinforced to carry the current she uses to zap people with, so he won't tear through them too easily. And really, if we're here long enough for that to be an issue, we're probably screwed anyway." He shrugged. "Should hold him long enough." He got up, dusting his hands off. "Now, let's see what the hell they're doing in here."

Chapter 11

HAVING DISPOSED OF THE TWO MERCENARY VILLAINS, Argent and
the Cobalt Rose looked at the corridor more closely. The hall was
white, and reminded Rose faintly of sets on Star Trek. It had a clean,
science fiction feel to it, aside from the damage where Argent had
dropped Brute. Looking at that, she said "Well you probably aren't
making friends with the maintenance staff, or whoever fixes that
stuff."

Argent walked down the hallway, away from the door they'd
entered by. "One advantage to fighting in the bad guy's base.
Whatever you manage to damage is more or less a good thing." He
walked along to a corner, and cautiously peeked around the edge.
"Nothing here. More hallway." Argent moved forward and glanced
upward, seeing some conduits. He jumped up and clung there,
touching the edge of one, then dropped. "Lotta power humming along
here. What the hell is he doing?"

They crept along farther, and found a large door in the middle of
the wall. "This looks like the right way." He tapped it. "Thick, heavy
metal. Must be something good behind it." Once more he raised his
wristband and flipped it open. It made a few beeps, and then suddenly
shot out a series of sparks and a small curl of smoke. Cursing, Argent
waved his hand back and forth.

"What happened?" Rose asked, torn between concern and trying
not to laugh.

"I told you, not a tech guy. Doc would know. I guess there's
some kind of disruption field or something. Cooked this thing, I
guess." He looked at it and then showed her, the display dark now.
"Guess we do this the old fashioned way." He raised his hands, the
faint ripple of his power surrounding them.

"Wait a sec, won't that kinda give away that we're here?" Rose
asked.

"I think they know that already, but you have another idea?"

"Maybe." She walked forward and focused her attention on the keypad next to the door. "I've been reading up on these things." Rose studied the pad. "The numbers are more worn on some of them, so those are likely the right numbers, right?" Bemused and a bit impressed, he nodded. "So, we have a 7, a 4, a 3, and a 0. Any of that sound familiar?"

Argent shook his head. "No. Should it?"

"They usually have some kind of meaning." She rubbed her chin, unconsciously mimicking a gesture she'd seen him use several times. "I was reading his file. Let me think." She paced back and forth a few times, and then snapped her fingers. "Got it. I think. Long as it isn't booby trapped or something." Quickly, she leaned forward and punched in 4703. A very tense moment later, there was a muffled click and the door swung open.

Rose tried to look nonchalant as she walked forward, and Argent asked, "Ok, what was that?"

"Birthday of his first son, according to some of the HeroNet stuff anyway. Figured with the whole Latin culture macho bit, it was a good shot."

The two moved stealthily through the door, finding themselves in a short hallway. At the end of it, they found a large room, several stories tall, roughly shaped like a cube, taking up much of the space of what should have been the center of the building. They saw many workstations with men in full-body white suits working with various vials of powders or liquids. A few heavily armed men who must be guards roamed the edges of the large space. Off to one side, to the rear wall from where they crouched behind a computer station, was a large, walled off space.

"What do you think is back there?" Rose whispered, indicating the enclosed area.

"Either something they need extra protection for, like a big bomb or something, or that's where we'll find El Tigre." Argent answered, surveying the room, looking for a way to get to the area without being seen. "I don't see a good way to do this, we may just have to fight through."

Rose studied the layout of the work areas, guards, and a few cameras, and nodded. "Yeah, I think it's designed that way. There is no good way to get anywhere unseen. Clever."

"Ok then. Drop the guards, keep moving fast, and get to whatever's back there?" Argent asked her.

"I don't see a better idea, so yeah, I guess so." Rose shifted a bit. "Before we possibly rush off to our deaths, do me a favor? Roll up your mask a bit?" Argent looked at her, shrugged, then did so, pulling it up to his nose. Before he could ask why, she grabbed him, pulled him in close, and gave him a long kiss on the lips. "Partially for luck and part because I've been thinking about doing that for a while," she said after she let him go.

He pulled his mask back down, but not before she saw a smile on his face. "Well then, I guess we really have to try extra had to not get killed here. We need to talk about that more." He drew in a deep breath, focusing on the task at hand. "Ready?" The Cobalt Rose nodded, and he said "Ok, I'm going to get as close as I can to the first one, and, if I'm lucky, drop him before they know what's going on. Maybe we can take a few that way."

Argent slunk off to the right, managing to stay out of sight with a skill born of long practice. Rose moved to the left, and realized she had the easier route to take. Part of her wanted to take issue with this, but she was realistic enough to realize this was too important for such games right now and, really, he was more experienced. Crouching behind a computer console, she waited until the worker at it turned to look at a side display, and then moved to the next station. Hiding behind a large tank of some sort, she had a passing thought of hoping it wasn't filled with something explosive or acidic, and then pushed the thought from her mind.

She focused on the guard closest to her. He was wearing grey fatigue style pants, a black shirt with several oversize pockets, and carrying some kind of assault rifle. His belt had a few other weapons and pouches that projected an air of menace. "Ok, he looks the part, but can he actually use any of that shit?" she thought to herself. He turned to look at something and Rose sprang forward, moving her hand up and then down sharply in an arc that brought a back-fist down on his neck with smashing force. She'd hit the nerve cluster she was aiming for, and he dropped with a very faint gurgle. Rose pulled him back behind the tank she'd been using for cover and checked him quickly. He was still alive, which was good, and one of his toys was a tazer, which was even better. There were too many people with too many guns to play games, and this could make things a lot easier.

She shocked the guard she'd taken down to try and buy more time, and make sure the tazer was working. It seemed to be, from the way he stiffened and then collapsed again as Rose applied it to him.

The Rose looked over to where the guard had been that Argent had been stalking, and saw no sign of him. Since no alarms had gone off and no shots fired, she decided that was a good sign, and moved on to her next target. After a few moments, Rose found herself caught behind a large computer station. It had been unoccupied when she first ran to it, but someone had sat down in the chair after she moved to it, and she hadn't been able to see a way to get out without attracting attention. Just as she had made up her mind to take a chance on the computer geek (she still couldn't tell if they were male or female) seeing her, the decision was made for her with a series of shouts, gunshots, and a crash.

Chapter 12

"FIRST THINGS FIRST," she thought as she leapt out from her hiding place, swinging one arm to stun the computer tech (a woman, she saw now) with the tazer. The woman let out a muffled squeak and fell as Rose tried to see what was happening and where the remaining guards were. Chaos was springing up on the far side of the work area, as Argent kicked a guard hard, driving him backwards. The man smashed into the wall, and bounced off it, staggering forward. Argent met him coming in with a punch to the man's head and he fell. Two more guards raced to find clear firing positions as scientists, researchers, whatever they were ("Henchmen?," she wondered) either milled around, ran away, or went to see what was happening.

Feeling like her head was on a swivel, trying to look every direction at once, Rose finally located the closest guard, separated from her by a knot of white-coated lab workers. She moved in among them, using them for cover as she worked closer to the man who had his rifle out and was clearly angling for a better shot at Argent. Passing the last of the lab workers, she lunged forward, wrapped her hand around the gun's barrel, and heaved upward. The would-be sniper, his attention on the other hero, was completely unprepared for this, and rapidly rising metal struck him in the forehead. He staggered and tried to focus on his new assailant, but Rose followed up with a left to his stomach, doubling him over, and brought her knee up to meet his descending chin. There was a loud cracking sound and the man fell. One of the lab rats (she finally decided on that name) belatedly reached for her and she distractedly zapped him with the tazer. He fell and the others backed off quickly. She saw another guard near the door who seemed like he might be about to shoot her partner, and inspiration struck. The Cobalt Rose spun to face the group of now nervous techs and yelled at them "Who's next?" while triggering the tazer, sparks arcing off it. They turned and ran for the door, trampling the gunman, who was taken wholly unawares by the small stampede.

The next guard had finally noticed her. He pulled his pistol, but hesitated to shoot, with too many of his co-workers (co-henches, she decided) in the line of fire. Looking almost scared now, he quickly drew a wicked looking knife. Rose almost smiled to herself- he was panicking, and still had the pistol out, although he didn't seem sure what to do with it. He slashed at her wildly once, twice, in huge, looping arcs. When his arm was at the end of its circle of motion, Rose leapt forward, her left hand locking around his right wrist. She stepped past him forcing his arm back and then brought her weight down into a low crouch. The guard backpedaled furiously but couldn't keep up and fell, landing heavily on his back. Rose quickly punched him the stomach, rose as he curled up, and brought her foot down on his nose, breaking it and knocking his head back to the floor.

Streaks of luck come and go, and Rose's easy run of things abruptly ended. One of the guards on the edges of the melee around Argent finally noticed her. He brought his rifle to his shoulder and began sighting in on her. Rose took two fast steps to her left and then slid, like a baseball player, behind a computer station. The roar of gunfire filled the room once again, and more of the civilian looking scientists began fleeing for the exit. Sparks flew from the work area as wisps of smoke began coming out of the computer tower. "I hope they hit save before they left," Rose muttered as the monitor flickered and went dark.

She saw a sturdier looking work area nearby, that appeared to have several large components made of some kind of metal. Another burst of bullets chewing away at her cover helped make up her mind. She moved to a crouch, balancing on the balls of her feet. Cobalt Rose drew a deep breath, focusing on her next haven. Figuring she was as ready as she was going to be, she shoved the desk chair from the station back the way she'd come as hard as she could, and then took off in a sprint. The gunman, as hoped, fired several shots at the moving chair before realizing what was happening. Most of the way there, Rose tripped over a dropped coffee flask. She turned her fall into a forward roll and managed to get under cover just as a few rounds zipped past her head. Bullets slammed into the work area with a satisfying thud, making her think she had chosen her new spot well.

Rose heard a distant grunt and the gunfire stopped. Peering around the edge of the desk, she saw that Argent had managed to flip one of his assailants onto the man who'd been trying to shoot her. "Ok, we're even," Rose muttered as she ran toward the smaller area they'd noticed before. Looking back, she had a rare chance to see Argent in action when she wasn't similarly engaged. She had to admit, although she might not say it to him directly, it was impressive.

Argent still had three guards to deal with, but she was fairly certain he'd be done before she could get there, so she watched the fight, keeping an eye out for more security forces. She saw one rifle with the barrel deformed, and no sign of the other guards. She guessed he had managed to disarm them somehow or other. One of the remaining guards leveled a pistol at him and fired from near point blank range. Argent's hand moved in a blur, his power shimmering around it, and a faint spark showed where the bullet arced away. She'd heard him talk about being able to do that, but had thought it was some manner of joke or boast. The guard was even more surprised, and the distraction cost him as Argent stepped in and drove his fist hard into the man's nose. The guard went down in a shower of blood as his nose broke. Argent kept moving, spinning low and leg sweeping another man as he moved in, knife drawn. As he fell, Argent continued his circle, moving his leg in a higher arc. The man managed to barely block the kick that would have connected with his head, dropping his blade, and Argent followed up with a series of punches to the stomach and head, and then a smashing downward hammerfist to the back of the guard's head. The first one started to try to reach for his weapon, and Argent kicked him once in passing. The scientists had fled by now, and the guards were all defeated. He sauntered over to her, dusting his hands off and said "What, you don't have the door open yet?" It was impossible to tell with his full face mask, but she was fairly certain he was smiling at her, if not winking.

"I thought I'd wait for you, hotshot," Rose said, bowing, indicating the large, heavy looking, metal door.

"Thanks." Argent regarded the door. "They probably know we're here by now, unless they're deaf or something." He focused, his body tensing slightly, the subtle distortion of his power appearing around his feet, building for a few moments. "Ahhh... fuck it." He brought his foot up and kicked out hard, bringing the door down with a reverberating crash.

He walked forward almost before the door had finished falling, wary, prepared for whatever trap or ambush he had just sprung. Rose, who had jumped a bit at the sound of the crash, shook her head and muttered "'the wizard will see you now...'" as she followed her impulsive partner into the heart of the villain's lair.

Chapter 13

SENSING MOVEMENT, Argent dodged to one side of the doorway and out into the main room just as automatic weapon fire ripped through the space he'd just been in. Behind him, Rose ducked back to the outside of the doorway, pieces of the entry falling to the floor around her. Argent jumped forward, deflecting several more shots with his powers, before closing with the gunman. The silvery hero managed to yank the weapon from the man's hands, tossing it aside. Rose raced into the room, and saw another guard aiming for Argent with his rifle. She snatched up the weapon Argent had just thrown aside, and hurled it with all her strength. The spinning rifle struck the man in the head and he staggered, raising one hand to the wound. Rose crossed the space between them in an instant and struck, doubling him over with a punch to the stomach, driving her knee up to his face, and then finishing with a roundhouse kick that caught the falling man alongside his temple. With a groan, he fell to the floor, and Rose kicked his weapon away, grabbing his tazer in what was becoming a habit and zapped him.

The man Argent had disarmed swung a quick punch at Argent's head. Argent blocked, and the man launched a low kick towards the hero's feet. Argent stepped back, kicking in turn at the man's stomach. That was parried as the guard leaned in and drove his elbow at Argent's temple. Fading back, Argent feinted at the man's head, and, when he blocked a blow that wasn't actually coming, Argent punched him in the stomach, swept his legs out from under him, and then slammed the man's head down against the floor as he fell. Breathing a bit heavier, Argent paused a moment and said "Ok, that one was pretty good."

With no more attacks being directed against them, the two heroes looked at the space they found themselves in. The large room was lavishly appointed, with artwork on the walls that Rose knew was fairly expensive. There were three enormous cages that held, naturally, a large white tiger in each one. Farther into the room, past the cages,

WAYLAND SMITH • 51

was a large, heavy wooden desk, with a series of computer screens on it. Behind the desk was a man in a white suit, with a black tie, belt, and handkerchief in his jacket pocket. A large cigar was in his mouth, and he put down a brandy snifter to applaud. "Very well done. Do you know, you have moved from a minor irritant to actually significantly affecting my business ventures in a remarkably short time? Very impressive, Argent." He turned his gaze to Rose, the light from the computer screens flickering over his black hair. "And you must be La Rosa. I must say, your surveillance pictures do not do you justice." He acknowledged her with a slight bow of his head. "I do not suppose you would be willing to discuss this like rational people over cigars and brandy? It's quite good," he added, taking another sip to illustrate his point.

"No way, Tigre. You're going down this time, and you're not buying us off," Argent snapped.

"Are you quite certain? What would it harm to actually listen to me before resorting to mindless violence that, really, is not terribly likely to accomplish much?" His voice was accented, clearly cultured, and irritatingly calm, given the circumstances.

"What would I have to talk about with a drug dealer? End of the day, that's all you are, no matter how fancy you make your little hideout." Argent waved his hand dismissively at the luxury around him.

"I do sell drugs, true. It is quite lucrative, and the people so enjoy them. Venus is doing quite well, and I will be introducing a new product, Mars, next week. Just as Venus enhances pleasure and desire, Mars dampens pain and increases aggressiveness. Variations on a theme, I suppose, but I suppose that is one of the perils of a classical education." He shrugged. "All of this is, of course, a sideline to finance my work in the field of DNA and genetics. To think, all of this could have been avoided by a research grant from the government. Ironic, is it not?" He sipped his brandy again.

"You'll be in jail next week, Tigre, not causing even more chaos on the streets," Argent said confidently.

"I find that unlikely. A pity we could not work something out, you seem quite talented. Both of you, actually. I had rather expected that my little diversion with the Bright Fang Clan of ninjas might be sufficient to, if not eliminate you outright, distract you for a time." He rose slowly and took off his jacket, then began unbuttoning his shirt sleeves and rolling them up. "Still, I suppose there is some appeal in doing things the old-fashioned, direct way."

"Let me guess, your new Mars crap is in your brandy, and you think it's going to give you an edge to fight me?" Argent sounded bored almost.

"Oh, no, I believe you might best me even that way. You are very formidable, sir." He took off his tie and laid it on the carefully placed jacket that was draped on the back of his chair. "I gave the Mars to them." He pressed a button on the desk and the cages began opening. "I have been trying something much different."

Argent and Rose exchanged quick glances, and he said, "I have the pets, you take him." She nodded, her eyes a bit wide. This was her first fight with an actual villain, and also her first brush with killer animals. Somehow, not a combination she would have asked for.

El Tigre moved out from behind his desk. "It truly is a shame, you are quite lovely. But, I fear, as stubbornly, narrow-mindedly moralistic as your comrade there. I am afraid I can not allow my sense of aesthetics to influence my business decisions."

"What is it you're actually up to here, if you're not just a drug kingpin?" Rose asked, stalling for time, doing a hurried mental inventory of what she had on her for weapons that might be of use.

"As you two have so aptly demonstrated, with so many so-called 'super heroes' interfering in the lives of simple businessmen, the era of conventional security has passed. So, to my thinking, a fortune lies for the taking for the man who solves this problem. If one can reliably imbue soldiers with powers to put them on par with these powered annoyances, I would imagine the process to do this would command a high price, no? I am not a petty peddler of drugs, Rosa, I am a visionary."

"And you think you have a way to do that, huh?" Rose wondered if she could just try and zap him with her captured tazers before he sprang whatever surprise on her he had cooked up, but they were still fairly far apart.

"Ah, well, I suppose you will have to tell me," Tigre said as he moved closer. His eyes were a lot lighter than she expected. In fact, they were a brilliant green. Even the whites, she suddenly realized, and the pupil was vertical now, like... well, a cat. His form swelled suddenly, his carefully tailored shirt ripping as muscles stretched and grew beneath his skin. His fingers lengthened, claws emerging from the ends of them, and pale fur was sprouting all over him. "It is not merely an affectation, my nom de guerre," Tigre's voice had deepened, roughened. "My mother believed in many old ways, and had a shaman pray over me. The shaman said the tiger was my spirit guide, my totem. I thought it only fitting that I seek to integrate that into my business, and now, into my very being." He was nearly growling, eyes narrowed. "Let us dance, senorita, and see what you have learned under the tutelage of your mentor."

Rose eyed the much more feline man that approached her, and one thought crossed her mind— she really considered herself more of a dog person.

Chapter 14

ARGENT PULLED TWO OF HIS TAZER DARTS from his belt and muttered, "Here, Kitty, Kitty," as the tigers began stalking towards him. He didn't think they usually hunted in groups, but wasn't sure about that. "Shoulda watched more Animal Planet or something," went through his mind as he moved carefully, trying to draw them away from Rose and also find a better position for himself. One growled at him, and he felt the hairs on his neck rise. This was far from his usual territory. He threw a tazer dart at it, which made it shake its head but had no other real effect. "Great, too big or too amped up on whatever he's been feeding them," he thought.

One lunged at him suddenly, and he flattened himself, letting it pass over him as he rolled to the side. Another tiger landed on the spot he'd just been in, claws raking the floor as he turned his roll into a leap to his feet, just in time to kick on his powers and jump straight up, evading a third cat lunging at him. "Ok, this is not working too well," he said as he hung from the ceiling, held in place by a flutter of his power. An idea came to him, and he smiled beneath his mask. "This is either gong to work or go down in history as one of the worst ideas ever." He studied the cats' positions below him, swung his legs, and then launched himself downward, landing astride one of them. The startled tiger jumped, bucked, and spun, trying to dislodge him, but Argent held on with strength, super power, and desperation in equal measure. The other two tigers were confused, watching the first's antics but not sure what to do. One came too close, and the near- frantic beast paused in its attempts to dislodge its rider long enough to swat at it, claws out.

That was enough of a clue for Argent. As if he were riding a horse, he jammed his heels into the sides of the tiger he had landed on. Startled more than hurt, the beast lunged forward, running into its fellow feline. Already agitated from the fight, and from the scratch it had just received, that animal, in turn, growled and attacked. Argent leapt high, tucking into a somersault in midair and landing lightly on his feet, then dodging to the left as the third tiger landed where he'd just been standing, claws drawing sparks from the floor beneath the carpet they cut through effortlessly.

Necessity is the mother of invention, but desperation can be a close second. The proverbial light bulb went off over Argent's head. He cast a quick glance over his shoulder to check his positioning, and dodged a few more lunges as the other two beasts fought. Finally, he was as ready as he was going to be, and faced the tiger. Its tail lashed, eyes narrowed, a long low growl coming from deep within its throat. "C'mon, Kitty, let's get this over with," he said, line thrower held tightly in one hand. Just before it leapt at him, he added, "I really hope this works."

The tiger sprang, roaring, front paws extended, claws glittering in the light. Argent timed his move with precision and hope, and fell on his back, bringing his legs up, uncoiling them and pouring as much power as he could into his repulsion field. The surprised beast flew over his head in a low arc and crashed in a heap on the floor of one of the cages. Argent fired his line thrower, hooking the cable to the bottom of the cage door, and hauled on it, triggering the retractor, anchoring himself in place with his power. There was a slight groan of stressed metal, and he had time to think, "Well, crap, now what?" when the over-stressed grate gave way and crashed down. It was far from seated perfectly, but it would keep the now-infuriated beast inside. Argent lay there a moment, panting. There was a difference between super strength and what he could do, and his quivering legs were reminding him of that very loudly.

However tempting it was to simply lie there and twitch, he knew both that the other two tigers wouldn't keep fighting forever, and that Rose would likely need his help. Suppressing a groan, he rolled over and pushed himself to his feet. From the way his legs were feeling, any more springing or leaping was probably a bad idea. Standing wasn't seeming like a great idea either, but he had limited choices just now. Rest later, he promised himself.

He lurched a step forward, and allowed himself a wince, glad once again for his full-face mask. Damn, he must have pulled about everything in his legs. He then realized that the slam of the gate on the first cage had gotten the other two tigers' attention. Both were staring at him with far from friendly expressions. Argent briefly wished he had a steak or something to toss into one of the other cages to lure them in, then realized the closest thing to that around at the moment was him, and banished the thought. "Don't suppose you wanna just step in there and call it a day?" he asked, pointing at the other two cages. A low rumble answered him, and he frowned under the mask. "No, didn't think so. Guess we do it the hard way. Soon as I figure out what that is."

He mentally ran through a quick inventory of everything on his belt in his head and dismissed it all as not useful for this situation. When he was creating and updating his usual equipment, fighting oversize predators wasn't something he'd had in mind. "Ok, no toys, no jumps, no brilliant ideas." He paused for a moment, looking around for inspiration. "This sucks."

With a loud snarl, one of the tigers pounced, jaws snapping. Argent sidestepped and drove his stiffened fingers just behind the hinge of the cat's jaw. It snarled, shaking its head, backing off a pace. "That woulda knocked a person out, ya know." Argent commented, limping back a step or two. The beast focused on him again, snarling and spitting. It swiped at him and he dodged backward, a bit too slowly this time. The claw sliced through his armored costume, and he felt a burning pain from the cut. Looking down, he saw a thin line of red welling up down the length of his arm, stopping just above his wrist. Inspiration struck finally. Backpedaling again, he yanked his wristband off. As the great cat snapped at him again, he timed his move carefully and jammed the wrist band into the animal's mouth. It stumbled backward, confused, unable to close its mouth, the "Exterminator" lodged in place. It wasn't choking, but couldn't get it loose. Argent looked at his bare wrist, shredded sleeve, and the empty spaces on his belt where the tazer darts had been. "I better wrap this up before I end up naked," he thought.

The third tiger looked towards the one trapped in the cage, and the other that was shaking its head and pawing at its mouth. It turned its green eyes on him and made a sound that was part hiss and part growl. It swiped at him with one massive paw, and he ducked, feeling the rush of air, followed by a faint tugging sensation. The sleeve of his costume fluttered free and he grabbed at it from force of habit. "Great, special flex-armor from the Doc and you're still just shredding through it. Bad Kitty!" It snarled, stalking him. He brushed his hand along one of the pouches at his belt and then had an idea. "Ok, let's see if staying old-fashioned has its advantages."

Argent emptied the contents of the pouch into one hand and yelled "C'mon, furball, let's do this." It reared back, preparing to roar again. As it drew in a breath, Argent flung a hand-full of grey powder into its face. The roar became a confused sneeze, followed by several more. Eyes tearing, it rubbed at its face with a paw. Argent jumped forward, hissing in pain from strained muscles. Deftly, he wrapped the reinforced sleeve around its head, making it harder for it to open its jaws and pinning the paw to the side of its head. It glared balefully at him, hopping unevenly. Argent gave a tired chuckle. "Ha! Let's see a digital fingerprint reader do THAT, Doc! Old fashioned powder to the rescue."

He wanted to just lie down and rest, but couldn't let himself. Now that he wasn't about to be mauled, he turned his attention back to El Tigre Blanco and Cobalt Rose, reeling a bit, trying to psych himself up to plunge ahead and help out his partner against the man behind all this.

Chapter 15

ROSE STEPPED TO THE LEFT as El Tigre circled the desk, keeping it between them. "I'm guessing that's more than just a make-over?" she asked, her mind racing.

"So very much more, yes. We have worked on this for so very long, to refine this process, perfect the complications along the way. We went through a great many millions of dollars, courtesy of all of those desperate drug users, and more than a few test subjects, many from that same source." His voice was lower, hints of a growl on many of the words. "Fortunately, no one will miss them, I do not think. Street scum, junkies– one could argue that I am doing more to 'clean up the streets' than you two and all your kind."

"I bet their families don't see it that way." Rose scanned the desk, looking for anything that seemed as if it would be able to help. Nothing seemed particularly promising.

"That is why men of vision are reviled in their own time, Rosa. We have the strength to do what needs be done, to not allow ourselves to be swayed by cheap sentiment. Are you certain you will not join me? You have strength, and a certain force of will, or you would not be here now."

"What is this, your 'Come to the Dark Side' speech? What would I be in your version of my life? Bodyguard?" Rose kept her voice mocking, not caring what he actually said as her mind raced, trying to come up with something approaching a plan.

"Of course not. Not only are you far too lovely, but, practically speaking, I could not trust you to that degree. But I am certain we could find something for you." Even with feline features, that smile made Rose's skin crawl.

"Not interested. I'll take my chances. And so far, you're not really impressing me. The plans were good, you're tricky as hell, granted, but here and now, you and me? All talk. And fur." Rose was coming up with the bare bones of an idea, but wasn't sure at all how well it would work.

The smile was certainly gone now. "Then allow me to remedy that, Rosa." With a casual grace that bespoke no real effort at all, El Tigre vaulted over the desk, his claws slicing through the spot Rose had been in just a moment before. Using her parkour skills, general agility, and a healthy helping of "Oh, shit!" near panic, she evaded the claws, barely. Rose had learned to be realistic in the arena of combat, even in her comparatively short time on the streets, and she had to admit to herself that this might be a bit out of her league right now. He seemed to have strength and speed at the very least on her, not to mention those talons on his hand. Realistically, she would be willing to swallow her pride and let Argent deal with this one. But, he seemed to be busy, as she risked a quick look and saw him fighting the three large beasts. "Right, on my own. I can do this."

El Tigre clearly seemed to feel he was in complete control, and was toying with her. Maybe the change was more than skin deep, Rose mused. She dodged two more swings, those wicked claws whistling near her. Finding herself behind the desk now, Rose flipped over the chair, landing with her hands on the back of it, and threw it at him. Without bothering to move aside, El Tigre knocked it aside, his claws slicing it into smaller pieces. "Yeah, more than skin deep," Rose thought.

Drawing a deep, centering breath, she took up a fighting stance. "Ok, let's see what you got," she said, sounding cocky.

"I always try to oblige a lady," he snarled, jumping forward again, claws out. Rose rolled to the side, sweeping her hand back in a blow that had no real power behind it, but didn't need to. He howled in pain, hopping backward, anger and confusion on his face.

Rose held up her hand, triggering more sparks from her captured tazer. "I think these might be this girl's new best friend," she said while waving it back and forth. Roaring, he swung again, and she ducked, striking with her other hand, zapping him again. "Two-for-one sale," she taunted.

She spent the next few moments parrying and dodging a flurry of blows, suffering a variety of small cuts on her arms, the wrappings that held her thorns tearing on one side. He paused, clearly about to launch into some speech again, and she dropped, sweeping at his legs. He leapt up, easily avoiding her leg, landing lightly, mockingly making a "no, no" gesture with one finger ticking back and forth. Rose moved to attack, and actually made him dodge back as she attacked high and low with the tazers in her hands and followed with a driving kick to his chest that made him stagger slightly. She followed up with a low kick which he avoided, and landed a tazer-punch to his upper chest in almost the same spot as her kick. He flailed at her, hissing in pain this time, and she fell back, keeping his claws from parting her skin as easily as they did her armored costume, strips of it falling aside along her ribs. She saw his eyes drop to the exposed skin and thought "Men!" as she stepped back, swinging the tazer in an arc more to keep him off her than actually try and connect.

"I have the power of my totem, and you have tricks. You can not hope to win this fight, Rosa. Surrender, and I will spare you," El Tigre said, displaying his claws menacingly.

"Yeah, you look really merciful," she answered. He's got the speed, strength, and claws. So how do you beat someone stronger than you are? She remembered her different studies in the various marital arts disciplines so far, and something from akido went through her head– "Turning your enemy's strength against him." Rose had her light bulb moment while she dropped to the floor and rolled under another strike. She came to her feet quickly and stabbed at him with her right hand, tazer extended. He blocked her, striking the inside of her wrist, sending the tazer sailing off.

"You can not beat me. You will die in great pain. Your partner will be scraps on the cage floor of my guardians. Yield, Rosa. It doesn't have to end this way." She stomped low at his feet, making him give ground. She sparked the tazer, thrusting it forward, making the fur on his arm rise with her near miss. El Tigre flashed a smile of triumph, moving in close to her, claws raised.

Rose brought her right hand back up, tazer gone but something new in it. El Tigre howled in pain as the cloud of pepper spray enveloped his head, hands flying to his face to rub at his eyes and nose. He swung blindly, roaring, choking on the gas. Even partially incapacitated, he was dangerously fast, and Rose felt a stinging pain along her shoulder. She sprayed him again, and then drove her remaining tazer into the cat-man's shoulder, discharging it once more. She dodged his answering swing, and kicked out hard, catching him in the groin. The growl died off into a strangled yelp as El Tigre bent, clutching himself. Rose kicked him hard in the chin as his head came down, reversed her kick to catch him in the temple, and then brought the tazer down hard between his eyes. With a hissing yowl, he fell to the floor. Rose grabbed several heavy plastic ties from her belt and carefully fastened them, pinning his elbows together behind his back, then his wrists, then his legs at the ankles, knees, and upper thighs, linking a few together for his leg muscles. "Doesn't matter how strong you are, you don't have the leverage to break those."

Rose turned to see if Argent needed help, and saw him limping towards her. "Caught the end of that. Nice. What'd you do to him?" the obviously wounded hero asked.

"Well, if he was all about being a cat, I thought I'd use that. Pepper spray can drop most normal people from that close. With sharpened senses? He had a real miserable time of it. You ok?" Rose looked at him, seeing the tears in his uniform and a few traces of blood.

"I'll live. Had worse. How about you? There was a bit more to that costume, last I looked." He pointed down to where she'd been cut, and she saw that she'd lost several sections of her uniform, and had various cuts all over her, but was still decent by most standards.

"Nothing too bad, but I'm kind of a mess." She answered.

"Looking good to me," he replied. He moved over to her, pulling up on his mask, and they kissed again, much longer this time, arms around each other. After what seemed like a very long time, they broke apart, looking at each other. "We better get some of this neatened up before the cops get in here." Working carefully, mindful of each others injuries, they managed to get the tigers back in their cages, and even got what was left of Argent's wristband back. He looked at it and shook his head. "This thing's trashed. I wonder if the Doc has the next version designed yet." A thought struck him. "Hey, where'd you get the spray? I know that wasn't one of Doc's toys."

She smiled. "I'm a woman living on my own in the big city. Of course I have pepper spray. Doesn't everyone?"

Chapter 16

THE CHAOS THAT FOLLOWED was familiar to Argent, but another new experience to the Cobalt Rose. Argent had called a contact of his at the police department, and soon, a special unit of the police arrived. The Parahuman Crimes Unit had special training and advanced weaponry to deal with criminals that had metahuman powers or high tech weapons. Argent had dealt with them a lot, and he spoke to Lt. Driscoll with an easy familiarity. Driscoll was a short woman with raven black hair and a very take-charge attitude. Rose had seen them argue several times already tonight, but it seemed to be one of those relationships made of friendship buried in mock-antagonism. Argent wasn't the only one used to dealing with the PCU (an abbreviation they hated, and there were rumors afoot of a coming unit name change), and shortly after they arrived, the press started showing up, somehow always managing to learn when the unit had been dispatched. A large scale police operation that included superhuman restraint vans and evacuating an apartment building wasn't something that could be kept quiet.

Driscoll pulled out a cigarette, lit it, and blew out smoke, sighing once. "So, you done recklessly endangering the public? Superheroes are irresponsible untrained vigilantes, blah blah blah. That's out of the way, thanks."

Argent made a mock bow. "Most welcome. Those things'll kill ya, ya know."

Driscoll looked at her smoke. "With this job? Please." The last three people before her to lead the PCU had died in the line of duty, and department superstition now had it that this was a deathtrap, a "promotion" to get troublesome officers out of the way. Driscoll had managed to hang on for six months now, and was closing in on setting a record. Argent hoped she made it, he kind of liked her.

Driscoll tilted her head slightly, her helmet ear piece buzzing slightly, and said "Press is out front and asking for you."

"Great. You guys done with me?" Argent asked, sounding half hopeful.

She laughed. "No such luck, hero. We don't need you. Shoo." She made a flicking motion with her hands, illustrating her point. As she did, another of her officers came up.

Doug Page was about 6'6, 270 pounds, with incredibly dark skin and massive muscles. He looked like he should be playing for the NFL. His true gift was actually computers, which surprised people when they first met him. "LT, we got what must be 500 pounds of Venus so far, and about as much of some new shit. Most of the computers are even still logged in. I guess the research types left in the middle of their work."

Argent spoke up, "The new stuff is called Mars, it's some kind of aggression stimulator or something, be careful with that crap." Doug, whose nickname was Tech (of course), nodded and spoke into his mic. Argent looked around for the Cobalt Rose and said, "C'mon, we're not done yet." The two threaded their way through hordes of police who were taking pictures, studying the room, and doing the hundreds of things involved in processing a crime scene this large. Argent exchanged handshakes and taunts with various cops, a few of them giving Rose second or third looks. She was attractive enough on her own, but her originally revealing costume, now ripped and torn, was getting admiring glances from many of the officers.

As they left the hidden lab and re-entered the actual apartment building, even more police were interviewing bewildered tenants, befuddled at being awoken in the middle of the night and told they were living in a villainous lair. Taking the stairs down, they exited the lobby and were greeted by an array of lights and an instantly sprouting field of microphones. The media had arrived in force while Argent and Cobalt Rose had been running the police through what they'd found.

A tall blonde man spoke up loudest and clearest. "Jeff Brody, News 9- Argent, can you tell us what happened in there tonight?"

Argent spoke in a voice that surprised Rose, louder and clearer than she was used to, "Well, this was the headquarters of the drug dealer El Tigre Blanco and his gang. With the help of the Paranormal Crimes Unit, we're sorting out the extent of the operation. But, if you want to talk to who ran the investigation, to the one who took El Tigre down? That'd be her." Argent pointed at the very surprised Rose. "The Cobalt Rose. I was just assisting."

The camera shifted to Rose and she felt a rush of gratitude, excitement, and pleasure. "Hello, Jeff it's nice to meet you. This all started a few months ago..."

Some time later, after many questions, the heroes made their escape via line thrower, providing some suitably dramatic footage for the news cameras to end the interview. Alighting on the roof of the next building over, Argent asked her, "Everything you hoped?"

Rose shook her head, smiling. "It was a blast, and I'm grateful you let me do that, but no, I don't think that's what this is about." She paused. "Jeff is cute, though."

Argent laughed. "I'm sure he'd love to hear that."

Rose moved closer, smiling at him. "So... is that hot tub still open?"

Argent put his arms around her and answered, "Depends. Who's asking?"

She pulled his mask up enough to kiss him again, and then whispered "My name is Laura."

He smiled, lowering his head to her ear. "Then yeah, Laura, it is." He kissed her just under her ear and she shivered at his lips' touch on her neck.

"You going to carry us there?" she asked in a breathy voice.

Argent let out a low, pained chuckle. "My legs are shot. That's why I used the line to get away from the reporters. It's going to be a slow hobble across the rooftops to get there tonight."

"You're such a romantic," she teased, as they began making their way across the city. After a longer time than Argent was used to taking, they arrived at a building that looked like any other to Rose. She peered over the side. "The Dark Knight? You're taking me to a bar? Wait, wasn't this one of the ones I thought was hinky on my search a while back?"

He moved over to the skylight and tapped in a code on a keypad next to it. "Kinda." He unhooked a cable and dropped it inside, climbing down. As he dropped from view, he asked "Coming?"

Wondering what she was getting into, Rose waited until he was clear and then followed. She dropped lightly into a large empty space. After a moment, she recognized it as a small dojo. The floor was covered with mats, the walls bedecked with various styles of weaponry. One corner held a large, clearly well used punching bag, with a set of weights and jump rope nearby. She looked around, impressed. "Nice set up. This all yours?"

"Actually, I own the building. Well, me and the bank, but I'm ahead on payments."

"Nice. The bar down there yours, too?" She was slowly turning, taking in the room and all the items in it.

"Yeah, that's why I'm ahead on payments. We do okay down there." He moved closer, pulling his mask off completely. "But that's not why I asked you over, and I hope not why you came."

"No, not really." She smiled, turning and gave him a much longer kiss, pressing herself against him. He put his arms around her and pulled her to him, their bodies tight together. After a few moments, she pulled back long enough to ask, "Where?"

Argent took her by the hand, grabbing his mask with the other, and led her out of the dojo to a large tiled room. A luxurious looking shower was set up in one corner, with a heavy duty washer and dryer on the far side. Between them, dominating most of the space, was a large spa hot tub. "Ooohhhh," Rose let out, staring at it in a moment of covetous wonder. It's huge, she thought.

"You can still change your mind if you want," Argent said. "I know you can get a hell of a rush after a take down like that, if you want some time to think about this," was as far as he got before she interrupted by grabbing him and kissing him again, hard, her body pressed to his, leaving no doubt at all about her desires at this point.

Chapter 17

ARGENT SMILED AT HER as they broke from their kiss. He pulled off the top of his costume, looked at the shredded mess where the sleeve used to be, and tossed it aside. Rose let her eyes play over him. He was well-muscled, which she expected from seeing him in action and the brief glimpse before when they had changed. What surprised her was the network of scars all over his torso and arms. Argent looked like he'd been hurt badly and often. Was this what she had to look forward to?

He crossed to a cabinet, typed in another code on yet another security panel, and opened it, taking out a small vial which he turned and poured into the tub. "The mighty Argent likes bubble baths?" she teased, watching. The water slowly took on a brighter quality somehow, glowing on its own. "What IS that?"

"Something the Doc cooked up. Helps speed up healing, longer you're in, the better. If you think we can come up with a way to pass the time." He was smiling now, with a definite wicked bent to it.

"I'm sure we can think of something." She crossed the room to him and kissed him again, hands running along his body slowly, fingers feeling the change in texture over his scars. He returned her kiss and she felt his fingers moving over her, undoing what was left of the upper half of her costume. Laura shivered at the feel of the air on her exposed skin, contrasted with the incredible warmth coming off Argent's body. They both paused long enough to get their own belts off-- the perils of booby-trapped heroic gadgets in the midst of passion. JT's hands worked lower, pulling the rest of her costume off, tossing her boots aside. He admired her body, toned and fit from constant training. Laura knelt, pulling his boots off one at a time, and then stood, arms around his neck. Pressing her bare skin to his, she whispered, "Didn't you say something about us needing to be in there?" and inclined her head towards the tub.

"Yeah... musta got distracted somehow." JT smiled at her, leading her around to the stairs up to the raised tub and then lowering himself into the water slowly, letting out a small sigh of enjoyment.

Laura started to follow and then stopped as her foot dipped into the water. The hot water felt great, and she couldn't wait to feel it on her sore muscles and various wounds, but there was something more. "It tingles. Why does it feel like that?"

"Side effect of Doc's stuff, something to do with the healing properties." His voice dropped lower, huskier. "Now get in here," he added, giving her a look of need and want.

Laura slid into the water, feeling the tingling all over. She moved towards JT, and then stopped for a moment, ducking under all the way in the deepest part, enjoying the feeling playing over her skin. "Oh, that feels great," she said. Moving closer, she punched him lightly in the shoulder. "And that's for not telling me about this sooner." Then she kissed him again, next to him on the bench, the water covering most of their bodies, her tongue moving over his lips.

They broke from their kiss and she moved her lips down his neck, over his throat. In a much different voice from how he usually sounded, JT asked, "And what was that for?"

"Because I want to," Laura said. She ran her hands down his body, beneath the water, and found he was definitely ready. She stroked him slowly, once, twice, making a sound between a sigh and a moan come from his lips. Laura moved her hands to his shoulders, pressing him back against the side of the tub. "Your legs are hurt, keep still," she said, moving herself to straddle him, sitting in his lap, facing him, arms around his neck, stopping for another long kiss. Laura straightened herself, rising more out of the water, and JT put his arms around her waist and pulled her to him, his mouth finding her breast. She moaned as his tongue moved over her taut nipple, then louder as he sucked her sensitive flesh into his mouth. Her head rolled back slightly, eyes closing as she enjoyed his attentions, the strange additive in the water definitely increasing her sensitivity. Finally she moved lower again, locking her eyes with his. She moved herself just so over him, and then reached down, guiding him as she came down, slowly taking him inside her. They both shivered, keeping their eyes on each others as she lowered herself. With him fully inside her they both stopped, enjoying the sensation, not moving but shivering slightly from the pleasure.

As one, they started moving. Laura rose and fell, each motion bringing another sigh or gasp from them, JT thrusting up to meet her. Her arms were around his neck as he held her at the waist, hands stroking up and down her back as they moved together. Their time of mutual desire, the long night, the euphoria from surviving yet another near-death experience, and the added sensations from the concoction in the water combined to bring a rush of pleasure that climbed to ecstasy in practically no time at all. Crying out in mutual release, the heroes lost themselves in a virtual explosion of shared pleasure. After a few moments that seemed to last forever and yet go by too rapidly, Laura leaned her head on JT's shoulder, her breath still ragged, heart pounding. "That was worth the wait," she panted out, smiling.

Her expression was mirrored by JT's. "Oh yeah. Never done that with this stuff in the water, that was…" he shrugged helplessly, "wow."

She chuckled. "Yeah, that's about right." She kissed him softly, hand running along his scarred shoulder. "So, do I get a collection of these too?"

JT looked down at his shoulder. "Probably not. Doc's stuff seems to work really well. Even the nasty shit that should scar forever goes away pretty quick with that stuff."

"Then why do you have so many scars?" she asked, kissing the rough skin. Knife wound, she thought.

"Because I did this for a good while before I met her, and this stuff is relatively recent. New wounds won't scar, but it's not a miracle in a bottle." He shrugged again, still smiling, as she lightly kissed his neck. "You won't end up looking like me."

She leaned back, still in his lap, held in place by his arms, mock sternly. "I would hope not! I worked hard to get this body. I'll keep it, thanks."

He smiled "Yeah, I like the differences, too," and ran his fingers lightly over her breast, causing her to shiver again. After a short time, caresses and kisses led to more, and they made love again, slower, starting to learn each other's bodies until they exploded once again.

In the months that followed, Argent and the Cobalt Rose became a well-known team, patrolling the city, going after the kinds of crime major league teams like Freedom Squad, New Citadel, and the Wardens never seemed to get around to. They fought gangs, super villains, and even teamed occasionally with Freedom Squad, both refusing full time membership.

The Dark Knight's finances gained a new accountant, and began turning over more of a profit. And the wait staff increased by one, a lovely woman who showed up occasionally and gained a reputation for a ready wit as she bantered with her customers. Everyone who worked there noticed that the boss was in the best mood they remembered seeing him in. The dojo upstairs saw a lot more use as a master fighter gained an enthusiastic new student. And the hot tub was used a lot as well, with and without Doc Lydia's additives.

THE END

Murphy's Hero

By Dara Hannon

Chapter 1

TIGER IRON CROUCHED ON THE EDGE of the tall apartment building, eyes closed, listening. He hoped tonight would pay off so he could get this mission over and go back home. He hated staying in hotels. He could never get a decent night's sleep in strange surroundings. Besides, he just knew Azure was not feeding his rats and plants correctly. He'd probably get home to find Fluff and Puff too fat to do more than waddle, and water stains under all of the potted plants.

Unfortunately, the whole team had agreed that he should be the one to make contact with this new hero that had been in the news lately. It had even been put to a vote. They had assured him that it had been thoroughly discussed when they had called him up to tell him about the vote and its result.

To be fair, though, he would have voted for himself too. He usually had the best results when making a new contact. Due to his training and abilities, he was better at honestly assessing a new hero or heroine. His even temperament put people at ease so there were none of those stereotypical "hero meets hero, hero misunderstands hero, hero fights hero" situations that provided so much fodder for late night comedians. Some of them still made jokes about the last time Azure went to meet a new heroine and the two of them managed to ruin a national monument. In fact, Soulforge, the Wardens' resident builder, was supposed to be finishing up the repairs this weekend.

Taking a deep breath, Tiger Iron pushed those thoughts out of his head. The sooner he tracked down this new hero, Murphy, the sooner he could go home. Focusing, he found a calm center and listened to the noises of the night. According to the news reports, Murphy liked to hunt a nearby park that backed up against a warehouse district. It was a favorite meeting place for drug dealers, and they seemed to be his preferred prey.

Tiger Iron didn't have much else to go on. According to his research, Murphy attacked small groups and had, so far, managed to move fast enough that the criminals were unconscious before they got a good look at the hero. The closest thing Tiger Iron had to a description was "the shadows came alive and swallowed him." Too bad thugs were not required to take classes on basic observation. Of course, if they were smarter, it would be harder to stop them, so he guessed it was a decent trade.

After Murphy disabled his targets, he always tied them up, called 911 and left a note. That was how everyone knew Murphy's chosen handle. The drugs and money were always found near the bound criminals along with a memory card containing film of the crimes. However, when the money was tagged for evidence and the amounts mentioned to the suspects, they all claimed that some of it was missing.

Not much to go on, but Tiger Iron had speculated about a few things. One, Murphy was either a hero or wanted to be if he was targeting criminals and not taking the drugs. However, since he appeared to be taking some of the money, there was a question about exactly how much of a hero Murphy was. Tiger Iron was going to find out.

Faint sounds of combat just at the edge of his hearing drew his attention. He could discern punches, grunts and curses. Grabbing onto the rope he'd secured earlier, he quickly rappelled down the side of the building. Without pausing, he ran out of the alley and into the lightly forested park, doing his best to stay off the lighted paths while at the same time, traveling in more or less a direct line.

The fight ended before he arrived but that didn't bother him. His real purpose was to get there before Murphy had a chance to disappear. The trees gave way to a picnic area with a metal picnic table bolted to the concrete under a worn tin roof. Four thuggish looking men and one weaselly one were unconscious and tied up to the posts holding up the roof and the table. Murphy had been careful to keep them separate so they wouldn't be able to help free each other if they woke up before the cops arrived. He had stacked two duffel bags on the table and was closing one of them, humming a happy tune. Murphy slipped something under his long black cloak.

At least, Tiger thought the cloak probably explained the 'shadow coming alive' description. If properly used cloaks and capes added a certain dramatic flair.

Murphy was pulling out a notepad and pen when Tiger Iron decided to reveal himself. He hadn't meant to be quiet, but he definitely surprised Murphy.

The other hero's head popped up and he brought his right hand back in a throwing arc just as Tiger Iron stepped forward. The throw was wild, and Tiger Iron dodged out of reflex rather than concern. As he shifted to the side and out of the way, the soft ground gave just enough to throw off his footing. His knee and ankle tried to go the wrong way, and he had to take a stutter step to keep upright.

Unfortunately, the adjustment moved him back in the way of the improvised missile and the pen bounced off the bridge of his nose. It didn't do any real damage but it surprised him and he blinked. When he gathered himself back together, he was more surprised to see that Murphy hadn't disappeared.

"Ooh! I'm sorry. I thought you were...well...I guess it's kind of obvious what I thought you were." Murphy's voice seemed rather high for a man, more a nice alto than a baritone even though it was muffled. No wonder Murphy didn't trade barbs and quips with criminals. Tiger Iron hoped he wasn't dealing with a teenager.

Quickly regaining his composure, Tiger Iron smiled, though it couldn't be seen very well under his gold and red mask. "No problem. Understandable," he said as he studied the younger hero.

Murphy wasn't that tall, probably closer to 5' 6" than 6'. He was slim even with the cloak obscuring most of his body's detail, though Tiger now saw it was a dark purple not actual black. Murphy had on a deep hood that shadowed most of his features and a burgundy scarf over his lower face.

"Uh, I was just going to finish my note and then go." He lifted his hands and then, remembered he wasn't holding the pen. "Oh, oops, did you see where the pen went?" He nervously walked forward scanning the grass, muttering, "And my other one's out of ink."

Tiger Iron wasn't listening. He'd been watching Murphy approach and was startled enough to do something he rarely did - speak without thinking. "You're a woman."

Murphy laughed softly and glanced over from the great pen search. "Yeah, last time I checked." From this angle, Tiger Iron could tell her eyes were blue and she had smeared gray makeup on her face to further hide her identity.

Taking a deep breath, he continued to watch her look for the pen. She eventually pulled a flashlight from one of the pouches on her belt.

"I'm sorry. That sounded bad. I was just surprised," he said.

"Yeah, I know...ah, there it is." Crouching, she retrieved her pen and traded the flashlight for her notepad again.

"I have to admit that it's a clever way to hide your identity... making everyone think you're the other gender."

She shook her head ruefully. "That was all an accident actually."

"Well, my name is Tiger Iron. I'm a member of the Wardens."

"I know who you are. I mean, you don't really get into this without being a little bit of a superhero fan, right?" He could hear the smile in her tone as she finished her note and placed it on the duffel bag.

"I'm not sure I would put it that way. However, I came here to get to know you. We like to help out new heroes." He left out the part about keeping an eye on new people and making sure they were what the seemed to be. A villain in hero's clothes or even a corrupt hero was not a good thing and the Wardens preferred to try to head situations like that off before it was all over the front page. "I scouted out a quiet rooftop nearby once you're done here."

She slipped the pen and notepad away under her long cloak and turned her shadowed face toward him. "K, I'm ready." She walked over to him and he could hear the laughter in her voice. "Just don't try anything funny 'cause I've got my pen and I know how to use it."

He chuckled as he turned and led her back to where he'd left the rope.

Chapter 2

TIGER IRON QUICKLY CLIMBED to the apartment building's roof and stepped out of the way before turning to look back. There was no one there. Frowning, he waited a few more minutes. Still no Murphy. He grumbled, reproaching himself about how he should have made her climb up first to be sure she didn't rabbit. It was a rookie mistake and he'd never hear the end of it if the rest of the Wardens ever found out.

Of course, she hadn't seemed hesitant about talking to him, his pride argued. How was he to know she'd run the moment his back was turned? Well, actually not the exact moment. He knew she'd been with him at the base of the wall before he started climbing. Maybe there was a chance he could still catch up to her.

Resuming his crouch on the edge of the building, he scanned the area and immediately found her. She was on the ground below about thirty feet farther along the wall, trying unsuccessfully to pull down the fire escape ladder.

He shook his head. Tiger had thought the invitation to use his rope had been obvious. Apparently, she was either too shy or polite to just follow him up without an explicit invitation. He watched as she studied the iron ladder that was just out of her jumping reach and had, so far, resisted her efforts to snag it with her scarf, which had left her face exposed.

He took a moment to study her even as he made a mental note to chastise her for taking such a risk with her secret identity. The gray makeup evenly covered the upper half of her face, smudged along the lower half where it had met the edge of the scarf. Her skin was pale. Not unhealthy ghost pale, but it was obvious she was not a fan of the sun. He was pretty sure the dark red of her lips was due more to lipstick than nature but the color was striking and emphasized her rueful smirk as she stared up at the fire escape in what he could only describe as amused frustration. Her black hair was held away from her face by a double ponytail but he couldn't tell how long it might be since it disappeared under the color of her cape.

He sighed. Tiger didn't normally object to the chance to study a beautiful woman. However, this was not getting his mission finished. It took him only a few moments to climb back down the rope and stride to her side. He did his best to keep any impatience or reproach out of his voice. "You can use the rope if you'd like."

With a small sound that sounded suspiciously like an 'eep', she turned away and hurriedly rewrapped her scarf around her face before pulling her hood back up. He found it funny that she should suddenly take so much care to hide her face. He was pretty sure, at this point, he could recognize her out of costume. It was all rather careless of her.

She must have realized the same thing since her first words once she was properly masked and cowled again were, "Okay, let's just pretend that didn't happen."

Tiger Iron was glad his face mask hid his broad smile and took a deep breath to keep from laughing. He didn't want to offend her. "So," He couldn't think of a clever segue so he decided to go with blunt, "Now that that's settled—"

"What's settled?" The cowled head tilted a bit in question.

"That you don't have to mess with the fire escape, you can just use the rope."

"No, I can't."

Tiger stared at her for a few moments, confused. He decided to stick with blunt before he got a headache. "Why can't you use my rope to climb to the roof so we can talk?"

"Because I can't." She looked down and fiddled with her combat belt which moved her cloak out of the way so he could get a better look at her. She was wearing a black body suit with obvious pieces of armor sewn in over the stomach and leg muscles and probably in the arms though those were still hidden. Black combat webbing encircled her waist and looped over her shoulders, covered in small pouches. Her body was athletic, not skinny, but she was carrying the extra weight in the places a woman wanted to be curvy. His eyes continued down to her boots to check if she was wearing spike heels which could explain her resistance but, no, she was wearing sensible black boots that he would guess were steel-toed.

Apparently it had to be some kind of obscure reason, personal or maybe cultural though he couldn't detect any kind of accent. He tried blunt again though he was losing hope it would help him avoid the headache. "I gave you permission."

She laughed, not a giggle but a full laugh. "That doesn't really help in this case."

"What?"

Murphy shrugged. "You could give me permission to fly but it doesn't change that I can't. So, giving me permission to climb a rope... kind of just as useless."

"You can't climb a rope?"

"Nope, guess I was sick the day they taught Heroic Rope Climbing 101." Tiger continued to stare at her and she must have sensed his disbelief. "Look, I'm working on my upper body strength but...it takes time, OK? It's not like I don't have other things to work on too."

She was running around in costume fighting bad guys and she couldn't even climb a rope? Tiger barely restrained himself from shaking his head. What was she even doing out here? He looked around and saw a park bench in a fairly large clearing. "How about there?" He tried his best to keep his voice even and noncommittal.

"Yes, I do believe I have enough strength to walk over to a park bench without falling." His thought that apparently he had failed at his attempt at a nonjudgmental tone had failed was interrupted by another of her unembarrassed amused laughs as she headed over to the bench, leaving him to follow.

Chapter 3

THEY WERE SEATED ON THE PARK BENCH and Murphy pulled her cloak tighter around her. It really wasn't that cold but sitting on a park bench with one of the Wardens was kind of intimidating, especially for an amateur. She firmly reminded herself that, no, she wasn't an amateur, she was a heroine.

Of course the sarcastic part of her mind wasn't silent. 'Yep a heroine that throws a pen at a world famous martial artist and can't climb a building...oh and let's not forget that everyone thinks you're a guy, right?'

Murphy was grateful for the makeup and scarf that hid her blush. At least, she hoped they were hiding her blush but the way this night was going... who knew? She decided to rush on to a new subject before they could discuss her climbing failures. "So... ummm... I told you I'd tell you why people think I'm a guy."

Tiger Iron nodded, his face impossible to read behind his full face mask with its stylized tiger head design. She'd always found it interesting that the overall tiger design of his body suit was done in flame colors such as gold and red instead of the typical yellow and black or the almost overused black and white. Though how he managed anything resembling stealth in it, she wasn't sure. He was also taller than she had expected. His body was lean like most martial artists but she was sure he could easily bench press her.

"Well, it's not really my fault."

"I don't remember blaming you." His voice was somewhere between a low baritone and a high bass, unusual but nice to listen to.

"True, but you gave me credit and that's kind of the same thing only in a nice way." She was babbling and she was fully aware of that fact. That didn't make it any easier to stop though. "Well, I was actually going to go by Lady Murphy but my first note sort of fell into a puddle and the 'Lady' part got smeared and I heard the police coming so I didn't have time to rewrite it. I'm not sure what happened to the second note. I mean, I left it on top of the cases completely away from the mud just so it wouldn't get smeared... but the news called me Murphy not Lady Murphy. Then the third note... I thought I put it on a dry case. It's not my fault. It was so dark that I didn't see the blood splatter that soaked through the 'Lady' part again."

"And the cops were almost there so you, again, didn't have time."

She smirked in amusement. "No, actually, that time I did have the extra time... I just forgot my notebook so I didn't have any other paper to replace it. But, by that time, I'd been in the news enough to be known as Murphy and, well, I figured fine, I'm Murphy. I mean, obviously my luck wasn't going to let me change it and it had taken me more than a month of constantly thinking up names to come up with Lady Murphy. All the others were so much worse that I burned the lists out of embarrassment. So," she shrugged, "I just stuck with Murphy and here I am."

He nodded. "Well, it's still a good way to protect your secret identity. It would help that anyone looking for you is looking for a man."

She shrugged. "Yeah, I guess... so... ummm, you said you were supposed to get to know me for the Wardens. Do you have a checklist or anything?"

"No. Usually it's just a matter of talking. For instance, why did you become a hero? You mentioned something about being a fan..."

He let his words fade leaving the question open. She shook her head slightly. "No, I'm not some fan girl hoping to grab glory and autographs from the big names. I mean I really do want to help people."

Tiger Iron nodded though she couldn't figure out if he believed her or not. "There are many ways to help people. What made you choose this way?"

She softly bit her lip as she considered what to say. It wasn't like she had a dramatic origin story. No dead parents or secret labs. No tragic childhood trauma or accidental radiation exposure. According to articles she'd read on the Wardens, Tiger Iron did their questioning and some criminals claimed he'd used some power to invade their minds to tell when they were lying. The accusations were never confirmed or denied but it gave her something else to think about before she answered.

"Well," She decided to go with the truth. It was boring but at least she wouldn't have any trouble keeping her story straight later.

"Like I said, I want to help people... but I hate paperwork. So, that kind of ruled out police or medicine. I mean, I'm sure the paperwork is necessary but... really it's completely ridiculous... ummm... anyway." She cut off her rant before she revealed how familiar she was with the subject. Being a court clerk was not the most prestigious job or an overly sensitive one, but she still didn't think that volunteering that information would be in her best interest. "So, anyway, I like my MMA classes, gadgets and helping so... hero just seemed the thing to do." She didn't mention her luck power. It had always been too hard to explain and she didn't want to get into it now.

He nodded in apparent understanding. "Why do you take the money?"

Chapter 4

"WHAT MONEY?" Murphy tilted her head in a convincing display of curiosity.

Tiger Iron wasn't buying it. Even if she wasn't taking the money, if she'd read enough of the news articles to know they were only calling her Murphy instead of Lady Murphy then she knew what he was talking about. The criminals who had managed to give interviews were telling every reporter that would listen that the money in evidence was short, accusing Murphy of being a thief or dishonest in an attempt help their defense attempts.

"The money that doesn't make it to the evidence lock up."

"Oh, that money." She took a few moments to tuck her cloak tighter around her. "Criminals lie, you know. So what does it matter what they're claiming?"

Her tone no longer had the easy amusement it had once held and he was convinced the criminals hadn't been lying. "It matters because heroes don't steal. I was sent to make sure that you are what you seem to be."

"Right, yeah. Can't be having me do any good without a stamp of approval." The growing bitterness in her tone disturbed him more with each moment.

"It's not like that--"

She cut him off, standing up. "No, it's like that or you wouldn't be asking me about the money, just whether or not I give the cops enough to successfully prosecute. Just for the sake of argument, if I was taking some of it, and I'm not saying I am, if I was, what's the harm? Where's the cash going to really go, huh? To bunches of administrators before it gets anywhere else. And who does the money really belong to? Most of it is probably stolen anyway and, you know, not everyone gets paid to do good. Not all of us get to live in some big base and being a hero costs money. So, just for the sake of argument, why don't you tell me how to get out of the catch-22 that you have to be a big hero to be picked up by a big rich superteam, but you can't be a big hero if you don't have either money or some big awesome cheap power!"

She didn't give him a chance to answer before turning in a swirl of a cloak and striding off. It took him a moment to respond. Her change from friendly with a great sense of humor to angry and offended had shocked him. However, they still needed to have a discussion, so he went after her.

She disappeared into a tangle of trees. He followed and ducked under a set of branches when a rock beneath his right foot gave way. He twisted as his training took over. He grasped one of the thicker branches almost out of instinct and shifted all of his weight to his left foot. By the time he realized that he stood at the crumbling edge of a ravine which had been hidden by the undergrowth, he had already started swinging back to solid ground.

Unfortunately by the time he had recovered his footing, Murphy was gone.

He scouted the area for signs of her, but he didn't find any clues. He wasn't surprised to find she had disappeared. She obviously wasn't interested in continuing the conversation.

Sighing, he gave up the search and went back to his rope. Once he was on the apartment roof, he pulled up the rope and unhooked the grapple, stowing them in his small backpack. A few leaps between rooftops and he reached his hotel. From the hotel roof, he had a view of a highway off ramp instead of the park. He sighed again.

He hooked the grapple onto the edge of the hotel roof that he had marked earlier and rappelled down, carefully counting windows. Breaking into the wrong room would be embarrassing at best. Once he reached his room, he carefully pried open the window and climbed in. After checking to make sure the room was empty, he reached out and tugged the rope with a practiced move that unlatched the grappling hook so he could roll up the rope again, replacing it in his backpack. It didn't take long and wasn't difficult, but he was glad that his teammate, Soulforge, had designed them so they wouldn't break a window. If he missed one of the swings and the grapple happened to bounce off a window, it would have sounded more like a bird hitting the glass. No one would be the wiser as long as he pulled it up fast. More embarrassing than entering the wrong room would be a hero that caused property damage while trying to be stealthy.

He quickly shed his costume and stowed it away in the false bottom of his suitcase. No matter how well designed, armored costumes were uncomfortable and hot to wear. His costume had armor plates over the chest, legs and arms, like Murphy's actually when he thought about it. It left him sweaty and in need of a shower, which he started once his gear was stowed away. He probably could have waited to pack up the costume until morning, but it was better safe than sorry.

As he stepped under the hot water and washed off the night, he thought about what he was going to do now. It was obvious to him the papers were right. Murphy was taking some of the money. She wouldn't have reacted the way she did if she wasn't. That would need to stop. Heroes shouldn't steal, but it didn't disqualify her from being a hero depending on her motives and what she was doing with it. He needed to catch up with her and talk to her more.

Unfortunately, he was sure that wouldn't happen tonight. He doubted she was going to be out in the park again after their encounter so that meant he had to spend another day in the hotel.

He sighed as he dried off and put on a pair of old jeans and a t-shirt. Running a hand through his short black hair, he picked up his Warden's Communicator. The name wasn't his choice. Soulforge was a bit of a Trekkie. Lying back on the bed, he dialed up Azure.

"Hey, Ti, how's it going?" Azure's light alto answered after the first ring. "You catch up with Murphy? Is he cute? Did the dating pool here improve?"

He smiled as he answered. "Fine. Yes. Not a he. Don't know."

"What do you mean, not a he?" Her demanding tone used to annoy him but now, he just accepted it as part of her personality. Although she was pushy, she had always come through for the team and she was an effective field leader.

"Murphy is a woman. She was supposed to be Lady Murphy but the name got covered up on the notes through different accidents so everyone just assumes that Murphy must mean a guy."

"Okay, so you got to talk to her, I'm assuming. What's the verdict?"

"I'm still not sure. Accidentally hit a sore spot that interrupted the meeting. I'll have to catch up with her again."

"Why didn't you just stop her from leaving? I've seen you do it with crooks so don't tell me you don't know how."

"Azure, think about her name for a minute."

There were a few moments of silence. "You think she's got luck power?"

"How often do I trip?"

"You don't."

"Well, I almost did tonight. Twice."

"Ah, well, be more careful next time you catch up to her."

"I will." Now that his report was complete, he decided to change the subject. "How're Fluff and Puff doing?"

"I had to go and buy more of the flavored chew toys today and picked up some more food for them."

He rolled his eyes. "I don't give them the flavored chew toys. You know that."

"But they like them."

Yep, pushy with people, softie with animals, that was Azure. "And I left enough food for them for another week."

"No you didn't. The poor things were starving. Fluff keeps stealing Puff's food so Puff never gets to eat."

"They are not starving. It's a game. Puff doesn't like people to watch him eat but if you pay attention, Puff steals the food back from Fluff."

"There was no food in there after I was done watering your plants." Her voice reflected her stubbornness. "Fluff ate it all and poor Puff couldn't have had any and he was just lying there, skinny and pathetic with wide little eyes. He was hungry so I've been giving them more."

"Azure, I've told you, animals lie and Fluff and Puff are excellent liars."

"They do not."

He shook his head in amusement. "I'll prove they're not starving. Go to my room."

"Okay, but I don't know how you're going to prove it."

"Just trust me." He heard some doors open and close before she spoke again.

"Here."

"Open the cage and check under the two wooden houses."

"I don't know what you think I'll find. Yes, yes, I know you're hungry, I'll feed you in a minute." Tiger knew the last wasn't meant for him so he just quietly waited. "Now, let's see... Hey! You little tricksters."

"Find it?"

"Yeah yeah, I see what you mean. They have enough food hidden away for at least two days. You don't have to sound so smug. Now, I need to go and do some actual work. Call me when you find out more." The words would have sounded clipped except he could hear the suppressed laughter at his rats' antics.

"Will do." He turned off the communicator with his own chuckle It was late but he still wasn't tired. Checking the time, he decided to get out and see what kind of food places were open nearby.

Chapter 5

MURPHY CROUCHED IN A SHALLOW CAVE she had discovered and used for her changing room, counting to 1000. There was no movement to indicate Tiger Iron had followed her so she quickly pulled a folded backpack out of one of her pouches and began shoving her scarf, cape and combat webbing into it.

Moving a couple of rocks, she unburied another pouch and opened it, sliding the chain with her keys over her head and using the wet wipes to clean off the gray makeup until it was just around her eyes so anyone who saw her would just think she liked dark eye makeup.

Her eyes burned. She told herself it was from the fumes of the wet wipe but she didn't believe herself. She'd never been much of a liar. Still, she pushed it away for the moment. She'd deal with the disastrous events of the night later.

She pulled out a long skirt, decorated with cartoon skulls and roses and slipped it on, covering up the lower half of her body suit and then added a lace choker and her favorite silver bracelets. A black velvet short jacket completed the look of a young woman with goth-vampire tastes. Well, technically it wasn't a look, but she was glad that her preferred clothing style tended towards dark and layered.

Pausing a few moments to make sure no one was around, she reburied the pouch and left her shelter, striding purposefully across the park towards the apartment building Tiger Iron had led her to before. Running her fingers through her hair, she smirked at the coincidence. That amusement lasted until she'd walked up the two flights to her apartment and gone inside, to be faced with her favorite poster of Tiger Iron.

She sighed and leaned back against the closed door, locking the deadbolt out of habit. She hadn't been lying when she said she was a fan of heroes. She just left out that it was specifically the Wardens and even more specifically him. She'd finally gotten to meet him and hadn't even gotten an autograph. Nope, she'd had a little temper tantrum and stomped off. Great going there. Brilliant really.

She muttered a soft, "Shut up," to herself and tossed her backpack onto the couch before heading into her kitchen to grab a bottle of water before taking her shower. The cape and costume might look cool but it was hot and she didn't need to deal with dehydration on top of everything else.

An hour later, she was feeling cleaner and more comfortable in a coffin and rose decorated tank top and black jeans. Unfortunately, she was not feeling more relaxed. She paced back and forth with nervous energy, still annoyed at herself. She understood that it wasn't the most heroic thing to take part of the dealers' money but she'd seen what happened to it. It went into evidence and then it was supposed to go to the department for more equipment and the schools. However, a large chunk of it, well larger than she thought was fair, got eaten up by administrative costs. Meanwhile the cops who'd done the busts still had to worry about mortgages while being ridiculously underpaid for the jobs they did.

Yes, she took the money but not for selfish reasons. Part of it went to her gadgets but she also used it to buy the digital cameras she used to take videos of the deals before she attacked. She then left the cameras with her notes so the cops had evidence. Another portion of the money was anonymously donated to families of cops that had been injured in the line of duty. The rest of it, she donated to other cops, teachers and rehab programs. Never a large enough amount at one time to be suspicious but a couple hundred here and there helped the people that needed it without filling the coffers of the politicians and the paper pushers who seemed to always come up with more paperwork to justify their existence.

It was stealing, but it was for a good reason. Of course, sitting there face to face, well scarf to mask, with Tiger Iron, she'd felt like a selfish thief. How could she explain it to one of the Wardens, especially him? Tiger Iron was known for being the most straight arrow honorable member. At least according to all the articles she'd read and interviews she'd seen. He was always calm and polite to even the nosiest, pushiest reporter and was the one to reassure the public that, yes, the Wardens would fix any major property damage that came from their fights with various villains.

She had really not wanted to hear disapproval in his voice, not directed at her. So, she'd panicked, let her temper carry her away and probably made sure he thought she was a nut case. Just perfect.

Tired of dealing with herself, she slipped her ID, credit card and cash into her back pocket, grabbed her keys and headed out to her favorite dance club. Maybe loud music and any friends that might be there would help her forget. At least it would wear her out so she'd be able to sleep tonight. Luckily, she didn't have to work the next morning.

It kind of worked.

Her favorite DJ was working the club that night. He was an old friend and when she waved to get his attention, he'd played a couple of her favorite songs which put her into a much better mood. However, it was on her third trip to the bar that she really forgot about her problems that night by acquiring a new one.

She didn't mind the guy in the suit offering to buy her drinks. It certainly saved her money and, judging by his suit, he could afford them. He wasn't bad looking even if he was dressed more for a board meeting than for a club. However, his insistence that she keep up with his drinking was definitely a turnoff especially since it seemed he wanted another drink after every other song. She started off with polite refusals and proceeded to outright,"No, I'm not drinking that." None of it seemed to penetrate his alcohol induced armor. When he asked her back to his place for a nightcap, she agreed. Not from any interest in him but from a worry that if she didn't go with him, he wouldn't get to his hotel safely, or maybe even at all and she didn't want that on her conscience.

Which was, of course, how she ended up in front of a hotel door pushing the guy against a wall so maybe he'd remain standing while she searched his pockets for his room key. It took a little while since she kept having to slap away grabbing hands from the drunk who insisted on misinterpreting what she was doing.

She had just managed to open the door and was about to help him in when he clumsily grabbed her from behind, groping her as he slurred. "I like a woman that's so eager enough to open the door herself. Get ready for the time of your life."

She was thrown off balance but managed to brace herself on the doorway. "Oh for... Get off me."

"Ooohhh, you wanna play shy?"

"I am not shy but I don't feel like dragging you into your room or getting crushed by you if you pass out here. So, go in there and lie down." She elbowed him in encouragement, but he was too drunk to pay any attention.

"C'mon, it'll be fine." He placed a sloppy kiss on her ear though he had probably been aiming for her neck.

She was working on how to get away without leaving him unconscious in the middle of the hallway when another player entered the comedy.

"You need any help?"

Chapter 6

TIGER IRON HAD NOTICED THE COUPLE when he had returned from his late night snack. Usually, he would have been mildly curious since the two of them were dressed so differently. However, he recognized the face of the woman, Murphy.

He wasn't completely sure why he had decided to follow them and he certainly didn't understand why it annoyed him to see her with the drunk. He hadn't known her long enough to form any opinions about her taste but, for some reason, it bothered him that she would willingly go home with a guy so obviously looking for a drunken one night stand. He decided not to study that feeling too closely.

It soon became apparent, especially from her sharp slaps at his wandering hands that she was just trying to deliver her companion to his room. She seemed to have things in hand until her date almost literally fell on her. Watching her stagger under the weight prompted him to action. "You need any help?"

The annoyance in her blue eyes changed to gratitude. "Yes, if you could get this gorilla off me and into his cage, I'd really appreciate it."

Tiger grabbed the drunk's arm and pulled it off Murphy and over his shoulder, his knee pushing at the other man's knee just enough to throw off the man's balance and cause him to lean more on Tiger.

Murphy's date was not grateful. He glared at Tiger. "Hey, who are you?"

"I'm here to help." Wrapping an arm around the drunk's torso, Tiger began to half drag the other man through the door Murphy was holding open.

"We don't need any help. The girl and I'll manage fine without you."

Tiger had serious doubts about that since the man's voice was getting sleepier and his steps were more unsteady with each moment. He figured arguing was pointless, so he simply made a noncommittal noise.

Murphy had followed them in and was checking the air conditioner when Tiger got her date to the bed and dumped him on it. The hero frowned. Had he misread the situation?

She walked over to the bed and grabbed the pillows and the extra blanket. "Help me get him lying down on his side. Don't want him choking on his own vomit."

Tiger Iron did as she asked, glad the guy had finally lost consciousness. Murphy shoved the pillow and blankets along the sleeping man's lower back as fast and firmly as she could.

Tossing the room's key card on the dresser, Murphy started for the door. "Let's get out of here before he wakes up."

Tiger Iron followed her and made sure the door locked behind them.

She smiled up at him, blue eyes sparkling. "Thanks for the assist. Wanna cup of coffee?"

He considered for a moment. It was late but he didn't want to turn down the opportunity to talk to her. Maybe he could find out more this way. "Sure unless you need to get up early."

She made a motion as if waving away a fly. "I'm not going to be sleeping anytime soon. In fact, I'll probably stay up all day just so my sleeping schedule isn't completely screwed before Monday morning."

He frowned. Patrolling while short of sleep was never a good idea. Of course, he decided to ignore the many times he'd done just that before he had become a Warden, back when he had to maintain a full time job to pay for his rent, food, etc. "I saw a Starbucks a couple of blocks away."

She looked away. "Ummm, maybe someplace a little cheaper if you don't mind. I don't really budget for brand names."

"I would pay."

That earned him an amused glare. "You trying to get me in trouble? I invited so I have to pay. The feminazis would have my head."

"There is always my room. It has a coffee maker."

She laughed. "Oh no, single woman safety 101, no going to some stranger's room for coffee especially when you meet him in the middle of the night alone and no on my apartment either. I don't know if you're normal or not and I wouldn't feel safe if someone normal knew where I lived."

Although her answers were amusing, he noted that they were running out of options.

"I was about to suggest this nice little 24-hour cafe I know if you can stand having normal coffee." She slipped her hands into her back pockets, and he couldn't resist taking a moment to admire what the move did for her chest.

"That sounds fine."

"K, follow me." She turned and led the way to the stairs, and he thought for a moment he heard her hum something from a Disney movie. However, she stopped after only a few seconds so he wasn't sure.

The cafe was located in a strip mall. The counter was in the back corner of the open main room. The middle of the room was taken up by two glass topped tables and one large one with outlets set in the surface at regular intervals. Couches and low tables were scattered along the walls. Next to the counter was a bookshelf full of a wide variety of books, battered from repeated readings. Overall, it felt relaxed and welcoming.

At the counter, Murphy put in an order for a hot chai tea and Tiger smiled in amusement.

"A normal coffee?"

Murphy shrugged with a smile. "I changed my mind. Now what do you want? Oh and do you want a donut or anything?"

He shook his head. "A small coffee will be fine."

"It's okay to get something else. I mean I'm not poor or anything. I just don't like paying extra for advertising."

"I like coffee."

She shrugged and paid for the drinks. They took a break in the conversation until she led him over to a couch in the corner. He watched her sit back against one couch arm, one leg curled under her. He sat down on the middle cushion, careful not to crowd her but close enough that they could talk in quieter tones. He wasn't sure where this conversation might lead but he didn't want eavesdroppers.

She smiled as she took a sip from her cup. "My name's Mara." She waited for a few moments before smiling in amusement. "And yours?"

Chapter 7

MARA SMILED AS THE MAN GRIMACED in amused embarrassment.

"Sorry, was surprised for a moment. My name's Jace."

Her smile widened into a grin. "Why were you surprised? Exchanging names is a common custom."

He nodded and took a sip of his coffee. "Yes. But, since we are already past the custom of invitations and purchasing drinks, I had forgotten we had skipped past the name custom." He gave a low chuckle and Mara joined in, laughing at the absurd twist the conversation had taken.

"So are you from around here?" It was a stupid question considering she had met him in a hotel. She defended it to herself by pointing out that it was a common conversation starter.

To his credit, he didn't laugh at her or give her a strange look. "No, I'm just in town on business."

"What kind of business?" She'd always been a curious person. At one point, she had even thought of going with a cat motif for her hero ID. However, she had worried about what would happen if she got a chance to meet Tiger Iron. There had already been a real chance that she might act like a fangirl. She didn't want to be creepy stalker copycat fangirl. Not that her meeting with the hero had gone well but at least she hadn't acted like a fangirl. Score one for embarrassment. Pushing away the memories, she focused on Jace's answer.

"I'm an independent security consultant."

She smiled. "Let me guess, if you tell me more, you'll have to kill me?"

He chuckled again. "No, nothing like that. So, are you from around here?"

Mara had the idle thought that she would prefer to learn more about him. She liked his voice and it seemed familiar but she couldn't place it. She probably needed either more coffee or more sleep. Odds were that she would figure it out right before or right after she fell asleep. Still, he was waiting for an answer. "Um, yeah. Strange as it might sound, I've lived here pretty much my whole life."

"You never wanted to live anywhere else?"

She shrugged. "As bad as it may sound, not really. I mean I like it here. I'm not against moving in general, I just never really found a reason to."

His head tilted in curiosity. "Do you still live with your family?"

She laughed. "No, definitely not. My parents were planning a really nice home theater in my old room and getting quotes the same time I was planning my graduation party."

He joined in with her laughter. "I can understand. My father made sure I knew I was welcome to visit any time but that he had raised me to be a man and he expected me to be one. So, have you had a chance to check out your parents' new theater yet?"

Mara looked down, running a finger along the edge of the cup. "It was never completed. There was a car accident."

"I'm sorry."

"My dad survived, but he couldn't handle the house by himself. He's living in a good place though. I mean I would have helped out, no problem, but dad wouldn't put up with it. Said he didn't need his daughter making excuses to put her life on hold just cause she was scared to live on her own." She looked up, smirking. "That wasn't it and he knew it. Just his way of telling me he'd be okay."

Jace nodded. "Sounds like something my own parents would say. So, what did you do to get on with your life? Are you in college?"

She laughed, grateful for the change of subject. "No, not that young. I work as a file clerk at the court."

"You like it?"

She shrugged again. "It pays the bills and can get frustrating. I mean, for a paperless society, it's ridiculous how much paper even the smallest parking ticket requires." She shrugged in frustration. "I mean I'm grateful for the job, but it's such a waste and wouldn't be needed if more people would just do what's right."

He nodded in sympathy. "If everyone did right, that would put a lot of people out of work, cops... heroes."

She rested her cheek in her hand. "I think they'd be happy to be out of work."

He took a sip of coffee, his green eyes meeting hers. Mara noted he had really nice eyes, set off by his short black hair and tan skin. She was only half paying attention when he asked, "You think your local hero, Murphy, would feel the same?"

Her distraction caused her to answer before thinking about it, so her tone was harsher than she would have liked. "What do you know about Murphy?"

Chapter 8

JACE SHRUGGED NONCHALANTLY. It might not have been the most subtle way to introduce the topic but he was tired and she seemed a rather direct person. "Just what I've read in the newspaper and online."

She tilted her head in curiosity though he thought he could still see some suspicion in her eyes. "You read up on heroes regularly? Like a fan or something?"

He smiled softly. "I told you. I'm an independent security consultant. Crime rate and law enforcement are both areas of professional interest to me." He took a long drink of his coffee. "All I know is a few of the more recent stories. He is a vigilante that works mostly against drug dealers. The people he's had arrested claim that he steals part of the money, and the police aren't giving any statements at all. So, it just makes me curious as to what kind of hero he is. Does it make you feel safer to know he's out there?"

She frowned and stared down at her cup. "You know, you can't really trust drug dealers. They're not upstanding citizens out to help their fellow human... more like opportunistic, manipulative..." She trailed off but her breath was coming faster and she was frowning. "Anyway, who cares if they lose money?"

Definitely a sore spot. He considered her for a few moments. "What about the police department that made the arrest? Seized money is to be distributed to the department for more equipment or to the local school system."

She made a very unladylike sound of disgust. "Yeah, after who knows how many years of appeals and motions and legal wrangling? It just sits there for all that time, taking up space, not doing anyone any good and, then, when it finally gets out, how much of it really gets to the police and the schools? I mean to the real police and the teachers, not the administrative level that fills out the paperwork and makes decisions from nice insulated offices based on numbers and theories produced by companies that only really make money if they can think of something wrong with an existing system that can be fixed without the entire community actually getting off their couches and doing what's right to begin with." She took a deep breath and stared at him, studying him, probably trying to figure out his reaction.

Jace remained quiet as he thought through her explanation. Her frustration was palpable. From what he could piece together, her intentions seemed to be benevolent. He still wanted to know what she was doing with the money. Was it, perhaps, how her father was living in the community she had mentioned?

He decided to quietly probe a bit further. "So, you approve of Murphy's actions?"

"Well, I--," Her words cut off, and she stared closer at him. "You." She lowered her voice to a forceful whisper. "I know who you are. You're Tiger Iron!"

He looked around. The nearest person was at least twenty feet away and was listening to headphones. Still, he leaned in closer and kept his voice soft. "What makes you think that?"

"Your voice. I knew I recognized it." Her expression seemed to be caught between victory, apprehension and anger.

He wondered how close she would come to admitting who she was. Taking a long sip of his coffee, he quietly asked, "And how do you know Tiger Iron's voice well enough to think you recognize it?"

Her eyes narrowed. "You know very well how I know what your voice sounds like. I never thought you were stupid so don't insult me by thinking I am."

She was not happy, but she hadn't walked away yet so he proceeded. "So, do you want to explain what you do with the money?" He didn't think there was anything to be gained by denying the truth. She had been aware enough to figure it out, and he had never agreed that such things should be undermined with manipulation, unless the person being undermined was malevolent. By this time, he was convinced that she might be misguided, but she was trying to be on the side of good.

"Why do you want to know?"

"I gave you the reason earlier."

She rolled her eyes. "Well, remind me."

"My group likes to help newcomers to the business."

Her blue eyes hardened. "But only if the newcomer meets your standards."

He shrugged slightly, not bothering to deny it. She was clever. "Our standards are not that difficult to meet."

"Oh really? And here I thought the War--" She cut off as he gave a short sharp jerk of his head toward the rest of the cafe. "The big names had high standards."

"For being part of us, yes we do. For helping people... well we help those that need help... as long as they're not part of the problem."

"Part of the problem?" She raised an eyebrow, and he read the unspoken question in her expression.

"The problem of crime, corruption and the strong preying on or taking advantage of the weak."

She leaned in closer. "And you think because the scum are claiming to be victims that I'm taking advantage of them?" Her voice was lower than before, and he could feel her breath across his cheek.

He kept his expression neutral. They probably appeared to be a couple sharing an intimate moment, and his body seemed to think the same thing. He could feel himself responding to the soft scent on her skin. He couldn't place it but it was unusual and seemed to fit her. He tried to take a few steadying breaths, the kind his grandfather had taught him to focus. It didn't help as he breathed in more of her scent. "I'm trying to find out what you're doing."

"Well, why don't you look at it this way—they're accusing me of taking money not excessive force and the cops don't have a warrant out for my arrest and the cases aren't getting thrown out of court. Put that in your little standard equation and see what you get." She abruptly stood up, her body tense and then she turned back and leaned in again, laying a hand on his shoulder for balance. "And don't expect me to jump through hoops for you, and it's supposed to be innocent until proven guilty, you know." With that, she turned away and stalked out of the door.

Jace didn't try to follow her. He'd learned his lesson the last time and did not want to have to arrange for payment for any tables, chairs or doors that might break due to bad luck. Besides, he now had a good idea where to look for her. Their paths would cross again.

Chapter 9

MURPHY KEPT HER HEAD UP and her eyes roaming as she walked back to her apartment. She was annoyed, but that was no reason to be stupid. Walking around the city after midnight and not paying attention to her surroundings would definitely qualify as stupid. Her luck should mean she would get home alright, but she had never seen a reason to push it... especially considering the cost.

Once she arrived at her small apartment, she quickly let herself in and locked the door before throwing herself on the couch. Turning her head, she stared up at the Wardens poster on the wall above her TV. She should have recognized Tiger Iron's broad shoulders and his lean muscled physique. She'd spent enough time staring at him on posters. She had been considering how to get his phone number or slip him hers as well as figuring out how to fit a date in her schedule when she had realized who Jace was. She glanced from the group poster to her poster of just him and was very glad she hadn't invited him home.

"Lucky for me... as usual." She sighed softly.

The logical part of her mind pointed out that she could have told him what she was doing with the cash. Explain why she thought it was necessary.

Of course, she knew that she didn't want to be logical. She wanted him to just trust her.

She rolled onto her back and stared at the ceiling. "He doesn't know you, so why should he? All he knows is those stupid interviews about you, and it wouldn't be the first time a villain has pretended to be a hero and you know it."

But she still just wanted him to trust her, to instinctively know that she was trustworthy.

Rolling her eyes, she pushed herself off the couch. She headed down the hall to the bathroom and turned the water on in her tub. While it filled, she lit some scented candles and grabbed the book off her bedside table. Hopefully, she would relax so she could get some sleep before waking up and finding out this whole rotten night was just some weird dream.

Tiger Iron, on the other hand, was pleased with the progress so far, mainly because there was progress. He wanted to bounce his impressions of Murphy off a third party, but he realized that he'd have to wait until the morning.

He finished his coffee on the way to his hotel, tossing the empty cup in the trash can by the side door. Once safe inside his room, he checked to make sure everything was the way he'd left it then set the window and door alarms that Soulforge had made for traveling team members.

He lay down, but he couldn't fall asleep. It wasn't his usual hotel room insomnia. Sparkling blue eyes kept dancing in his head. She definitely had fire, warm and alluring when she laughed, fierce and dangerous when she was angry.

He was attracted to Murphy. And that meant that he needed to question his judgment. He would have to be careful to keep his emotions from blinding him. More importantly, he needed to speak to his grandfather. The old man had trained him in all levels of combat, including how to battle his own emotions.

His grandfather came from a long line of Shifus, or teachers, carrying martial arts secrets passed from father to son. However, his grandfather was the only son of an only son of an only son and had not produced a son of his own. Though, as far as Jace understood, his grandfather had not shown any disappointment in his daughters or tried to turn one into a substitute son but the lack of a son meant that his grandfather's knowledge would die with him.

His grandfather had been born in America and was an odd combination of tradition and adaptability. In addition to never showing disappointment in having only daughters, he had not objected to Jace's mother dating and eventually marrying a man who didn't have a drop of Chinese blood in him. He had welcomed Jace's father as easily as any other son-in-law.

Jace's mother, though, had made a very strict demand of his father before marriage. They had to always make sure she lived near her father so her first son could be trained. She wanted the knowledge to continue to pass down the family line. Jace's father, out of love for his bride and respect for her father, agreed and enforced the training, even during those times Jace had complained. Becoming Tiger Iron hadn't been easy.

He resolved to call his grandfather in the morning to seek advice. After all, as both his father and grandfather were fond of saying, no man was ever too old to benefit from wise counsel.

Chapter 10

JACE WOKE UP AT DAWN. He was short of sleep, but that meant he needed to focus past it. He spent the morning the usual way, exercises, stretches and technique patterns followed by a period of meditation to the smell of brewing coffee. More than once, thoughts of the previous night tried to break his focus. He finished his meditation, finding peace despite the distractions. He stood and went to the window.

Standing in the morning light, he dialed his cell phone, smiling in amusement. Many of the Wardens made fun of him since he never stored numbers in his phone. His grandfather's training made him think of it as a cheat. It was more work memorizing the numbers but he never had to worry about not being able to contact people if he lost his phone or if its power died.

His mother answered on the second ring. "Jace, what have you been up to?"

"I've been on a fact finding mission that I need to discuss with grandfather."

"In other words, you don't have time for your poor mother whose only grandchildren are two fuzzy rats that never write."

He smiled in amusement at her overly melodramatic tone. "Mom, I sent their thank you note for your last care package out before I left. It should arrive today or Monday." It was a long standing family joke, and he really had sent a thank you note that held Fluff and Puff's footprints. It was a messy project to have the rats run over an ink pad then over the card, plus give them a bath to clean up their paws, but it was worth it for the laughter it brought. "I would also be more sympathetic about your longing to be a grandmother if I couldn't hear my nieces and nephews in the background."

"Well you're wrong there. It's just nieces, no nephews. Your sister Lily is visiting with her daughters. However, before I release you to Father, are you doing okay?"

He smiled. "Yes, I am fine." He couldn't resist a little teasing. "Just like I was the last time we talked... three days ago."

"Yes, and how many times were you fine one time I talked to you and calling me from a hospital bed two days later?"

"Once... twice at the most."

"And that was two times too many." She sighed. "I trust in your judgment but humor me and make sure to tell me you're fine as often as possible."

"I will, Mother. I'm fine, and I'm being careful. I promise."

"Good. Now, here's your grandfather. I'm being summoned off to cookie baking duty."

Jace could hear her laughter fading in the background as his grandfather's deep strong voice came over the line. "Hello?"

"Good day, Shifu." His voice took on the softer, more formal tone it always did speaking to the man that was teacher, family and wise elder.

"You have something to discuss with me." It wasn't a question.

"Yes."

"It has to do with your calling?"

"Yes. I seek counsel to ascertain that my logic and awareness have not been undermined by emotion." His grandfather said nothing, but Jace had known he wouldn't. "I was sent to evaluate a new heroine. She has targeted drug dealers and leaves notes with details of the crimes and a digital camera with the activity recorded. She does not maim or kill but uses tasers and other means to incapacitate the targets and ties them up for the police. The interviews of the incarcerated say the money confiscated is much less than should be there, however there is no mention of a corresponding shortfall in the drugs. I've met with her twice. She is passionate when she speaks of helping others and shows distaste when talking of procedures such as paperwork. I have asked her about what she does with the money both times. Both times she has become offended and stalked off. My impression is that she is not taking the money for malicious or selfish reasons and that she is an honest and earnest new heroine." He fell silent.

Now was the time for his grandfather to speak and for him to listen.

"She is pretty?"

"Yes."

"Fiery?"

"She is passionate when she speaks and freely shares her frustration with unfairness. She seems to face obstacles with more humor than frustration." He smiled as he remembered her staring up at the uncooperative fire escape.

"She does not deny taking the money?" His grandfather's voice was calm as ever, making it impossible to determine what he was thinking.

"Not directly. She becomes upset and redirects the conversation."

"It is simple. She is committing theft."

He frowned. "It is not simple. I commit assault. You have always taught that laws are guides to acceptable behavior but should never be an excuse not to do what is right."

The other end of the line was silent for several moments. Jace practiced calming breaths as he waited.

Finally, his grandfather spoke in the same unreadable voice. "You have already made your decision. Why have you called me?"

Jace took a few more calming breaths before answering. "To seek your guidance. Is my judgment sound?"

"You already know the answer, once-tiger. Remember your father's birthday is next month."

"Yes, Shifu. Thank you."

His grandfather hung up, and Jace felt a strong temptation to growl and crush the phone. He resisted the urge. His grandfather wasn't being difficult out of any malice. There was something here Jace was supposed to learn or realize, and his grandfather expected Jace to be able to do it. His mind kept coming back to the phrase 'once-tiger'. His grandfather had never used it before.

Jace glanced at the clock. He still had a few hours before he could go out Murphy hunting again. He decided to see if he could catch a little more sleep.

It didn't work.

Chapter 11

MURPHY WOKE UP in what might generously be called the afternoon. She had not slept well and felt surly. "Good thing it's a patrol night," she muttered when she saw herself on the mirror. "Be a shame to waste monster Mara on work." She snickered softly as she put on her coffee and yawned.

She checked to make sure she had a digital camera charged up and ready to go. It wasn't really cheap to leave them at each crime scene but necessary. Working as a file clerk in the courthouse, she knew about too many criminals going free because of lack of evidence. Tying them up next to the evidence didn't work because, amazingly, all of them became innocent bystanders who were there by mistake and didn't know what was going on when the unreasonable hero attacked and tied up everyone in sight. Leaving a note detailing what the hero had seen wasn't enough either since any decent lawyer got it thrown out as hearsay and violation of the defendant's Fourth Amendment right to face his or her accuser.

She frowned. Funny how those 'innocent bystanders' never had anything to do with the drugs that were either just lying there or 'planted' on them while they were unconscious, but the money was a different story. They usually came up with reasons to be carrying around rolls of hundreds and bags of cash. It was interesting how they never denied a connection to the cash.

She shook her head in disgust as she shoved the camera into her bag along with a new pen. At least leaving the camera at the scene helped.

She made sure to take videos of the deal and left the entire camera so the date stamps could be checked, and there wouldn't be grounds for any tampering accusations. Her notes giving the cops permission to watch and use information on the videos made them admissible in court and, since there were a lot of precedents for allowing legally recorded images into evidence, it got around the

Fourth Amendment. Put all together, the cameras helped get convictions, but were completely beyond the budget of her paycheck. This was why she used part of the drug money to fund the cameras. Plus using cash made it harder to track where she bought them. Of course, she still had to be careful and change where and when and how many with each purchase. It was annoying but necessary.

Slipping her pack over her shoulder, she headed out to the park to finish getting ready. On the way, she wondered if she might run into Tiger Iron again. Part of her hoped yes but part hoped no.

The more hopeful part kept pointing out there had been chemistry between them and who knew what might happen. Her logical side pointed out that it might explode in her face because he would probably never approve of her.

She muttered a quick quiet to herself as she changed in the small cave. If he was good for her, her luck would bring him to her. If he was bad, her luck would keep him away. Though, if that was the case, she really hoped it didn't result in some disaster that needed the Wardens' full attention.

Murphy pushed those thoughts away. That was beyond her control and she needed to focus for tonight. She didn't need to be so distracted that someone had to be unlucky enough to break their leg or worse, their neck, to be prevented from sneaking up on her.

Carefully moving through the trees and sticking to the shadows, Murphy made her way around people enjoying the night air and each other's company. She stopped when she encountered any groups and took a few minutes of video, focusing on faces and distinguishing marks such as tattoos. Never could tell when something bad would happen and the police would need to know who had been present. She preferred giving them more information and potential witnesses than they needed rather than not enough.

Eventually, she found what she was looking for, tucked in a corner upwind from the public restrooms but near enough to them have a decent chance of flushing the evidence if he spotted trouble. Quietly settling herself in the deep shadows, she scanned the area. There were two men farther up the path talking quietly and scanning the area carefully, probably the dealer's spotters. She didn't see anyone else so she brought out the camera and started recording. As before, she used the zoom to focus on the three men's faces and tattoos then returned to a wide shot, hands carefully cupped around the softly glowing screen. She always set the brightness as low as she could, but it was better safe than sorry.

It was a slow night for the dealer and Murphy's left foot threatened to go to sleep before a customer showed up along the path. She wiggled her toes to encourage blood flow as she focused on the face of the would-be buyer.

After exchanging a few words with the sentries, he was waved through, and Murphy focused on getting a good shot of the deal, almost holding her breath to keep the camera steady. A twig snapped behind her.

She tried to turn and block with her arm, but it was too late. She felt a sharp blow to her head, a burning sensation near her shoulder, and then nothing.

Chapter 12

As Murphy woke, the first thing she was aware of was a burning pain in her shoulders. She kept her eyes closed. More details followed. She couldn't feel the ground beneath her feet and her arms were stretched above her head. She was hanging from her wrists. Her scarf and hood were still in place for some reason, and she could feel the straps of her combat webbing digging into her skin.

She tentatively wiggled her fingers and toes. Nothing seemed broken and, with that, she had pretty much come to the end of what she could find out without advertising that she was awake. Slowly opening her eyes, she peered out from under her hood.

She was still in the park not more than ten feet from where she'd been spying on the dealer. She didn't see him. Rather than look for the dealer, she decided to study the two men in front of her

One wore a dark blue costume with an elaborate web of lightning strikes across his chest in whites, blues and purples. She didn't remember any villains with his costume, but he obviously had some power. Otherwise, he wouldn't be wearing a colorful skintight suit in the middle of the park this late at night. Over in the red light district? Yes. Here? No.

It occurred to her that she should have done more to get hooked up with the HeroNet information network thing that a lot of costumed heroes mentioned in interviews. Maybe she'd know more about her electrical-looking friend. Of course, she couldn't manage to get through a conversation with her favorite member of the Wardens without storming off. Oh well, hindsight and all that.

The other man was taller and more thickly muscled with no neck to speak of. If he'd been wearing a suit, she would've looked around to see if she'd stumbled into the filming of a mafia movie. Instead, he wore jeans and a Bromston Wasps basketball jersey. His dark brown eyes were studying her with malice and, from the thick gold rings on his fingers and the thicker gold bracelet on one wrist, he looked the boss of people she'd been putting in jail.

Using her most pleasant voice she asked, "Now that I'm awake, could you please go ahead and let me down? Oh, and turn yourself in to the police of course."

The boss smirked at her. "You've got spirit."

She tried to shrug, but the motion only made the ache in her shoulders worse. "Not really. It didn't hurt anything to ask."

His smirk became more pronounced. "That's where you're wrong. I never said I liked spirit." He motioned to lightning strike guy.

The costumed man pointed at her. Electricity shot out and danced along her skin, stinging and making her muscles jerk involuntarily. She had expected this to be his power from the costume, but it didn't make it hurt any less.

After the current cut off and she could breathe again, she gave a short breathless laugh. "I wasn't wrong."

The boss' smirk turned cold. "Are you going to try to be really brave and claim that didn't hurt?"

"No, of course it hurt. That's why you had it done. It still doesn't make me wrong." She forced herself to keep her voice amused.

He cocked his head in curiosity.

"You were going to torture me anyway so my question really didn't change anything, did it?" She glared at him. "I'm not stupid. You want something, or I'd already be dead."

He nodded and stepped closer to her. "Yes, I want my money back."

"I don't have it."

He motioned and his companion, once again extended a finger. Every muscle tightened in pain and she could smell burnt ozone. She wasn't sure if she screamed or not and, at the moment, she really didn't care.

The pain stopped suddenly, and her entire body went limp.

The boss leaned in closer. "You've been amassing quite a bit of my money including two shipment payments. You give it back to me and no more pain."

It took a few moments to get her breath back to answer. "I can't give what I don't have. It's gone."

She tensed, anticipating another bout of pain. The boss crossed his arms. "You call yourself Murphy after Murphy's Law, right?"

"Yeah."

"You do realize your luck's turned against you, right? That things just took a turn for the worst?"

"Luck is a matter of perspective. You don't know if it's good or bad until the end." After all, she wasn't dead yet and that meant her luck had a lot of room to work.

He laughed at her. "How philosophical. You really think this is gonna be anything other than a tragedy for you? You took my money, and someone's gonna to pay for that. I can give you a hint who it is."

"Tragedy is in the eye of the beholder. If there was any chance you were gonna let me live, you'd have already stripped off my equipment and costume."

"No." He stepped back and gestured to his companion again.

Murphy wasn't sure if she screamed or not but she knew something was very bad when she tasted blood and smelled something burning.

"I haven't removed your costume because I'm not interested in breaking some faceless nobody. I can do that anytime I want. No, right now I have an opportunity to break a real live superhero. You're going to die, Murphy, but I'm not going to go after your family. I really don't care about them so you're not protecting them by remaining silent. All I care about is my money... well that and making an example of you. However, you don't have to make it difficult. Tell me what you did with my money, and I'll have Spark kill you quickly. Otherwise, well, he can go all night. Can you?"

"I gave it away."

She didn't see him motion to Spark, but he must have because every muscle in her body spasmed in agony.

"I doubt it. Not that much. What did you buy with it? Think I can get refunds?"

She didn't have any more breath to trade quips with him, and she didn't have any other answer to give him. She let her head fall forward and waited for the next punishing bout of electricity. She didn't see what happened next.

Chapter 13

When Tiger Iron heard the scream, he was sure of two things. It was a woman and that woman was Murphy. His first instinct was to run as fast as he could directly towards the sound. He fought the urge. His training told him that getting himself caught wasn't going to help her.

He took a single deep focusing breath and scanned the direction the scream had come from. There was a stand of trees cutting off his view. They would serve as cover and let him approach undetected. He took an extra moment to make sure no one was watching before running to the trees.

Crouching in the shadows, he listened carefully, part of him hoping not to hear her cry out again and part of him listening anxiously for it since it would mean she was still alive. As he approached as silently as possible, he heard the conversation and was unable to resist a smirk as Murphy taunted that tragedy was in the eye of the beholder. He could see them and started counting. There were three men over at the path apparently keeping watch, another guy flanking Murphy, the man that seemed to be the boss and Spark, electricity powered torturer for hire.

Murphy screamed again.

It took every ounce of the will that his grandfather had painstakingly instilled in him to stay still. Impulsiveness steals strength and increases trouble. The old mantra played easily in his head but it didn't make it easier to wait until the moment was right. Spark had to be his first target.

Thought turned immediately to action as he rose to his feet before launching into a jump kick aimed at Spark's side. The force of the blow sent the merc stumbling into his boss, sending shocks through the other man since Spark had created a protective field of electricity around himself as soon as he was hit. Tiger didn't pause. He still had four more men up and moving and Spark wasn't going to be down long.

He flowed into another jump kick, landing his foot squarely in the face of the man flanking Murphy. The guard went down in the middle of drawing his gun. Tiger immediately grabbed that hand, planted a boot on his opponent's ribcage and twisted forcefully. Ribs broke and the shoulder popped out of joint. Tiger continued to pull on the arm, shifting his grip to grab the man's coat, yanking the thug upright and then bodily throwing him into the rising Spark, moving towards his next targets even as the thug convulsed from Spark's electrical field.

He ducked under one gun swinging in his direction and dodged a badly placed punch as he positioned his back to the path and maneuvered his opponents so their backs were to Spark. The electrical villain was pushing the unconscious gunman off him. Tiger's three opponents were not used to fighting together and kept getting in each other's way which suited Tiger just fine. He landed a foot into a solar plexus, knocking the wind out of one, while twisting another's arm, using Fen Jin techniques to tear the tendons into uselessness. A quick kick to the knee and the ankle broke both in the third man, and a strong front kick to his face sent him falling back into Spark who seemed to be looking for an opening through Tiger's human screen.

Apparently, having another body fall on him broke the limits of Spark's patience. Electrical bolts danced over both of the standing thugs. They fell as if hit by tasers, which was why Tiger had been throwing people at him.

Despite the electrical sparks flowing around Spark, there was no hesitation to Tiger's next attack. His uniform provided some protection from cold, heat and most importantly at the moment, electricity. The Wardens never knew who, what or where they would find themselves fighting, and they needed to be prepared. However, his costume had limits and Spark might be able to exceed them. Tiger needed to end this fast.

Spark lifted his hands, lightning flashing between them. Tiger struck with a punch to the chest, hitting the acupressure point that temporarily froze up the skeletal muscles, freezing Spark in position. It wouldn't stop the villain from unleashing the electricity, but it did mean he wasn't able to move when Tiger Iron used an upper palm strike to knock the man out.

He knew he should tie everyone up, but checking on Murphy was more important. She was still breathing, but she wasn't conscious. He drew a small knife and cut her down, resting her against a tree trunk. There was a charred scent around her that he didn't like. He pulled open his communicator, dispensing with any niceties. "Problem."

Azure's voice came back clear and quick. "What?"

"Murphy got hit by Spark. Unconscious. Breathing. Assailants down."

"Set up beacon." The line went dead. Azure didn't waste time when there was a problem.

Tiger pulled open one of his belt pouches and took out a short steel and copper cylinder. He pressed a button, and a small tripod extended out of one end. As soon as he set it down, a red light bathed the area as it scanned and then sent information back to the Wardens' base. When Soulforge had built their teleporter, she had made sure they all knew that the technology was very dangerous and chancy. The computer had to have completely accurate diagrams or someone could end up with their foot half melded with a concrete curb. Which was why the landing area had to be thoroughly scanned and Tiger Iron was careful not to move until the others arrived.

It seemed to take forever but, realistically, it was probably about five minutes when they appeared. Azure, in her scintillating blue costume, immediately issued orders, shortening everyone's code names as usual. "Chi, check Murphy. Salka, restrain the suspects. Ti, report."

Chi, or more accurately Chimera, crouched next to where Murphy lay against the tree, skin, clothes and hair shifting to match his background. He was their resident illusionist and medic. As far as Tiger knew, no one on the team had any idea what he really looked like as his cloaking illusions changed minute by minute.

Salka, better known as Rusalka, wore a gray, white and dark blue costume with ragged edges that made it resemble the breaking of waves on a beach. She whistled up some water golems to bring her the prisoners and stand guard over them, especially Spark, as she tied them up.

Tiger gave Azure the rundown on the events of that night, which wasn't much since he had arrived near the end of the questioning. Azure listened attentively, then asked, "So, what's your plan now?"

Chapter 14

TIGER IRON PAUSED AS HE THOUGHT through his answer. "It partly depends on what Chimera says. If Murphy is bad off, further questioning will have to wait. If she needs hospitalization, we should take her back to the base."

Azure's mouth turned down in a confused frown. "You're telling me that you still think she needs to be checked out but you want to bring her back to the base? You need to make up your mind."

Tiger tried to suppress his smile of amusement. "I said if she needs a hospital then we should take her to the base. If she's that bad off, she won't care where she is and won't be a threat."

Azure's disgusted glare made it clear he hadn't quite hidden his smile. "And if she is aware enough?"

"Then I stay here a while longer until she's up to answering my questions."

"You called us down for a--"

"For a downed heroine, yes. I don't know her power profile or her history or--"

"Or why she's taking money."

He nodded, not bothered by Azure's interruption. It was just the way she was. "Yes, or what she's doing with the money. However, I do know her motives are noble and she got into this business to help people, same as the rest of us."

"You're sure of that?"

"Yes."

"Then next step is to see how she's doing." Azure turned toward the team medic. "Chi?"

Odd patterns of light and shadows moved over and around Chimera and Murphy. The illusionist's amused voice emerged from a face that would be the envy of Hollywood. "She'll be fine. Spark got carried away, and she's got a nasty burn on her side and her shoulders where her combat webbing buckles got too hot because of how she was tied up. She won't be feeling good and would be better off if someone looked after her but she'll heal fine. Oh and, side note," Chimera was now sporting a long ponytail and golden fangs, "she's been awake for awhile now."

"Why didn't you say anything?" Azure demanded while Tiger immediately moved to crouch next to Murphy.

Chimera didn't pause his bandaging, and his illusions made Murphy's costume still seem intact. "I didn't see why she shouldn't know what was being said about her. My grandmother always said 'If you wouldn't say it to their face, don't say it at all.'"

Azure threw her hands up in frustration. She walked over to check on the prisoners that Rusalka had secured.

Chimera chuckled and addressed Murphy. "As for how I knew you were awake, unconscious people don't tense or flinch when I work on patching them up." He turned a reassuring smile toward her, the same smile used by the latest Best Actor Grammy Award winner. "Don't feel bad. It's almost impossible to avoid. It's not a failing. I gave you a mild pain reliever." He gave her some instructions on the wound care and Tiger Iron concentrated so he'd remember them. Once he was done, Chimera stood up. "The cops should be here soon to pick them up. We'll take care of it. You figure out your next step, and we'll help out." He chuckled again. "Even Azure."

Chimera walked away, but Tiger remained next to Murphy. "Do you need anything? Want to sit up?"

She shook her head carefully. "No, I'm okay."

He followed her gaze toward his teammates. "Don't worry. They'll make sure you get credit."

"I don't do this for credit." Her voice radiated annoyance. Tiger took it as a good sign. Her spirit wasn't broken.

"I know you don't." He considered how to phrase his next thought and decided blunt seemed to work the best with her. That was his preference anyway. "I'm going to stay in town a few days."

He didn't think she heard him as her eyes slid closed.

Chapter 15

MURPHY WOKE UP SLOWLY and completely against her will. Her body ached which meant the previous night happened, though the details were a blur she wasn't up to puzzling out. At least, she'd somehow ended up home in bed. She didn't know how and didn't care since soft bed trumped hard ground by leaps and bounds.

Sighing softly, she turned her head into the pillows to escape the dim light of the room. The pillows felt different and then it came crashing down on her. This wasn't her bed which meant it wasn't her home and that meant she had no idea where she was and that was a definite problem.

Pushing herself up, she became aware of several things all at once.

First, her body was not in agreement that moving was in her best interest. It expressed this opinion with pain in every muscle and joint, forcing her to grit her teeth not to cry out.

Second, she wasn't in costume. She was still wearing her pants and shirt. However, her cloak, scarf, boots and gear were gone which left her more defenseless than she liked. Of course, none of that had helped her earlier but still... it was nice to at least have around.

The third thing she realized was that she was not alone. There was a figure sitting in a shadowed corner. She reached for something to use as a weapon. Unfortunately, the only things at hand were hotel pillows. She grabbed one anyway.

A familiar chuckle answered her movement. "First a pen and now a pillow. You get full points for creativity, but you might want work on effectiveness."

Murphy carefully shrugged. "Yeah, well you're just lucky I recognized you, or you'd be in trouble."

Tiger Iron chuckled again. "I believe that. I haven't quite got it figured out but I'm convinced you have some kind of luck power."

Murphy gave a noncommittal nod, trying to think of a way to change the topic as she rearranged the pillows. Leaning back against the headboard, she asked, "Can I have some water or something?"

Tiger immediately stood up. "Oh yeah, sorry." He wasn't wearing his mask so she could see a light flush of embarrassment. "I've got water in the fridge and the room has a coffee maker if you prefer, or I can into something normal and get you a soda from the machines."

"Water works." She watched him as he moved over to the small room refrigerator, admiring the tightly muscled lines of his body and the unconscious grace of his movements. She really needed to come up with a new topic before he caught her staring like a schoolgirl with a crush. "So, I'm assuming this is your hotel room."

He shrugged as he handed her the still sealed bottle. "Seemed the safest place to take you. I didn't think you would appreciate being taken out of the city, and I don't know where you live so..." He let the statement trail off as he returned to his chair.

She smiled and thanked him as she opened the bottle and took a long drink. However, she couldn't resist muttering, "The whole shadowy man of mystery thing is a tad annoying," when she noticed his position had left his face in shadows again. She immediately mentally castigated herself as stupid and ungrateful. Heroes were supposed to protect their identities and considering the situation he had gotten her out of, did it really matter where he sat and if it was shadowed? Well, other than it prevented her from seeing his really handsome face that she probably wasn't going to be able to see much more of if she didn't stop acting like a temperamental nutcase.

While Murphy took herself to task, Tiger leaned over and turned on a nearby lamp. "Better?" His mouth was curved up just short of a grin, and his jade eyes were bright enough to make her suspect he was quite amused by her.

She nodded briefly and took another drink of water. "So, how did I get here? I mean with our costumes, I'm pretty sure it wasn't through the lobby. Even without the masks, still pretty noticeable. And when did you take off my mask?"

"Don't worry. No one else knows what you look like except maybe Chimera...and, actually we did come in through the lobby with Chimera providing cover so no one noticed."

She nodded. "Oh, I think I was a little out of it so well..." She let her words trail off, unsure of what to say at all. She had been a lot more than a little out of it. Everything after the second time she'd been hit with electricity was a vague dark blur. At least her luck had worked out okay. Being in a hotel room alone with Tiger was nice though the silence was starting to get on her nerves. "I've always wondered, why you picked the name you did. It's kind of odd because most heroes use iron as an adjective and would have made it Iron Tiger like Iron Wolf or Steel Dog or Cobalt Rose." It took her a moment after she stopped talking to realize how many mistakes she had just made.

Always wondered? Why not just tattoo 'fangirl' across her forehead? Especially naming other heroes off the top of her head. Oh, and one of them was a new heroine just on the scene. Yeah, might as well just get that tattoo. Oh and the unintentional inference that his name was weird which he could take as meaning she was calling him weird. Yeah, brilliant.

Her internal litany of errors almost caused her to miss his answer, but only almost.

Tiger briefly looked down, his smile turned rueful. "It was a youthful rebellion actually." He leaned back. "Do you really want to hear this?"

Murphy leaned forward with an eager nod before her body reminded her of her aches and the really sarcastic voice in her head muttered something about making that tattoo appointment right away. She carefully eased back against the pillows. "Please. I'm curious and you already know how I ended up as Murphy."

His smile didn't change. "My grandfather comes from a long line of Shifus, teachers of Chin Na, and he has trained me, literally, from infancy. When I had graduated high school, I wanted to go to college away from my family so I could have independence, and I wanted to be a hero to help people. I knew it would be impossible for me to become a hero and him not know it since he taught me everything I use in the field and many of the forms are unique to our family style. One decent video of me in costume and grandfather would know. He was already trying to keep me from going to college in another state and became more insistent when I told him my full plans. He told me I was too much of a tiger and tigers must stay at home until they grow into dragons."

"Tiger?"

"It's an old concept. Tigers and dragons are both respected for their strength and power. However, a tiger is impulsive and acts without thinking which usually gets a tiger in a lot of trouble. A dragon is more spiritual and mental. They consider deeply before acting. So, my grandfather, in calling me a tiger, was telling me I needed more training before I could use what he had taught me properly. I was doing a report for school on the cultural meanings of various gemstones and came across a stone called Tiger Iron. It's believed to bring vitality, power and confidence, attributes of a tiger. However, the vitality and power is supposed to be more mental or spiritual than physical." He shrugged, giving the impression of amusement at his younger self. "It seemed to me like its description was partway between a tiger and a dragon so I took the name as a way to tell my grandfather he was wrong."

"So, your grandfather raised you and doesn't approve of what you're doing?"

"It's a little more complicated than that."

She smiled, eager to have him tell her more, so she decided to softly prod him. "Well, I'm not going anywhere anytime soon unless you're about to throw me out."

Chapter 16

TIGER RAN A HAND through his short black hair as he stared at Murphy. Her position on the bed emphasized several of her curves and was, to say the least, distracting. She looked tired though, pale. He didn't really want to start interrogating her right now, feeling like it would be unfair of him after what she had been through. However, he was enjoying talking to her even though he was not used to revealing so much information about himself. The things she was asking were relatively harmless and, more importantly, perhaps if he opened up more to her, she would do the same.

"My father and mother raised me but my grandfather trained me. In China, there is a long tradition of martial arts and the various schools of Chin Na each have their own traditions and secrets that they guard. As I mentioned, my grandfather is the last in a long line of Shifus of his family's school. The school, though, was for family only and the teachings only passed down from father to son. All the men on that side of my family were killed during the Japanese occupation of China during World War II except for my great-grandfather who managed to escape to America with his wife and one daughter."

She frowned either in confusion or concern or maybe both, but he wasn't sure. She remained silent though, so he continued.

"My grandfather was born in America and is my great-grandfather's only son. My grandfather only had daughters and, by tradition, he can't teach the secrets to anyone not of his blood or a daughter." He held up a hand and shook his head to stop her protest. "Yes, I know it's sexist but it's a different culture and my grandfather gave his word during his training. No, he doesn't look down on women but he won't break his word whether he agrees with it or not."

"Did you give your word when you were being trained?" Her head was still tilted to the side, and he was happy to see more curiosity than condemnation in her gaze.

"Yes, though not the same promises as my grandfather made to his father. Part of the training is learning the importance of traditions and oaths. Martial arts are not just about fighting, at least not the way my grandfather teaches. It's a way of life. Anyway," he decided to steer the conversation back to what he felt was a safer topic, "My grandfather didn't have any sons but my mother told my father from the start that her first son would be trained in the family school by her father and my dad agreed. So, when I was born, my parents moved into a house with a guest house in the back for my grandfather and my dad and grandfather worked together and built a dojo for me in the backyard. So, my childhood was spent at regular school during the day, grandfather's school during the afternoon, homework during the evening."

"Sounds lonely." The words were soft, and he didn't think she meant to say them. When she immediately started talking faster, he knew she had said them without thinking. "I mean, it's great that your family was altogether like that but kids need to play... not that I'm saying you had bad parents cause you turned out great... I mean... you're a hero and you do good things and..." She looked away, a soft blush on her cheeks as she nervously took a drink of water.

He chuckled softly. She was cute when she was flustered. "I had time for friends. Dad insisted that I get to have most of Saturday free if I had all my homework and chores done. My grandfather even taught my friends some basic punches and blocks if they came over to hang out while I was training." He smiled. "It was tough sometimes but I think they did a pretty good job on me and it's nice to know you agree." His grin widened as her flush deepened. "So, what about you? Do your parents know that you're a hero?"

She shook her head. "No. I didn't figure they needed the worries when I first thought about it back in high school. And, after the accident, I didn't think my dad needed to know what I was up to. I really don't know if he would approve or not. Though he's always been fairly tolerant even when he doesn't agree with me."

"Oh?" He hoped she'd take the hint and continue.

"Well, yeah, he doesn't really like my music or the way I dress or anything but it's my life so he doesn't bug me about it. His main rule to me when I was in high school was don't break rules, his, the school's or the law's, 'cause if I did, he wasn't gonna get me out of trouble...especially if I ended up in jail for doing anything illegal and my mom agreed completely. They said they knew I'd do what I want but, whatever I did, I'd better be ready to deal with the consequences, no whining allowed."

"Does either of them know about your luck power?" He tried to keep his voice soft and hoped she'd answer without thinking. His conscience wasn't very happy with him questioning her, but he was curious and she was talkative. So, he did his best to shush it, promising himself he wouldn't press if she changed the subject or wanted to rest.

Her eyes seemed far away as she stared down at the bottle. "Yeah. My dad has the same luck I have. It's a family thing, sort of like yours I guess, except I was born lucky. But, I had to learn to deal with it."

His brows drew together. "Deal with it?" He had only heard of a few people with a luck power and, for them, it was just a matter of turning it on and off and choosing a target for the bad luck. So, her use of the word deal seemed a little odd.

"Yeah, I had to learn how to control the danger to others so I wouldn't accidentally kill or maim anyone."

Chapter 17

MURPHY ONCE MORE WISHED for the ability to rewind time so she could take back something she had just said. She had not meant to say that last part but it had been nice and comfortable talking to him and her mouth, as usual, had engaged before her brain.

She waited for him to jump on the comment about her power being dangerous. The curiosity in his face was obvious. However, he simply sat as if waiting for her to decide to explain or not. She sighed. Well, he had been open about himself and even rescued her after she'd yelled at him twice.

"Luck is kind of a balancing act. One person being lucky can mean another person being unlucky. It depends on how many people are involved in the situation and the stakes."

After a few minutes of silence, he admitted. "I'm not sure I understand. Do you mean for things to go right for you, something has to go bad for someone else? Like, every action has an equal and opposite reaction? Or is it an area effect?"

She shrugged. "Yes and no. Luck isn't simple and it changes. It doesn't really have any rules other than good luck makes you smile months or years later 'cause you got what you wanted or needed whether or not you knew it at the time and bad luck makes you frown at remembered pain for no good reason and even those aren't absolute laws."

Tiger was silent and still for an even longer pause. "I didn't follow that at all. I'm sorry."

Murphy shrugged and pain made her regret the action. "I don't completely understand either and I think that's part of it. If I could understand it, then it would be some kind of control power and not just luck." She pushed a strand of hair behind her ear. "Okay, let me give you some examples. A person wins the lottery, that's good luck. For the one person to win, a lot people had to lose, that's bad luck for them. However, since it's spread to a bunch of people, the bad luck doesn't affect those thousands of people as much as the good luck affects the one. However, in a smaller group, there's one job and two applicants. One gets the good luck to get the job. Not getting the job is bad luck but it all falls on one person hurting them more. Then, sometimes, there's no bad luck. You're late for work and you have the good luck to get all the green lights. That doesn't require bad luck on the part of someone else for you to have that good luck."

Tiger nodded. "Though all of those things could end up switching. The green light switching to give you the good luck of getting to work quickly could change at just the wrong time for someone else. The job might be a nightmare which makes the person who didn't get it the lucky one, and most big lottery winners seem to run into bigger problems."

She nodded, pleased that he saw those problems so quickly. She had always been sure he was smart. "Exactly. You don't always know if something is good or bad luck immediately and what if one thing that is good luck is followed by other things that are bad luck and on and on. At least I know things will always work out for me in the end but not what I might have to go through to get there."

"You mentioned maiming?"

She looked away. "Well yeah. If some guy decides to try to kill me or rape me, my luck will interfere. But I can't control or predict how. The guy could easily trip and break his leg or get hit by a car to make me lucky enough to stay safe and alive. There's no way for me to predict it. All I can do is try to minimize my risks...but even then...I wonder how much pain can be blamed on my ability...like dad and mom's death." Her voice trailed off. She couldn't swallow, and tears burned in her eyes.

The bed dipped, and she felt a strong hand resting on her shoulder offering comfort. "Are you worried your power killed your mom?"

She smiled sadly. "Tragedy is in the eye of the beholder."

Chapter 18

TIGER'S HAND ON HER SHOULDER was comforting and real. Mara gave into temptation and leaned into him, smiling when his arm obligingly slipped around her. Tiger, or rather Jace, since he wasn't wearing his mask, was off in his assumptions but the comfort felt nice. He didn't object when she laid her head on his shoulder.

Mara let herself enjoy the closeness for a few moments before trying to sit up and correct him. Jace's arm remained firmly around her, anchoring her to him.

She licked her lower lip nervously. "I wasn't in the car wreck with my parents. It wasn't my luck that affected it."

She felt him tense but he did not release her. His voice was calm when he asked, "What happened? If you'd like to talk about it."

She nodded, feeling comfortable but tired and sad at the same time. "A drunk driver hit my parents. Mom died at the scene. She had multiple injuries including a skull fracture and the paramedics said that she couldn't feel anything. That was a mercy considering the pain she would have suffered, but she couldn't feel Dad hold her hand either. He was badly injured as well. His spine won't ever be right. But they managed to say goodbye before she passed away. The other driver is still in the hospital, still in pain and rehab."

"You think your father's luck power killed your mother?" His arm tightened around her back and his other hand came up to stroke her upper arm.

She softly shook her head. "I think his luck power gave him time to say goodbye and protected him from seeing her in pain which protected her in a way. I mean, honestly, who were the lucky ones? The drunk that hit him? Even if he rehabs enough to live a halfway decent life, he knows he killed a woman and his friends and family know it. Any money he had is gone and will stay that way 'cause of medical bills, court costs and judgments. Meanwhile, Mom didn't suffer, and my parents got to say goodbye. Wouldn't you call that lucky?"

"What happened to your dad?"

"He's in a wheelchair in a good assisted living community and still has his job since it was a desk job to begin with." She pulled back so she could look into his green eyes. They were such a nice shade of jade, she thought. Too bad his mask hid them. "Luck doesn't make sense. If it did, it could be predicted and it wouldn't be luck." She smiled softly, feeling a little light headed. "Sort of like love and attraction." Once again her brain thought about her words after they were already said. She blushed and waited for the inevitable explanation that he was just being nice.

He just nodded and stared at her in silence for a moment before sighing. "I do still need to know what you're doing with the money."

Her mouth turned down in annoyance. Why did he have to keep harping on that? Well, other than he was a hero and it technically was stealing even if she preferred to think of it as a necessary shortcut for the money to do what it was supposed to do. Still! "What do you think I'm doing with it?"

Chapter 19

JACE TOOK A FEW MOMENTS to consider his response before speaking. "I think that you're doing what you believe is right, or at least what you think will help people."

"You think that, huh?" She had turned to face him and her lips quirked in amusement.

"From what I've seen and what you've said, you are passionate and dedicated to helping right wrongs. You're not in it for adventure or fame." He found his gaze sliding back down to her full lips and mentally took himself to task. Now wasn't the time. He had an assignment to finish.

"How do you figure that?" Her head tilted to the side in curiosity.

The part of him that was much too aware of the fact that Mara was still in his arms pointed how perfectly positioned they were for a kiss. It gave his voice a rough tinge as he answered. "You haven't shown any interest in Warden membership or help. A fame or adventure seeker would be going out of her way to try to impress me or justify herself when she found I was assessing her. You tend more towards telling me you're doing the best you can and to stay out of your business."

Her lips turned up in a full smile. "That's a nice way to describe what I've been doing." Her eyes weren't meeting his anymore. Her gaze seemed to be focused lower on his face.

A shiver went up his spine. Luckily for him, focus had been one of the first lessons his grandfather had taught him. He grasped at his slipping self control with both hands. "I still have an assignment too, though, and that assignment requires me to know what you do with the cash you take."

He felt her breath on his face as she sighed. Exactly when had they leaned in that close?

"You're very stubborn." Her tone made it sound more like an endearment than a complaint.

He smirked, "So are you."

She gave another sigh and his skin tingled where her breath flowed over it. "I use it to buy the cameras I leave and equipment like tasers and handcuffs when I can't afford them on my paycheck. The rest I give away anonymously as money orders to police officers or boxes of food and diapers and stuff to food banks and shelters. I don't use any of it for my bills or my dad's, just in case you were wondering about that."

He felt a small tinge of guilt that he had wondered just that. However, now that he had an answer the guilt and his focus both fled.

Without thinking, he closed the small space between them and pressed his lips to hers. They were soft and warm and parted eagerly against his. Her hands stroked the back of his neck and he regretted that his armored costume had prevented him from feeling them sliding up his chest. That thought slid away under a wave of pleasure as her tongue eagerly met his own. Arms tightening, he pulled her closer to him and smiled into the kiss as she molded her body to his. His fingers pressed into her back, rubbing and massaging, slowly becoming firmer until he could hear small sounds of enjoyment.

A small part of his mind, the place where his focus had slid into, commented that this was probably not the smartest move on his part. He acknowledged it and then told it to shut up. He had wanted to do this since shortly after meeting her and, now that he had completed his mission, there was no reason not to, especially not when Mara was willing.

She was more than willing and became more aggressive, her fingers sliding into his hair as she tilted her head further to deepen the kiss.

Giving in to his impulses, he slowly pressed her back against the bed, giving her ample time to protest. She did neither but gripped his shoulders pulling him down with her until his weight pressed her into the mattress.

Suddenly, she made a noise of distress and Jace immediately retreated, sitting up and away from her, confused and concerned. "What's wrong? Did--"

She cut him off with a quick shake of her head and a rueful smile. "No, my body just decided to remind me that I almost got electrocuted last night." She bit her lower lip briefly, reaching up to lay a hand on his chest. "I'm sorry."

He pushed the hair back from her face. "Don't apologize. Not your fault. I should have--"

She reached up and pressed fingers against his lips, cutting him off, "Nope, if you don't allow me to apologize you can't either." She smiled up at him though her eyes were wet. "Besides, it kind of is my fault, since I'm the one that's been busting the bad guys that got them mad enough to bring in the walking electric chair."

He smiled and nibbled at the tips of her fingers for a few moments before commenting. "And I can see you're just really torn up about that."

She laughed softly. "At least I got to meet you again." Her eyes went wide suddenly. "Wait! Today was Sunday." She pushed herself up to a sitting position, looking around. "Okay, I need caffeine and my clothes and my key and just what time is it anyway?" Mara winced as she strained to look around him at the clock on the hotel table. "And I only have four hours before I have to be at work!"

"Work? After a night like this?"

She glanced at him. "If I get enough caffeine and take it easy, I should do okay, not the first time I've had to function on caffeine." She winced again as she pushed herself up to her feet. She glanced around. "Do you have an extra shirt I can borrow and maybe a bag I can stick everything in so I can get through the lobby and go get my apartment key and things so I can get ready for work?" She laughed as he raised an eyebrow. "I figure a man's t-shirt won't look too odd with my pants and boots so it won't get me noticed going through the lobby which is my only choice," She glanced at the heavily curtained window, "Unless we're on the first floor 'cause, remember, I can't climb ropes."

Jace moved to the side to stay out of her way as she moved over to check on the pieces of her costume he had removed, folding them into a small bundle. "It might be better if you called in sick."

She shook her head. "No, I'll save my sick days for when I really really can't make it out of bed or when I've got a lead on something during the day I have to take care of. Just being tired and sore isn't enough of an excuse to stay home."

He slid his hand through her hair. "You're going to be stubborn, aren't you?"

She grinned, "Of course I am. I'm me. Besides, I'm not nearly as tired as you. I got a nice long nap."

Jace chuckled and proceeded to pull out his own luggage, tossing her a clean t-shirt and pulling out a set of clothes for himself. "You might have to put your stuff in a garbage bag for the moment. I don't have a backpack with me." Walking into the bathroom, he closed the door to give them both some privacy and quickly changed into civilian clothes.

Chapter 20

JACE WOKE UP IN THE EARLY AFTERNOON to the hotel alarm. A strong temptation urged him to break the plastic annoyance and, if it had been his, he probably would have given into the impulse. However, it did not belong to him, and Jace was not in the habit of breaking things that did not belong to him. Well except when those things were being used to take over the world or destroy the world or something equally catastrophic.

He forced himself to get up and used an abusively cold shower and hot coffee to finish waking up. Drinking his second cup whole waiting for room service, he let his mind drift over that morning.

Once both he and Mara were in civilian looking attire, he had insisted on accompanying her home. She had tried to be stubborn but he hadn't budged. She had finally relented muttering something about not having time to waste arguing with hard headed chivalry.

He had walked with her to the park and played lookout as she had slipped into her... he wasn't sure what to call the small dugout. Whatever it was, it seemed to work for her because she had reemerged after a few minutes with a backpack and keys on a chain around her neck. He was glad when she hadn't protested his decision to accompany her to her apartment. On the way there, her hand had slipped into his and he had decided not to comment on it, instead he had laced their fingers together and enjoyed the feeling of closeness without questioning it.

She hadn't invited him into her apartment. He wasn't surprised or offended. She still had to get ready for work, or come to her senses and call in sick. Either option would be easier without an audience. Besides, Jace had begun to feel his busy night. He had waited until she had unlocked the door and turned toward him to say goodbye before catching her chin in his hand. He had leaned down to press a slow sweet kiss against her very willing mouth then had asked her to promise to contact him that evening. A shiver went through him the present as he remembered her slightly breathless agreement before she had leaned up and kissed him again. The blush that had spread over her cheeks as she had ducked into her apartment had been very cute.

Finishing his cup of hot coffee, Jace looked over at the time. She had said she was a file clerk and so he assumed that Mara would be working typical 9 to 5 hours. It was only around 3 so he could easily assume that he had a few hours before he could expect her to get off work. He decided to use his time constructively.

He was about to dig out his communicator when his cellphone rang. Opening it up, his eyes widened as he recognized the number. "Hello?" Nervousness gripped him in the split second it took to receive an answer. He had talked to his mom and grandfather the previous day. Why would they be calling him unless something bad had happened?

"Have you made any progress or decisions?" His grandfather asked without any preamble or greetings.

"Yes, Shifu." His voice immediately shifted into the softer respectful tones. "May I ask how you determined I might have?"

"The news said that the Wardens were involved in an arrest of drug dealers in Bromston. Her territory."

"Yes, Shifu. She had been captured and I had to call in reinforcements for aid in tending to her health and the aftermath."

"She is well?"

"She seems to be. She said she was in some pain but insisted on going to work today." He knew that many of his Warden comrades would think it odd how much information he shared with his grandfather. However, his grandfather, as much as his parents, had been his guide in honor and behavior. If he couldn't trust his grandfather then he didn't know who he could trust.

"Honorable." The compliment from his grandfather took Jace back a bit but he was happy that Murphy had apparently gained some favor in his Shifu's eyes. "What decisions have you made about her?"

"She is engaging in a dishonorable behavior but for benevolent reasons and due to a lack of more honorable options. She does not use any of it for self advancement but in the pursuit of justice and defense of the majority. If given an honorable and feasible option, I believe she will end the dishonorable behavior."

"Will you and your comrades provide that honorable option?"

"I must still discuss that with them. Her ability has... unpredictable factors that must be taken into consideration. However, I will seek other options for her with or without their help."

"You are choosing to begin a relationship with her then? Or has it already begun?"

Jace closed his eyes and once more wondered if his grandfather possessed telepathy or precognitive abilities. He didn't think his voice had been anything other than calm. "I..." He hesitated. There was no use hiding anything from his grandfather. The older man had proved that repeatedly when he'd been younger. However, he didn't know what Mara was interested in. "I know what I would like. I am not sure of her feelings."

"You admit to your lack of understanding. Finally. I am glad to find you have finally progressed." There was a definite edge of amusement to his grandfather's voice.

"I...I'm confused."

"Of course you are. All young dragons and tigers are confused and ignorant. The difference is that a young dragon knows his state and will admit it."

"Shifu, you said a tiger could not grow to a dragon without guidance. I have not returned to you for further training so I do not understand." He remembered quite clearly his grandfather's lectures to him as a teenager that his duty was to learn, and he was to remain at home not some college or self-aggrandizing team.

"It is true, a tiger cannot progress to a dragon without lessons and trials. However, those trials and lessons are individual for each person and must be faced alone."

Understanding began to dawn on Jace. "You told me to stay home because you knew I wouldn't?"

"Of course. A tiger knows that he is wise and powerful and that no one is perfect or all knowing. Therefore, a tiger shows his individuality by throwing off the authority of others, asserting himself." There was definite amusement in his grandfather's tone and a hint of pride as well.

"So, you told me to stay and learn because you knew I would do the opposite?"

"I did my best to push you to rebel and go out into the finishing school of life without pushing you away from me or losing our bond. A tiger cannot transform into a dragon in a controlled environment. Now, though, you have shown that you know your own shortcomings and ignorance as well as your strengths. You seek counsel from those you trust as wise but you no longer take the wisdom or advice as true without questioning. I am proud of your progression."

Jace wasn't sure what to say or how to react to his grandfather's words.

The older man continued without Jace having to say anything. "I do make a request of you, now that you have progressed and are ready. Please arrange to come and see me regularly for continued education. There is still much I need to pass on to you and neither you nor I am becoming younger. Also, try to arrange for Murphy to accompany you for your father's birthday next month. I would like to meet the woman that made my grandson finally question my wisdom."

The phone went dead on that odd note, and Jace shook his head a bit ruefully. His grandfather might call him a dragon but that didn't give him any sudden enlightenment. He wasn't sure he understood everything his grandfather had said but decided there was time to think figure it out later. He still needed to talk to Azure.

Chapter 21

A ZURE ANSWERED ALMOST IMMEDIATELY. "So, Ti, do you have a verdict for me?"

"Yes and no."

"Thanks so much for clearing that all up. So nice to know that everything is all wrapped up there." Her light teasing tone suddenly turned serious. "Ti, I really don't want to ask this but if you're delaying... I mean I'm not blind and you —" She took a breath. "You'd tell me if your opinion was compromised, right?"

He sighed. He couldn't blame her for asking. After all, that same suspicion had been why he had called his grandfather the previous day. "Yes, I'm attracted to her. No, my judgment is not compromised. Yes, I would tell you if I thought it was compromised. Yes, I understand why you're asking and no, I'm not offended that you would ask."

There was a short laugh. "Okay. Now that we've got that straightened out, how about clearing up that yes and no bit?"

"I think that she's doing everything, even the wrong things, for the right reasons. She's not a glory hound. She just wants to help people. She's taking the cash, but she's using it to purchase the cameras to help with the convictions and giving it to people in need, particularly cops. She's not proud of stealing, but she doesn't see any other options."

"So, what are your recommendations?"

"That's where there's a bit of a problem. I talked to her more about her ability and... personality wise, I think she might be a good fit for us. However, power wise... it might be better to just give her assistance and leave her where she is. I want to discuss it more with you, Chi and, possibly, Soulforge. She knows more about math and probabilities and energy than any of us do."

"I'll put a call out to them and get us all in the meeting room. I'll beep you back as soon as we're ready."

He nodded and made some more coffee, ordering his thoughts.

The communicator beeped in less than ten minutes. As usual, when Azure sent out calls, people jumped. It made her a good team leader.

Jace had decided to sit at the small table in his room for the meeting. It wasn't as comfortable as the bed, but it put him in a more professional frame of mind.

Azure's voice was firm, as she called the meeting to order, giving the others a short rundown on what he'd already told her. "Ti says he has some... worries about her power that would affect her possible membership. Go ahead, Ti."

"Her luck power isn't a control power. She doesn't consciously control probabilities or targets. As far as she's described it to me, she has no control over it at all. She stated she doesn't understand it fully and doesn't believe it can be understood."

"So, she doesn't choose who is afflicted with bad luck?" Soulforge's clipped tones were easily identifiable.

"No."

"Does it affect a certain area around her?"

"I'm not sure."

"How did she explain it then?"

Ti tried to push away the feeling that he was back in school. Soulforge always seemed to have that teacher tone in her voice. "According to her, she just has good luck. Things always work out for her in the long run. However, she tries not to use her luck, tries to make sure she doesn't need it. She's afraid of what kind of bad luck might happen to others in order for her to have her good luck."

"Do any of you get that?" Azure's voice impatiently filled the pause.

"I feel I grasp the theory." Soulforge answered, and Jace wondered at Chimera's silence. "Tiger Iron posits the theory that her effects on probability might not be localized and could grow in proportion to-"

Azure cut her off. "Bring it down to non-multi-doctorate level."

"As I understand it, if Murphy is placed in the middle of large events such as the stereotypical heroic world saving, her power effects may mathematically grow in proportion to the situation which could possibly lead to a chain of events that--."

Azure sighed. "Okay, now I'm getting a headache so just give me the tired Azure headache version."

"At worst case scenario, if her beliefs are accurate and conservative--"

"Soulforge, I get it, worst case scenario, probably never happen, like the whole billion to one chance like a time rift at the OK corral that should never logically happen but does. What's the worst that can happen? Simple words please." There was the sound of a soda can and a medicine bottle opening. "Thanks, Chi."

Soulforge's voice was long suffering when she spoke again. "If an alien race wanted to blow up the world with Murphy on it, there's a slim chance Murphy's power would take effect on the small scale of Murphy being captured in order to save her life or it might have a large enough effect that the ship would malfunction and meltdown killing all hands on board in order to keep her safe. There's a chance her ability would not be strong enough to affect it at all and a chance that it could have even greater effects."

"Is there any way to know?"

"I would have to run tests. So far, this is all theory based on the little information we have. There is no point in further speculation without actual data."

"Ti, would she agree to the tests?"

"I don't know Azure. That's why I wanted to talk to all of you. If she had a simple power or at least one we'd seen before, I'd suggest recruiting her. But a power the user can't control? I'm not sure how to proceed."

"I don't really think we have to make any decisions or do anything right away." Chimera's voice came over the communicator, familiar and unfamiliar at the same time. "We don't even know if Murphy is interested in joining us. I think this is one of those situations where we can all take it a step at a time."

"Chi's right." Azure sounded more like herself. The pain meds Chimera probably gave her earlier must be taking effect. "Check on Murphy's thoughts and intentions then we'll go from there. When will you be headed back, Ti?"

He didn't want to think about leaving right now. "How soon am I needed?"

"Nothing odd on the scans and such right now, but you know how quick that can change."

"Yeah. If it does, I'll use the teleportation tech to get back fast. Otherwise, I'd like to stay here for a few more days."

He could almost envision Azure's amused smile. "Uh-huh, I bet. Don't worry, I'll spoil Fluff and Puff for however long you need to get things… arranged."

Jace was glad they couldn't see him blush as he quickly said goodbye and signed off.

Chapter 22

MURPHY WANTED TO HEAD RIGHT OVER to Jace's hotel room after she got home from work. Unfortunately, her heretofore cheap but reliable furniture had somehow become corrupted and turned traitor on her. She sat down on her couch for just one minute. Just long enough to take off the nice flats she wore for work so she could change into something more comfortable, more her. That's all. But her evil couch had done something because, as she woke up to a knock on her door, she found herself still in her office clothes, only one shoe off and the sky dark outside her window.

The knock came again, more insistent and she kicked off her remaining shoe as she called out an unfriendly, "Alright, alright, give me a minute here." She tried to run her hand through her hair and made a very unladylike comment as her fingers ran into her hair clip. Someday, she really needed to learn to wake up better. Covering a yawn, she blinked her eyes a few times then peered through the peephole to see who was bothering her when she needed to go get changed so she could head over to Jace's hotel and... Oh no! Oh no no no! Jace was here! Outside her door and she probably looked like hell in stupid rumpled boring office clothes and, oh no, not good. Her eyes moved around her apartment and her previously treasured superhero posters seemed to suddenly be aggressively mocking her. What was she gonna do?

"Mara, are you okay?"

Her heart did happy jumps in her chest at the concern she heard in his voice. Her mind, however, was thinking, 'oh, no, definitely not OK, he's going to think I'm a crazy little fangirl!' Her logical side noted that he was going to think she was crazy anyway if she didn't answer him...or that she was hurt which meant he would come in anyway. He was a hero after all.

"Mara?" His concerned voice was starting to take a determined edge.

It cut through her panic and she actually giggled at the comedy she was enacting, pressed to the door like something out of a cartoon. She was a fan. She was about to get caught because telling him to go away was not really going to get her anywhere good anyway. So, the only thing she could do was open the door, brazen it out and hope that he didn't immediately run for the hills. However, if he did, at least she gave it her best shot.

"Ummm, yeah, just getting the door unlocked and waking up at the same time." She undid the deadbolt and opened the door with the best smile she could muster under the circumstances. "Sorry about that, took an unplanned nap on the couch." Reaching up, she took out her hair clip and combed her fingers nervously through her hair, hoping she was making it better not worse.

He smiled at her. "You probably needed it. I brought dinner if you're up to it." He held up a bag from a local burger place.

Her stomach decided to answer before she could make a choice one way or the other, and she felt her face warm in embarrassment. "Ummm, yeah, that would be great..."

His smile widened and she appreciated him not laughing out loud as he asked, "Can I come in or do you want to have a picnic in the hall?"

"Oh, yeah, sorry, I don't wake up really quick." She stepped back and let him in, waiting for him to notice the large poster of him in costume. There was no way to miss it.

However, he didn't say anything as he turned pass it into her living room. "Where do you want the food?"

She pointed off toward the small kitchen area. "Plates are in the cabinet next to the fridge. Help yourself to whatever's in there to drink and do me a really really big favor of making some coffee while I get out of these clothes and into something that's more real me instead of work me?"

He reached out and caught her hand, pulling her close. "I will, in a minute." He shifted his hold before she could react and wrapped an arm around her waist, pulling her against him for a soft kiss. He had probably meant it to be short but she couldn't resist gripping his shirt and staying close for a longer kiss even as his arm loosened slightly around her.

When they eventually parted for a breath, she smiled up at him. "That was worth it."

"Worth what?"

"Staying in these clothes a few more minutes, but I really, really need to go change."

He slowly released her. "Well, go get in different clothes but no changing. I like you the way you are." He turned and walked into the kitchen, hopefully missing the really goofy happy smile she could feel on her face.

Of course, once she was in her bedroom looking at her clothes, she was suddenly faced with the dreaded what to wear question. Sexy? Casual? She put her face in her hands. She needed to get a grip. He didn't seem to mind her costume, her jeans or her work outfit so just grab a shirt and jeans and get back out there before he had the time to count how many posters had him in them.

She took a few minutes to brush her hair out after slipping into a comfortable but still attractively tight black jeans and a red tank top with a black cat and bats across the front However, she left off the make-up this time. She really was hungry and cold burgers were not that appetizing.

Chapter 23

WHEN SHE STEPPED BACK OUT, he was sitting on the evil comfy couch with the burgers and fries split between two plates and various condiments and toppings spread out. He looked up at her with a rueful smile. "I didn't know what you liked so I told them to put everything on the side so you could do what you wanted with it. Coffee's made but since I don't know how you like that either..." He trailed off with a shrug.

She nodded approvingly. "Smart." She didn't wait for the awkward silence, immediately going to the kitchen for her coffee and then quickly putting her burger together the way she liked it as she munched on fries to quiet her hunger.

They finished their dinner in companionable silence. Mara tried not to wolf down her food, but she was hungry and apparently, so was he. Dinner was over very quickly. They were sitting close enough on the couch that it seemed natural to lean back and cuddle into his side. His arm wrapped around her, his fingers stroking her arm.

"So, what now?" She regretted the words as soon as she said them since she would have more than enjoyed just cuddling with him for the rest of the night.

His fingers continued to trail up and down her bare arm. "We need to discuss some things and, afterward, well I have some ideas depending on how tired you are and how much time you'll have to sleep before work."

Mara tensed. "Okay. What did you want to discuss?"

He shifted slightly and the light stroking turned to a soft massage of her neck. "You, me, the future."

It was a funny feeling to be partially tense and relaxed at the same time. It also felt a little foolish. He wouldn't be letting her snuggle up against him if this was a "you're nice and maybe we can be friends and colleagues" speech. "Ummmm, what are you thinking about... for that I mean?"

"Two things actually. First, have you ever wanted to join the Wardens?"

She sat up. She couldn't help it. She was so surprised. Her gaze flicked from the large poster of the Wardens that he was directly facing and back to him to see if he was making fun of her. "You haven't gone blind in the last few minutes, have you?"

His green gaze focused on her. "No. Yes, I can see the posters but they don't automatically mean that you want to join a team. I admit I'm rather flattered, but that's part of the second thing. You still haven't answered me though. Are you interested in joining the Wardens?"

"Well, you guys help a lot more people than I do. I don't know if I'd be really useful to you guys." A nervous laugh escaped. "I can't even climb a rope, you know."

"You already said you were working on that. Just on your passion for helping people, you'd fit in fine. Although, there is a question about your power..."

She sighed and lay back against him, resting her hand on his stomach and smiling as he resumed massaging her neck. "Right. If I start playing in the big leagues, how many big league things will it affect?"

"Exactly. Soulforge thinks she can figure it out if you're willing to work with her on some tests. And we can do the tests for you even if you don't want to join, to help you understand what it is your power does, if you want."

"Is this an offer to join?"

His hand shifted to stroking her hair. "No, but it's a possibility, if that's what you want. If you don't want to join or find out more about your power then no one's going to hold it against you. But the offer's there to help you out."

She mulled that over and looked up at him. "So, you've decided I'm a not a bad person even though I steal."

He lowered his head for another kiss, and she decided that staring up at him had its advantages. "Of course you're not a bad person, but the stealing has to stop."

She glared up at him. "I told you--"

He cut her off before she could get too mad. "I know, and I understand. However, eventually, the cops won't be able to continue to ignore it, even if they're ignoring it now. You know that they might still be working on a case against you but haven't been able to do anything about it. Your luck may be defending you but how long before someone gets hurt? And, yes, I know that you need the cameras. I'm going to make sure that you get enough money to get the cameras and gear. If you want, I'll even talk to Soulforge about getting you better cameras."

Her eyes widened. "No. I mean, no on the better cameras. I use the ones I do because they're so simple the lawyers can't say I've tampered with the images. But...you'd help me out like that?"

"Of course. You're putting criminals in jail, and the Wardens are dedicated to helping people do that. Besides," his jade eyes were bright with amusement, "It would be hard for me to date you if you were in jail for theft, wouldn't it?"

"Date me?" The question was stupid considering she was snuggled against him and they'd been kissing. What did she think? He was just going to make out with her and then forget her. Well, he could but if he did she was better off without him but it wouldn't be a heroic or honorable thing to do and--

His words cut off her galloping thoughts. "Yeah, that was the second thing I wanted to talk to you about. I want to date you, and I'm pretty sure you don't find me repellant." His gaze flicked over to one of her posters of him in costume, and he gave a low chuckle that grated on her nerves.

She immediately forgave him though as his mouth met hers again in a long and deep kiss during which, somehow, she ended up on his lap instead of beside him. She wasn't really sure how it had happened or whose idea it was, but she was not going to complain in the least.

"So, you still haven't told me what you think about any of what I've offered."

She stroked the side of his face with her fingertips. "Hmmmm, sorry, brain becoming routinely disconnected."

His hand caught hers and held it still. "Not complaining, but I need some answers."

She took a deep breath and tried to order her thoughts enough to deal with everything that was being offered. "For joining the Wardens? Ummmm, not sure and won't be until I know more about if my powers would be a big problem so, yeah, I'll do the testing bit. No problem. As for the second part..."

"Yes?"

"I'm pretty sure you already know that answer."

He grinned at her. "I wouldn't mind hearing it."

"Maybe later." She freed her hand from his and slid her fingers into his hair as she indulged her fangirl self in another long deep kiss with Tiger Iron.

THE END

Hidden Strengths

By Harry Heckel

Chapter 1 - Scott's Moment

ABOUT THIRTY MILES OUTSIDE OF MEGALOPOLIS, Scott parked his car, turned it off and stared out the windshield. A dark sky broken by only a handful of cold silver stars stared back. In front of him, or rather in front and below, lay the abandoned Jackson quarry.

"Okay, I'm here," he said, stalling.

He was supposed to get out of the car and walk to the bottom of the quarry. The text message had suggested that he take his shirt off as well. His stomach twisted in protest. This was definitely the dumbest thing he had ever considered doing.

"Why am I here again?" he asked himself, even though he knew the reason. He was here because he was getting paid.

His thoughts raced back to "The Moment" as he thought of it, the instant when his life had changed, his super-powered origin. He had read comic books, played videogames with supers in them and watched more than his share of movies. Most of the heroes who gained their powers through an accident had something dramatic happen. "The Moment" for him had been a stupid prank.

He closed his eyes. Once again, he was Scott Miller, private university student with more loans than he could ever hope to pay, trying to find a major. He had signed up for a tour of the new cyclotron built as part of a recent science push and somehow, he had been selected and allowed the privilege of touring the facility and being on hand for the first big experiment. Sadly, he couldn't even remember what that experiment was now. He briefly broke out of his "The Moment" memory tour to consider using his phone to look it up, but he wasn't sure that he should use his phone.

In any event, he had been uncertain of himself and a bunch of students who knew each other had been giving him a hard time. Scott had gotten shuffled to the back of the tour group and after they had entered the cyclotron, the students ahead of him had shut the door with him inside. That's when it happened.

There had been a bright flash with every color in the rainbow plus some. He shook his head. He still couldn't put words around what he had seen. How do you describe a color that you can't normally see? White-black, but not gray? Reddish green? He sighed.

After the flash, he had fallen. The falling had taken a long, long time, so long that when it ended, he wasn't sure if real life was real anymore. He still wasn't sure that he wasn't in a coma somewhere. After he fell, he heard the voices.

"Get up. We only shut the door for a second."

"OMG! He fainted."

"This guy had a seizure or something."

He vaguely remembered the medical staff checking him. The nurse was a guy who kept shining a light in his eyes. "What happened?" the nurse asked.

"I felt something. I saw colors. Did it get turned on? Was I in there when…?"

The man had laughed. "No. They won't turn it on until later tonight and even then, it will be a bit before it's ready. You weren't actually going to be able to see it in action. Safety checks and such."

And that had been "The Moment." Scott sighed again.

He leaned his head back against the headrest. "Of course, Mr. Nurse-guy, there's a problem with quantum collisions," he said, "particles can go backward in time."

He heard a crunch as he snapped part of the steering wheel. "Damn! No, no, no. Please tell me that I didn't break something else."

A quick inspection showed him that the steering wheel was damaged, but it would work. The car would be fine. Super-powers were supposed to be cool, not make life difficult.

Scott stepped out of the vehicle before he did any more damage to it. The gravel shifted under his tennis shoes. The air was still, and he could hear his own breathing. He wondered if he was being filmed. Looking around, he couldn't see much, just his car, the treeline and the dim outline of the edge of the quarry. He cracked his knuckles and took another deep breath. Then, he balled his hands up into fists and started down the gravel and dirt road into the pit.

He had never really planned to be fighting anyone. As he was growing up, his mom had always referred to him as a gentle soul, more of a scholar than an athlete. He had played a little football until his parents grew concerned about concussions. He had never been great at it, but he wasn't the worst player. The biggest thing that he lacked was speed, but he'd tried to make up for it by lifting weights. He liked weights. Something about having metal in his hands felt right.

Of course, he hadn't been great at that either, not comparing to the massive muscle men who drank green and brown shakes that smelled like swamps and had arms the size of his thighs. Like everything else, he was okay, maybe mediocre. One of the trainers at the gym had once said to him, "Scott, you're a good kid, but you aren't tough enough."

So that was who he was, Scott Miller, not-really-an-athlete, not tough enough, a random accident of quantum-something-maybe, getting ready to go fight somebody he didn't know in an abandoned quarry. How many times had he been pushed around at school for not being cool? How many times had he avoided getting into fights? How many times had he quietly sulked off not wanting to get in trouble or to risk someone pulling a knife on him?

Okay, so there were some good things about superpowers. He was also going to get paid after this. It would be so nice to have some money, to not have to worry about rent, to go out to eat if he wanted, to pay for a date.

Chapter 2 - The Werewolf

HE REACHED THE BOTTOM. He took a few steps forward. Something growled, and he heard movement somewhere in front of him.

"Okay, no going back," he muttered to himself as he took off his shirt and folded it rather shabbily. The growling got louder. Scott's heartbeat quickened.

People die doing stuff like this, he thought.

Lights came on all around the quarry. Scott blinked and heard whirring as cameras suspended by propeller drones flew overhead. He could see his opponent who looked rather... furry?

"What are you? A werewolf?" Scott said.

His foe made a deep growling laugh sound. He certainly looked like a werewolf, not one of the old wolfmen of black and white cinema, but a modern CGI version brought to life, covered in muscle with gleaming teeth and sharp claws.

"Uhh..." said Scott, taking a step back. He hadn't been expecting this. Punches were one thing, but claws were another.

"Okay, rookies, you are about to go live worldwide via the internet. Unlimited Underground Fighting presents a fight to the finish, the Toughman against the Night Howler," announced a voice coming from multiple cameras.

"Wait, fight to the finish?" said Scott. "You didn't say anything about killing anyone."

"Scared?" rasped the Night Howler, narrowing his yellow eyes and licking his snout.

The voice spoke. "Listen, Toughman, or maybe I should say coward boy, the fight goes on until one of you submits or can't fight anymore. Listen, one of you might get killed. It happens, so don't let it be you. There are close to a million people watching. At the end of this, one of you goes viral and gets to move up to the big leagues. Thirty seconds. You better put that face paint on if you don't want everyone to know exactly who you are."

"Okay, okay," said Scott. He reached into his back pocket and started smearing black face paint on. He was sweating already, and he wasn't sure if he was covering his features well enough. He had no idea how any of this would work. When he had started the toughman competitions after "The Moment," he had been punched a million times. Getting cut or bitten was different.

However, it could have been worse. At least Night Howler wasn't radioactive or on fire or something.

Scott started hopping up and down and trying to look like he knew how to fight. He really wished that he had taken a boxing class or signed up for some martial arts. He'd thought about it after he'd found out about his powers, but he figured he'd kill someone trying to spar with them.

"Ten seconds. Make it good and brutal. Five... four... three... two... FIGHT!"

Night Howler threw back his head and howled. When he lowered his head, he flexed, showing off that impressive set of muscles covered with glossy black fur and his vicious-looking claws. He growled at Scott.

At this point, Scott realized that just standing there and watching while the werewolf was howling had been really stupid.

Night Howler charged and smashed into Scott, knocking him into the gravel floor of the pit. The force of the impact was tremendous, and Scott screamed as the werewolf bit into his shoulder. Claws tore into his ribs.

That's when Scott started glowing.

In that brief blur of pain, Scott remembered a conversation that had taken place almost two months before. He had gone to a physicist friend, Rebecca, to ask if there was any substance that got stronger when it was struck.

"There's a lot of work in body armor being done with what they call 'shear-thickening' fluids. Basically, they are liquids that solidify when struck. You should ask some of the Chem guys about that stuff," she had said.

"What about solids that gain energy when they get struck?"

"Lots. Are you talking about kinetic energy or something to do with the electromagnetic spectrum?"

"Um, both maybe? Not sure. Just curious. By the way, would you be interested in going out to dinner later?"

She had sighed. "Not interested. Sorry."

Once again, he had struck out. Searching on the computer had helped a lot, but he didn't have any real explanation for why he got stronger everytime he got hit.

At the moment, he was just thankful that he did.

He put his hand on Night Howler's nose and squeezed. It nearly exploded. The werewolf yelped and rolled off. Scott got to his feet. His skin was glowing orange and his wounds were glowing more brightly than the rest of his body.

Scott grabbed the werewolf by the scruff of the neck and flung him nearly ten feet through the air. Night Howler landed with a thud but scrambled back up, growling.

"Rarr rose roke," the werewolf said, putting a claw over his snout.

Scott saw a decent-sized rock on the ground. He grabbed it and flung it. "You deserved it, Scooby, for fucking trying to bite off my arm."

The rock landed nowhere close. A couple of flying cameras flew all around.

Night Howler charged and leapt with his claws wide. Instinctively, Scott pulled back and punched him. There was crack and the werewolf flew backward again. When he landed, Night Howler howled in pain. Slowly, he rolled over and tried to stand.

Scott wasn't about to wait. He ran over and kicked Night Howler hard in the midsection. Something snapped and the werewolf started choking.

So much power was flowing through Scott, far more than he had ever experienced in the toughman competitions he had tried. He felt invincible. He suddenly realized that every single time that he had been treated badly, every single insult that he had endured, including the crap that the guys had pulled on him at the cyclotron could all be avenged. He had power.

Scott lifted the werewolf's head and pulled back his fist. "Scared?" he angrily asked Night Howler.

There was a soft choking whimper, and the werewolf's yellow eyes looked back at him in agony.

Scott hesitated. What was he about to do? His skin was glowing. What had he become?

"Uh… blink twice if you submit."

Night Howler blinked twice.

"Good," said Scott, putting the werewolf down.

"There it is. The winner, the Toughman, the man unafraid to face a nightmarish horror… call him, Valor!" said the announcer voice.

The lights went out. There was a whirring, and Scott could hear the cameras flying away. At his feet, he heard the shifting of gravel and the sounds of choking. There was a guy where the werewolf had been.

"Want me to call 911?"

"No… I'm gonna be okay," said the werewolf, now in human form. He wheezed harshly. "I just can't breathe. Oh, God."

"Okay, going to get my phone," said Scott.

He ran over and grabbed his shirt and sprinted up the gravel path to the top of the quarry. He called 911 immediately. "There's a guy who I think fell into Jackson Quarry or something. Send help now!"

After answering a few questions, Scott hung up and ran back down. Night Howler was still rasping.

"It's going to be okay," said Scott. "Help is on the way."

When he heard sirens, Scott ran back up to his car. The ambulances had arrived at the other side of the quarry. Very carefully, without turning on his headlights, he drove away.

His cell phone vibrated. He picked it up when he stopped at the main road and glanced at it. He had received an electronic deposit.

"What have I gotten myself into?" he said.

Chapter 3 - Marisa

DEEP INSIDE AN ABANDONED CONCRETE WORKS, Marisa peeked out of a barely open door. She stared out at a crowd of the ultra-rich. Tuxedoed waiters carefully made their way around the tables which would have not have been out of place at a fine restaurant, gathering fine china and clearing the settings. Plasma televisions were carefully being removed from the walls after showing the public bout of the Toughman against Night Howler.

The host of the event spoke through hidden speakers. "Honored guests, we hope that you have enjoyed your dining experience. Please bear with us as we prepare for the next bout. You have certainly noticed the large cage in the center of the room. Those interlocking bars are made of Ultracite, the strongest substance known to man, but don't get too close. The cage itself was originally constructed as part of an American superprison to be used as part of a holding area, but we are able to bring it to you tonight thanks to none other than the U.S. Congress itself! You see, due to spending cuts, that superprison project was closed down and our fine operation was able to come in and help the government stay green and recycle."

Marisa never liked the announcements. She watched as the waiters increased the speed of their efforts. The dishes had vanished save for a few glasses of wine that their owners refused to relinquish. The televisions were off the walls, securely packed away.

"Ladies and gentlemen, I will remind you that with super-powered combatants, even though they will safely maul each other within the cage, you will experience shock waves due to the raw power that each possesses. We cannot guarantee that you won't feel the force of the battle. Of course, that's part of the thrill. The preliminaries are over. Now you will witness a combat between two of the most powerful beings on the planet. You are about to be as close to super-powered combat as possible without actually experiencing it. No more waiting! It's time!"

Cheers erupted in a dozen languages. Women dressed in red carpet gowns clapped their hands while men in fine Italian tailored suits shouted. The crowd wanted blood.

"Your first combatant is a metallic terror who sends even the mightiest of heroes into hiding. I present the destructive power known only as… Armageddon."

Marisa could see Armageddon, a colossal figure, rumored to be a demon trapped in dark fiery bronze armor. He was on the other side of the room from her partially blocked by the cage. He wore a mask, or perhaps helm was a better term, with a demonic face and curled ram's horns. As he stepped into the Ultracite cage, his skin burst into flame. Whatever he was, he certainly wasn't human.

"Armageddon has never been defeated, and none of his last three foes will ever fight again," said the announcer.

Marisa closed the door. She knew that she shouldn't have been watching, but she was too excited not too. She could still hear the announcer clearly.

"However, his opponent is like none other, unbreakable and also undefeated. May I present… Diamond!"

Marisa took a deep breath. She looked down at her glittering gem-encrusted leotard and wondered if they were cubic zirconias or real diamonds. This was the moment that she had trained for.

She stepped away from the door and then smashed it down with a single kick. With her best smile, she strode toward the cage, making sure that everyone got a good look at her. There were audible gasps from the crowd and murmurs, even a few whistles. It was perfect.

"Only one will walk out of this cage. The only rule is survival. Armageddon versus Diamond. Fight!"

Marisa could feel the heat from Armageddon's flames, but she knew that her skin wouldn't burn. She studied him as they circled each other, trying to locate any weak points. He was doing the same. He was at least two feet taller than her own six foot height and had longer reach, but she thought he was slower. She wasn't sure which of them was the stronger, though she assumed that based on size alone, Armageddon would guess that he was. Some of her previous opponents had backed off or hesitated when they realized they were fighting an attractive woman. Based on his body language, Armageddon didn't seem to care.

That was fine with Marisa.

She backed up against the Ultracite bars as Armageddon advanced toward her. His attacks came fast. She barely blocked his right fist, but she did and learned two things. First, she confirmed that the flames didn't bother her. Second, she was at least close to his equal in strength since her forearm didn't snap when she blocked. Despite himself, the monstrous Armageddon seemed surprised by the block and hesitated just enough for Marisa to kick his left knee.

Her foot made a loud clang when it struck his metal body.

Armageddon was slightly off-balance, so Marisa threw herself onto him, into the flames. Someone in the audience screamed. Fire raced all over her body as she slammed Armageddon to the ground. She found herself in a mount position and immediately went for his throat.

Her fingers found burning-hot solid metal as she tried to choke him, but she had a sudden revelation. Armageddon wasn't breathing. He didn't seem to need to breathe.

He caught her with a punch that sent her flying off of him and into the side of the cage. It actually hurt. Armageddon climbed to his feet. The crowd roared as she did a kip-up and flipped from the ground back to a standing position.

Gemstones fell from her leotard as she engaged Armageddon with a series of powerful kicks. He partially blocked one, but she struck home with her second, third and fourth kicks, leaving dents in his chest until he fell against the cage with a thunderous clang. He partially slumped against the Ultracite.

She moved in to grab the horns of his helm but realized that he wasn't as hurt as he appeared only as he embraced her in a terrifyingly tight bear hug. He lifted her off the ground as if she were an unruly child, and she couldn't get any leverage. Her arms were pinned against her body and his flames scorched her. Despite herself, she cried out as much in frustration and anger as in pain.

Attempting to wriggle free didn't do her much good and Armageddon's hands were locked behind her back. Unlike him, she needed to breathe and couldn't get her lungs open. The crowd started chanting, "Armageddon. Arm-a-ged-don. ARMAGEDDON!"

He head-butted her and then did so again and again. She had thought that her skin was unbreakable. As blood started dripping in her eyes, she learned that it wasn't true. There was only one thing that Marisa could think to do. She kicked at his knee again.

It was a wild kick and didn't have much force. She wasn't sure if she struck his knee or his shin, but whatever she hit gave way ever so slightly.

Armageddon stumbled and his grip loosened. That was enough for Marisa to get her arms free. She locked her hands on the horns of his helm and twisted. He flailed for a second before completely losing his balance and falling to the ground with a thunderous boom.

She landed on top of him and as she held on to the horns, she pulled his neck as hard as she could. He roared. The crowd was standing and going wild. He punched her in the ribs with one hand and in the head with the other, but she didn't let go. She managed somehow to get a foot on his abdomen and stand while pulling his head. She stomped on his stomach and his groin.

Something metal broke beneath her foot. She felt fire race up her leg, much hotter than the flames had been before. He convulsed and stopped punching her. She held his head for an extra moment and then dropped it.

He lay on the ground, bits of metal all around, gemstones scattered across his body. The fires had stopped burning. Marisa stepped away from him. She could taste blood in her mouth, and her entire body was glistening with sweat from the heat. There wasn't much left of her leotard, and she didn't think anything was left of the makeup that she had spent an hour working on before the fight.

It didn't matter. She had won.

The crowd chanted, "Diamond. Diamond. Diamond."

She raised her arms in triumph and enjoyed her moment, knowing full well that this was the best she could ever hope for.

"Your winner - the unbreakable Diamond!" said the announcer.

The cage door opened, and Marisa felt a terrible feeling of dread. It was time to return to her life.

Chapter 4 – Reality

MARISA DID HER BEST TO HOLD ON to the sound of the cheering and wrap it around herself like a warm blanket, even as she discarded the tatters of her leotard on the tiles of the shower room. Blood splattered on the tiles whenever she looked down. She had a ringing sound in her ears and bruises were starting to form along her ribs.

But she had won, and nothing felt better than that.

She closed her eyes and tried to fix the memories of the bout. She never wanted to forget anything again, but this was really important. She re-imagined the blows and the feeling of her foot crushing Armageddon. All of her training, all of her determination had paid off.

She smiled and looked around as she opened her eyes. Of course, she was the only one in the room. No one was here, which was reasonable. She was about to take a shower, but still she felt empty. Marisa didn't have anyone to congratulate her.

"You are the only one who matters," she said to herself.

Marisa got into the shower and turned it on. The water ran ice-cold at first. Although she hadn't seen any visible burns on her body, the cold water felt good. By the time it warmed up, she closed her eyes and just enjoyed how it felt. She put her face in the stream and let the shower remove all the blood. She touched her scalp, running her fingers along her forehead and through her hair. She found a hard scab.

"Looks like I heal quickly when someone does break the skin," she said.

She heard footsteps coming. Based on sound, it was someone in heels, probably Ivy.

"Marisa, how are you doing?"

That was definitely Ivy, her caretaker, her handler, and she sounded genuinely concerned. Ivy watched her, directed her and made sure she received the training she needed. When she asked for things like clothes or books or television privileges, Ivy provided them. She didn't like having someone run her life, but at this moment, she just wanted someone to celebrate with her.

"I won," said Marisa proudly. "I broke Armageddon."

"Yes, you did, but I saw you were bleeding. There's blood all over the place out here. Is this what's left of your leotard?"

"Did you hear me, Ivy? I won."

"Yeah, Marisa. You were great. The crowd loved it," said Ivy distractedly.

Marisa poured shampoo in her hair, lathered and rinsed it out. Ivy had said the right words, but she didn't sound like she meant them. Marisa suddenly felt like a little girl, desperate for approval. She tried to remember the crowd chanting her name.

Instead, memories of her family came rushing back. As always, they were shreds, ripped pieces of a torn painting, but they were all she had.

She saw a small house surrounded by many green trees. "Marisita, Marisita," said her papa, picking her up and swinging her into the air. He had bright sparkly brown eyes and a soft dark beard. Papa was wearing a hat. She knew that he always wore hats, even if she couldn't remember them.

Mama was showing her how to cook with a great big black pan.

She chased a giant blue and black butterfly on a dirt road.

Her brother had a red ball, and she was playing with him, kicking it back and forth.

She sang as loudly as she could in church.

The soldiers came, and she had screamed.

Needles and blue masks, bright lights and tubes with dripping liquid. "Flawless. Her DNA is exactly what we needed." The memory of the doctors made her shiver.

She pressed her palm against the tile wall of the shower. The wall cracked and pieces of tile fell next to the drain.

"Marisa, are you sure you're okay?" asked Ivy. "You can take a real shower at the mansion. We need to be out. Orders."

Marisa turned off the water and stepped out of the shower. Ivy handed her a towel.

"Clothes in your duffel bag?" Ivy asked.

"Yes," said Marisa as went over to her bag and unzipped it. She quickly pulled out her clothes and dressed in a sweatshirt and jeans. "Ivy?" Marisa asked.

"What?"

"Could I go out and celebrate? Like into the city and just talk to people?"

Ivy sighed. "Seriously? Do we have to go over this now? You are an undocumented alien with superpowers. If you are caught by the government, they will put you away for a long, long time. If you had too much to drink, you could kill someone. Think about it. You would never see your family or anyone else."

Marisa clenched a fist. Ivy was right, but she didn't want to hear it.

"Listen," said Ivy softly, stroking Marisa's arm, "we will help you get your memories back. We'll find out who you were and locate your family. The sponsors will make sure that everything's right... as long as you keep winning. Now, let's go back to the mansion. I'm sure Dominic has a celebration for you."

Marisa met Ivy's eyes. She wanted to believe that everything was going to get better. She wanted to believe that she would remember her family and find them. Yet, no matter how she tried, she just didn't trust Ivy or Dominic or any of the trainers.

But Ivy was right. She didn't have any other options.

Chapter 5 - Tyrell

SCOTT PULLED INTO HIS APARTMENT COMPLEX. His hands were shaking so badly that he thought he might tear his steering wheel off instead of just snapping another piece. Had he just killed someone?

He sat in the parking lot and stared up at the 5th floor of the Leonard Building where he lived. He found his window and saw that the lights were on. His roommate and best friend since freshman orientation, Tyrell, was still awake.

"I hope he doesn't have a girl up there," said Scott, checking the time on his cell phone. It was 1:17 am. Maybe it would be better if Ty had a girl up there. He might not ask Scott any questions.

"What have I done?" he asked himself.

He got out of his car and headed inside. His hands were still shaking as he carefully swiped his pass card. Scott purposely was as gentle as possible when he opened the door.

The night desk guy raised his head and started staring. Scott felt a surge of panic. Was he glowing? Was there a lot of blood on him?

"Hey, you have dirt or something all over your face and you look like a mess. Were you mugged?"

Scott tried to wipe his face and smeared some of the face paint on his hand. "Uh, I was doing a paintball after dark thing," he said. "Went way too long. Sorry, didn't mean to scare you or anything. It's me, Scott Miller, Apartment 513."

"Yeah, yeah. Just wanted to make sure you were okay." With that, the night desk guy went back to staring at his computer monitor.

Scott hurried over to the elevator, praying that no one else would notice him. He had completely forgotten about the face paint. The elevator doors opened right after he pressed the up button. He hurried inside, and they closed behind him.

The elevators in the Leonard Building were odd. They always bothered Scott. For one thing, the lighting in them seemed to be on the dim side. For another thing, they seemed to move between floors at their own individual rates, which Scott was sure varied from day to day. While he didn't consider himself to be claustrophobic, he always felt a slight sense of relief when he got off the elevator.

"So, you beat the crap out of a real life werewolf, but elevators scare you. Man, Scott, you are a piece of work," he said to himself. "And you talk to yourself way too much."

The doors finally opened, and he stepped out on the fifth floor, keeping his head down. He walked quickly over to his apartment, unlocked the door and went inside, shutting and locking the door behind him.

"Oh man! I've never seen anyone hit someone that hard!" shouted Tyrell from the living room.

"Rewind, I want to see it again," came a woman's voice also from the living room.

"Yo, Scott! Is that you?" said Tyrell. "Come see this."

Scott's bedroom was right off the foyer. He didn't have to go into the living room. "Uh, Tyrell, I'm out of it. I need bed right now. Sorry."

Scott slipped into his bedroom, shut and locked the door.

A moment later, Tyrell knocked on his door. "Man, it's some footage they caught of Argent. He's a bad, bad man. Criminals will volunteer to go to jail to avoid running into that guy."

"No, um, I'm really messed up. In the morning."

Scott thanked God that he had his own bathroom. He went in and started washing off his face. He was an awful mess. Dried blood was on his jeans and one of the legs was torn, well, slashed actually. He undid his belt and stepped out of the jeans while trying to scrub with a washcloth in one hand and pull his shirt off with the other.

There was another knock. "Scott?"

The black paint was mostly off now. It looked more like smudges. As he stepped back to take a look, he started staring at his own chest and abs. He looked absolutely ripped. He could see muscles in places that Scott didn't even realize had muscles.

"Scott?" said Tyrell.

Scott grabbed his robe. "Yeah," he said, doing his best to sound exhausted.

"Are you okay, man? Look, I've never seen you do much drinking or anything. You didn't try some pills or inhale some powder or something?"

What if Tyrell called the police or something? Although, Scott wondered if he should be watching the news to see if there was any information about Night Howler. He hoped the guy would be okay, even if he had sort of tried to eat Scott.

Scott tied his robe and opened the door. Tyrell wasn't the sort to drop something until he got an answer.

"Hey, thanks for worrying, but it's nothing like that," said Scott. "I've been on this fitness kick and just killed myself at the gym."

Tyrell tilted his head and examined Scott's face. "I've noticed," he said and quietly added, "so have some of the ladies. LaTanya has this friend…"

"That would be cool but not now. Really. I'm beat," Scott said.

"Okay, but there was some grease or something on one of those barbells you were lifting. It's all over your face."

"Oh," said Scott, "um, thanks. I guess I should wash that off too."

"One last thing, tomorrow's rent day. I know I spotted you last month, but, man, I can't do it again," said Tyrell.

"I got it. For both of us. I'm good. I called my parents."

Tyrell smiled. "Awesome. Get some rest then. You look like shit. I've got LaTanya waiting."

"Enjoy," said Scott, shutting the door.

He went over to his pants, pulled out his phone and called up his banking app. Ten thousand dollars had shown up in his account, bringing his balance to $10,138.53.

"Wow," he said to himself.

An appointment had also appeared for tomorrow. He didn't know the address but the description said "Career Planning. Urgent. Toughman."

Chapter 6 - The Party

THE SUV DROVE AROUND THE SIDE OF THE MANSION and Marisa saw the pool lights on. She couldn't help but feel a little excitement. It was her night, Diamond's night. Maybe Dominic and the sponsors were doing something special for her.

Ivy was right. She had everything that she could want. She just needed to accept and enjoy it.

What if she did find her family? She couldn't remember much at all about her former life, really about anything before the doctors. Would her family even know her? Could they understand what she had become?

Tonight, she resolved to herself, she would embrace her life. She was Diamond. She was unbreakable, and she had defeated Armageddon.

The SUV stopped. One of the guards, wearing a suit, walked up from the mansion and opened her door. She got out. Ivy followed.

Marisa could hear music and laughter. Guests from the fight were cavorting around the pool. She caught a glimpse of waiters bringing out drinks and food. There was a large screen showing images from her bout.

She felt a small rush of excitement.

Ivy nudged her away from the pool toward one of the discreet servant entrances to the mansion.

"I want to go. It's about me," Marisa said.

"I know," said Ivy, reaching forward to open the door for her, "but you need to get another shower and get changed. We'll head up to your room. You take a quick shower and I'll make sure that you have something magnificent to wear."

Marisa did as she was told, and as she did, her resolve to embrace her life seemed to crumble. She showered quickly, and when she finished, she discovered that Ivy had hung a gorgeous black gown with a long slit in the skirt in her bedroom. She wasn't sure what the material was, but it felt heavenly. A set of black flats rested on the floor beneath the dress.

She stared at them. She wished that she could wear heels, but Ivy said she was too strong for them and they'd snap. Marisa didn't believe her. She thought that it would make her taller than Dominic, and she suspected that he didn't like that.

Marisa did her hair and got dressed. When she was done, she left her room and stole down the hallway toward the pool. She tried to be as quiet as possible because she wanted to eavesdrop and hear what people were saying about her.

The first voices that she heard were those of Dominic and one of his assistants. They were standing in the great room that opened to the back pool.

"As you can see, sir, it's one of the most impressive things we've seen," said the assistant.

Marisa smiled. Making Dominic happy was important, although she didn't exactly know why she felt that way. Something about thinking about it made her uncomfortable.

"Yes, it is. Toughman though? That's a terrible name," said Dominic.

Marisa's mouth dropped open. How could they be watching Toughman against Night Howler?

"The announcer suggested Valor, sir," said the assistant.

"Perhaps. Still not what I want. I need to see him again. Set him up to come to the mansion. We are going to offer him far more money for his next fight."

"Done."

Marisa leaned back against the wall. Her eyes burned. She had won. She knew she should understand, but she couldn't. Not tonight. Clenching her fists, she stormed out of the hall to confront Dominic.

"I'm here," she announced.

Dominic glanced up from the tablet he was holding. He was a dark-haired middle-aged man with an edge to him that scared other men. She knew that he had once commanded soldiers, and a voice inside her head told her that she should always obey him. Tonight, he wore a black tuxedo. His cold blue eyes regarded her.

"Hello, Marisa," he said calmly.

She wondered why he always seemed so unafraid of her. She could tear him apart. She could destroy the whole mansion.

Her head started to hurt.

"What's wrong?" he asked. "Are you hurt? I don't think I've ever seen you bleed."

Marisa's cheeks became warm. Armageddon had made her bleed. Was that why Dominic was watching the other fight?

"I'm okay. I'm just… maybe I'm unhappy. Why are you watching the other fight, Dominic? I'm better than Toughman or whatever you decide to call him. I would have turned Night Howler into a throw rug."

He shrugged. "I'm fascinated by our new fighter. He does something that I haven't seen before, and after what happened with you and Armageddon, I need to keep recruiting."

Had she killed Armageddon? He didn't breathe. Could he die? She felt a strange visceral thrill at the idea, and at the same time, a twisting nausea. She hadn't even considered the possibility. Why hadn't she considered it?

"I want to find my family," she said, but she didn't know where the words had come from.

Dominic sighed. "That's up to you. Keep winning, and we'll have the resources from the sponsors that we need. Let's get you some more medicine for your brain. It'll help you remember."

"No," said Marisa, shaking her head. "I want to celebrate. I want to dance. I won. Did you see it? I won. I'm unbreakable. How much money did I earn tonight? All the other fighters get paid. What about me?"

"Marisa, you get to live here. With the way you are feeling tonight, I don't think you should go celebrate anything," he said.

Ivy had come up beside her. "Marisa, Dominic's right. You need to go to bed."

Marisa didn't want to do it, but she knew that she had to. What other choice did she have? "Okay, Ivy," she said.

She turned around and headed back to her bedroom. When she reached the door, she hesitated. "I don't want to go to bed," she said as she turned the doorknob.

The door was open. She was tired. She thought about all the men in the tuxedos out by the pool. She wasn't allowed to touch any of them, because Ivy said that she could kill them. Marisa felt so trapped and so angry inside. She wanted to be Diamond. She wanted to fight and hear the crowd cheer. She loved being Diamond.

Marisa went into the room and closed the door behind her. The memory headphones lay on her nightstand next to her pills. Maybe tonight she'd remember something important.

She kicked off her shoes, and they flew across the room. She shook her head and lay down on the bed without bothering to take off the dress. She saw the headphones out of the corner of her eye.

She flipped off her lights without taking her pills or putting on the headphones and cried herself to sleep.

Chapter 7 - The Meeting

WHEN MARISA OPENED HER EYES, she felt far better than she had expected. As she sat up, a pain in her side and a half dozen warm aches reminded her of the fight from the night before. Out of curiosity, she reached up and touched the scab on her scalp. It was nearly gone.

The headphones lay unused on her nightstand. "Oh, I forgot about them," she said for the benefit of anyone who might be listening.

She looked around her room, taking her time to let her eyes linger on the large picture of the new Megalopolis cityscape. She wished that she could enjoy everything instead of feeling like a prisoner. She dared another glance at the headphones. Were they really helping her remember anything?

She shook her head and realized that it was a mistake. "Okay, Armageddon hit you very hard. Even unbreakable superwomen need time to recover."

After a short prayer of thanks for the day to come, Marisa began her routine. She didn't want to disappoint Dominic and the sponsors any more than she had the night before. She wasn't sure exactly what she had done wrong before the party, but maybe she had been slightly concussed by the fight.

Her morning shower was followed by a change into shorts and a sports bra and a walk down to the basement gym. "Start light," she said to herself. "Warm up."

The gym itself looked more like a facility for testing heavy machinery to Marisa than the gyms that she had seen on television. There were mats on side of the room and lots of standard gym equipment, but everything was specially reinforced. On the other side of the room were the crushers, large concrete cylinders and a well-dented titanium steel wall. She loved that wall.

Marisa went through some stretches and decided that she was in the mood for a few katas before any lifting. Performing the katas always gave her a sense of peace. After she was done, she went over to the thousand pound barbell and started a series of warm up exercises. For her, a thousand pounds was a light weight.

She shot a look at one of the concrete cylinders. "Today is your last day on earth," she promised it with a smile.

"Marisa," said Dominic over the gym's speakers, "You are needed to escort a guest. Shower and change into your red bathing suit. You can do some laps after he leaves if you'd like."

She sighed, but there wasn't anything she could do. If Dominic needed her, he needed her. Thoughts of disobedience crept into her mind. What if she didn't listen? What would he do?

She contemplated it for a moment, but any man with the resources to provide her with a mansion like this and be able to arrange super-powered bouts could find a way to punish her. All he had to do was to tell one of the government agencies about her. The good mood she had been working on faded.

Half an hour later, Marisa had showered again. She changed into her v-cut red one piece bathing suit. She put light glitter on her legs, slipped on her silver barefoot sandals and finished the outfit with a thin silver chain belt.

She resented this part. One of the fighters or a potential fighter was coming for a visit, and Dominic liked to have her close just in case someone got out of hand. As Ivy told her, if she wore something skimpy, it only enhanced Dominic's image and distracted the fighter. More importantly, if an idiot tried something they wouldn't expect the woman in the bathing suit to stop them.

Marisa cracked her knuckles. Maybe this guy would cause trouble. It might give her a chance to reaffirm to Dominic how valuable she was.

She went to the side entrance. Ivy was waiting for her.

"What did you forget last night?" asked Ivy.

"I'm sorry. I got emotional after the bout, and I was tired. I didn't think," said Marisa. "Did you come in and check on me?"

"I always check on you," said Ivy, giving her a smile. "Walk him in by the pool. He's new to the mansion, so Nathan's playing the role of Dominic until we have a better feel for our friend. Dominic will be watching. You handle it." She walked away, leaving Marisa as the sole greeter.

"Fine," said Marisa, wishing she could get back to her workout.

A cheap compact car drove up and idled for a second. Marisa opened the door. The car window rolled down and a guy asked, "Do I park here or keep going?"

"Park there," said Marisa, smiling as brightly as she could muster and walking out to meet him.

The guy got out, fumbled his keys as he shut the door and half-gasped as she approached him. His mouth moved slightly, but he didn't say anything. He was wearing a dark suit, but it seemed tight on him. It wasn't a very expensive suit and certainly hadn't been tailored.

"Um, I thought this was like a job interview. I certainly... um, as you know I'm Scott. Hi." He extended his hand for her to shake.

"Hi, Scott," she said, taking her hand, "I'm Marisa."

"Marisa," he said, as if he was trying to make sure he knew how to pronounce it. He then followed with, "I'm pleased to meet you."

Scott had a good solid handshake, but Marisa made certain to be gentle. He was about her height, maybe a half-inch taller, and nothing about him reminded her of the other fighters she had met. He had some muscle definition, but she had seen plenty of stronger-looking men. He was definitely nervous, and most of the fighters came in with an arrogant swagger. None of them had dressed in a bad suit. A sliver of doubt stuck in her mind. What if he was an insurance agent or something?

"Are you... ?" she started to ask slowly.

"I'm Toughman. Well, I was last night. I hate the name though. Am I going to be Valor? Oh, wait. I'm sorry about the questions. I mean, you should probably be asking the questions. I didn't expect you to..." He stopped and looked down.

"Hey," she said, this time with an honest smile, "take a breath."

Scott raised his head and looked her in the eye. He had soft blue eyes the color of the sky on a summer day. There was something about his eyes that was different than those of anyone else she knew.

Kindness. He had kind eyes, like her father's. They were a different color, but she could see it. Her mother's face appeared in her head. Mama was wiping her mouth and cheeks. Mama's eyes had that softness too. She looked away as she released his hand.

If he had noticed anything unusual, he didn't show it.

"How is Night Howler doing? This morning I heard that a man who had tried to commit suicide at the Jackson Quarry had been taken to the hospital. I also heard that police were investigating. I was ready to fight him, but I did't want to kill anyone."

"I don't know, but we can find out," she said. She wanted to repeat what Dominic always said. They are super-powered battles. People die. Just make sure it isn't you. "I think we should go inside."

She turned around and headed back toward the pool. She opened the gate for him. He looked a little flushed. "Are you okay?" she asked. "Are you still recovering from your fight?"

"I'm fine. You just aren't what I expected."

"What do you mean?" Marisa asked.

"I don't know how to put this, but I thought I'd be talking to some older man, not a woman in a bathing suit."

She laughed. "I'm not in charge. Dominic is. I'm just your escort."

"Oh. I thought this was your mansion."

"I live here," she said.

They walked by the pool, and Scott took it all in, staring down the length of the Olympic-sized pool out to the manicured lawns beyond. He seemed so overwhelmed by it all.

She couldn't stay quiet. "Why are you doing this?" she asked.

"Because I have the power, because I need the money, because I don't think I could be or know how to be a superhero," he said.

Before she could respond, the glass doors to the mansion opened.

Chapter 8 – The Interview

A THIN MAN IN A BLACK SUIT stepped out of the mansion. "Mr. Miller," he said, "Please come in."

Scott shrugged slightly at Marisa and followed the man. He adjusted the knot on his tie as he stepped through the doors. His eyes were immediately drawn to a fully stocked wet bar done in black marble with gold taps. He wondered if his apartment might fit in the sitting area. It made him think of a high-end furniture store showroom, but the sets of comfortable looking recliners and couches matched. One wall had an inset giant aquarium filled with corals and multi-colored fish, while another had the largest HD TV that he had ever seen.

He was still trying to take everything in, when Marisa gently touched his arm and guided him over to a couch. She took a chair caddy corner to his and shifted slightly to face him. Scott had to remind himself not to stare at her.

The man who he assumed was Dominic sat across from him on the end of another couch. He gave Scott a slightly disapproving look. "So, let's discuss your future."

"Yes, sir," Scott said, shifting as he tried to decide if he should attempt to look relaxed or sit up straight. He stole a glance at Marisa. She seemed amused.

"You did well in your first bout, very well. I was impressed and our sponsors were impressed. The video went viral. That's the good news."

Scott nodded. He decided that it would be best to stay quiet. He wanted to ask about Night Howler, but he thought it would be better to let Dominic make his point.

Dominic sighed. "The bad news is that people are viewing it because they want to see a werewolf getting his ass kicked. No one wants to see you. We have a problem."

"How is Night Howler?" asked Scott.

Dominic sat back after he heard the question. He raised his hand to his ear and tapped an earpiece that Scott hadn't noticed before. "He's alive."

"Thank goodness." Scott breathed a sigh of relief.

Another woman, dressed far more than Marisa and very attractive entered the room. She was holding a small bag. Scott tried to stay focused on Dominic.

"Thank goodness?" said Dominic. "What kind of fighter are you? Scott, you have potential, but we need to be able to market you. Valor isn't the worst name, but it doesn't say much. Toughman is abysmal, but we were desperate. I need to know who you are. We want to build a future for you. Looking that relieved that a werewolf who tried to eat you survived your fight makes me wonder if you have what it takes to win."

The woman Scott didn't know sat down at the far end of his couch. She began opening her bag.

"Maybe he's not a fighter," said Marisa.

"I am. I won," said Scott, "I just haven't hurt anyone that badly before. Usually there are doctors around or something."

Dominic spoke, "If you are scared of hurting someone, why did you participate in toughman competitions?"

"I wanted to make some extra money, and I knew I could win."

"No, that's not it," said Dominic. "There are lots of ways to make money with your strength. As one example, you could have gone into tree and stump removal. Instead, you started fighting. Why?"

"I'm not sure that I want to continue fighting," Scott said. He had said it. He wasn't sure that he was going to be able to say it, but he had. He waited for Dominic to thank him and say goodbye.

"That's not what I asked," Dominic said instead. "Why do you fight? Be honest. You just said that you aren't sure you want to continue. I'd like to know the truth. You might want to know it too, Scott."

Marisa sat forward. She was watching him carefully, waiting to see what he would say.

"I guess I wanted to prove something to myself."

"What?" asked Dominic.

"I'm not sure. That I could do it I guess."

"Have you ever been great at something? Don't answer. We both know that the answer is no."

Scott turned to look at the woman on the couch with him. The bag was a medical kit. He turned quickly back to Dominic. Marisa flinched as if she were about to get out of her chair.

"Who is she?" Scott asked.

"She's a medical professional. Back to what I was saying, the point is that you can be great. One of my sponsors believes that you have the potential to be the best fighter we've ever had."

Marisa turned her head to look at Dominic and then shot a questioning glance at the woman with the medical bag. Scott tried to ignore her and concentrate on Dominic.

"You also need to make a lot more money. I'm thinking 100 Gs for the next bout."

Scott froze. The reality of that much money struck him. He had planned to come here and quit. He wanted to say that money wasn't important, but instead he asked, "Wouldn't someone notice?"

The woman on his couch said, "We'll give you a list of banks that handle offshore accounts. There's a lot we can do for you."

"Ivy, what are you doing?" said Marisa. "If he doesn't want to fight, why are you trying to make him? As…" she paused and gestured toward the man across from Scott, "As Dominic said, he wasn't even popular."

"Thank you, Marisa," said Ivy, in a tone that indicated Marisa had said more than enough. "Now, Scott, what do you want?"

Scott thought as Ivy and Dominic watched him patiently. Somewhere the conversation had changed, and Scott realized that he was out of his league. Marisa seemed slightly irritated and somewhat disdainful. She was a beautiful athletic woman, the sort that would never even glance at a guy like Scott.

What did his future hold? Did he want to be a landscape guy? A mover? Could he be a personal bodyguard?

This was his chance to do something amazing. The "Moment" had changed him. He could live out his fantasies. He would be like an Olympic hero or an NFL star, well, perhaps more like a pro wrestling or MMA champion, but still…

He remembered his original plan, the one he had created in his mind before Night Howler. This was his training. This would be his way of testing himself. This would his way of gathering the resources to be what he really wanted to be… a superhero.

That seemed so naïve now.

The silence had lingered. Scott gazed over at Marisa again, taking in her legs and the way the red bathing suit clung to her. He looked at the colossal TV in wonder. He thought about the size of the mansion and what it would be like to lounge at the pool outside.

"You're right. I do have something to prove. And that kind of money sounds great. I'll do it, but I have no idea what sort of name to use."

"We'll think of something," said Ivy. "Now, I need a blood sample." She slid over to him with the syringe. "Take off the jacket and roll up your sleeve."

Scott did as he was told. "I don't think it will work. It takes a lot of force to break my skin."

"Make a fist for me. Good veins and nice arms. You look like you're a little better conditioned in person. Don't worry, it has a diamond tip." Ivy pressed against syringe against Scott's forearm and it pierced the skin.

Scott looked away as Ivy drew blood.

Marisa smiled and crossed and uncrossed her legs. "Are you afraid of blood…," she asked, "….or diamonds?" She had a strange playful sparkle in her dark eyes.

"Never liked needles, actually," Scott said. He felt rather stupid as he asked, "By the way, why do you need the blood sample?"

Great job, Scott, he thought to himself, let them take your DNA without asking what it's for. An army of Scott clones marched through his mind.

Dominic answered. "HIV, things like that. We have audiences at a few elite events, and as you know, there's blood spilled in our fights. We strive to make sure that everyone is as safe as possible."

"Done," announced Ivy. She put away the syringe and taped a piece of gauze over the wound. "For those we decide have potential, we assign handlers. I'll be working with you."

Marisa made a sound like a startled gasp. "You'll be his handler?" she said.

"In addition to my other duties," she said, "yes."

Dominic stood up. "That's it, Scott. We'll contact you about your next fight. In the meantime, you'll receive information from Ivy about offshore accounts and we'll set up how you'll receive payment. If there's anything worrisome about your blood, we'll let you know. Marisa, go ahead and escort our guest out."

Scott offered his hand to Dominic. "Thank you, sir."

"Sorry," Dominic said. "No one here shakes hands with people who can break steel."

Scott paused as he remembered shaking hands with Marisa. Maybe she had made a mistake. He picked up his jacket, still not exactly sure how things had progressed the way that they had. They hadn't even asked him any real questions.

Marisa led him out.

As they got to his car, Scott said, "It was good meeting you. I'm sorry that you don't think I can be a fighter."

"I didn't say that," she said. "I'm just not sure that I want to see you get hurt. You seem like a nice guy."

Scott nearly rolled his eyes. How many women in his life had told him that he was a nice guy? It was up there with being told what a good friend he was. He looked her in the eyes. She seemed confused. He decided to try something stupid. After all, he had just agreed to keep fighting super-powered opponents and gave a blood sample to a woman he had never met. If something bad was going to happen, he had already laid the groundwork.

"Would you be interested in getting together for coffee or a drink? Dinner perhaps?" he asked.

Marisa blinked at him. He thought that maybe she had seen a ghost. Her mouth was partially open.

"Just a coffee sometime? I can pay," he said, managing a weak grin.

"I can't. I really want to, but I can't," she said, glancing around nervously. She shifted her weight from one foot to the other and folded her arms across her chest.

"It's okay," Scott shrugged. "Believe me, it's the answer I expect. Thanks though."

Yes, he was still himself, despite the superpowers.

He got in the car and pulled away. As he looked in the rearview mirror, he realized that Marisa hadn't moved. She was still standing by the mansion in her red bathing suit, staring after him.

Chapter 9 - Secrets

SCOTT DROVE BACK HOME. He felt relieved when he saw the Leonard Building. The trip to the mansion had been like a strange dream. Now, he was back to reality, back to his world.

"One hundred thousand dollars," said Scott. That kind of money seemed inconceivable. He'd have to be careful with it though. He couldn't buy a really expensive car or anything, but it would help take a chunk out of his student loans. He wasn't going to let himself be like those professional athletes who spent all their money during their career and went broke. "Investments," he said to himself.

He went into the building, waved to the daytime lady manning the desk, and pushed the elevator button. He tried to tell himself that he didn't have to go through with fighting, but he really didn't see any reasonable alternatives. He kept thinking about that pool in the rear of the mansion and Marisa. Didn't he deserve to have some luxury?

The elevator doors opened. The elevator was empty. Scott stepped in and pushed the button for the fifth floor. He undid his tie and slung his jacket under his arm. "I don't need a roommate anymore," he said to himself as the doors closed. It wasn't that he didn't like Tyrell, but they hadn't been roommates long. His old roommate, Brian, had left for a job in California shortly after the "Moment." Scott had been desperate for funds which was why he had decided to try his first toughman competition. Thankfully, he had won the $1000 prize and his parents had spotted him the rest. Tyrell had answered the ad at just the right time.

However, not having a roommate would make things much less complicated, especially if he was fighting.

The elevator seemed to be moving slowly again. Scott was growing concerned when the doors suddenly opened. "I could move out of this building," he observed as he stepped into the hall.

He reached the apartment and started to unlock the door. Before he could finish, the door opened from the inside. Tyrell stood in front of him. "So, we need to talk."

"What?" asked Scott, "I paid the rent before I went to my interview."

"Come in to the living room and sit down. Like I said, we need to talk." Tyrell indicated a seat on the couch. He looked annoyed.

Scott went over to the couch and sat down. "What's wrong? Is it the bills? I didn't take any leftovers out of the fridge, I swear."

Tyrell sat on the arm of the living room recliner, a reclamation project from a secondhand store. He crossed his arms, tilted his head and stared at Scott. "You tell me."

"I don't know," said Scott.

"I'll give you a hint. Your father called. He wanted to know if you needed money since he hadn't given you any this month. Since I didn't want to cause you any family issues, I told him that I thought you were okay. That was when you were in the shower. So, you know what I did when you got all dressed up and headed out to your job interview?"

"What?" asked Scott.

"I followed your ass, that's what. Nice mansion. I think you told me that it was a healthcare company. Hmm… pharmaceuticals, I bet."

"Huh? No," said Scott.

Tyrell looked over at Scott's sleeves. "Arms… now."

"Look," said Scott, "It's not what you think. I had a blood test." Scott rolled up his sleeves. "I have tape and gauze."

"Jesus, Scott! What kind of idiot do you think I am? You paid rent for both of us. You lied to me about the money. You looked like shit when you came home last night. Let me show you something."

Tyrell turned on the TV. Before this morning, Scott had thought that the TV was okay sized at almost 40 inches. Now it seemed tiny. Tyrell went to the DVR and started playing the news.

"You see that. That's Argent in silver there, punching the hell out of that criminal. See it. This is what a security camera caught."

Argent, Megalopolis' resident crimefighter, flipped in front of a man with a pistol. Argent performed a lightning fast strike to the man's chest and the guy collapsed.

"Boom!" said Tyrell. "You know who that guy was?"

"Argent?"

"No, the criminal who needs to learn how to breathe again."

"No," said Scott.

"He... is... a... drug dealer. You got me? Do we understand each other? That is what happens to drug dealers." Tyrell folded his arms again, having made his point. "I'm putting it on replay. Watch it. Scott, you've got to stop."

"No, Tyrell, it's not like that. I had an accident. Look, you wouldn't believe me."

"Okay," said Tyrell, standing up. He walked over to the window and stood with his back to Scott. "I'm sorry, man. I tried to help you."

"Ty, listen, it's crazy..." Scott didn't feel well. This wasn't what he had expected, and he didn't know what to do. Should he tell Tyrell?

"Scott, the feds know about you," said Tyrell.

"What are you talking about?"

Tyrell turned around to face him. He turned the scene of Argent off. In a low voice, Tyrell said, "There was a lady who approached me yesterday. Pretty lady, really fit, decent suit but not too expensive. She showed me a badge. She was some part of Homeland Security. She asked me to watch you carefully and report anything unusual. She told me that you weren't in trouble necessarily, but that they were worried that you might be getting involved with the wrong people. She was a federal agent. Scott, I'm telling you that your only hope of not going to jail for the rest of your life is to tell her everything."

Ty handed Scott a card. "Call her."

The card was for an interior decorating company. This was crazy.

"Yeah," said Tyrell, "I know about the card. The number is what's important. Call her, and use this phone."

Ty reached into his pocket and gave Scott a small and extremely thin phone.

Scott held the phone and hesitated. What had he done wrong? Did he need to talk to anyone? What about the money? Superheroes fought supervillains all the time. They didn't have to report to federal agents.

"I'm not doing drugs. I'm not selling drugs. I'm in some semi-amateur fights, and I won some prize money."

Tyrell didn't say anything.

"I'm not calling anyone. I haven't done anything," Scott said. He stood up. "Thanks for worrying."

Tyrell shook his head and sighed. "Fine. They told me that I wouldn't be implicated, so it's just you. Keep the phone and the number. If you decide that something isn't right, call them. Deal?"

"Deal."

Chapter 10 - Going Forward

MARISA WATCHED SCOTT DRIVE AWAY. She wasn't sure how to react. She was used to the fighters who came for their interviews leering at her, not stealing glances. They'd come up to her and brag about themselves and their prowess. They'd offer to let her do them. She was used to graphic sexual offers.

No one had ever asked her if she'd like to have coffee. No one had ever asked her for a date.

Why did he bother her so much? That swift look of disappointment when she told him that she couldn't stung her. It hurt inside, and she was angry because she wanted to go but couldn't. Dominic wouldn't let her. She wasn't allowed.

Marisa made a fist and studied it. She wanted to be fighting. She wanted not to think about anything and just fight. She wanted to feel the adrenaline rush and hear the crowd. She wanted to struggle and triumph.

"But I can't… I can't fight this… this…" she said, looking around at the mansion. This what? Was it the mansion? Was it Dominic's rules? Was it the laws of this land of the free that would lock her up for not having papers and being taken from her home? Was it that for all the power she had, she didn't even get to go on a date?

"I'm not allowed to go have coffee," she said quietly and released the fist. She remembered the smell of coffee. It was a smell of her home, lost so long ago. Ivy never let her have coffee. She said that caffeine was bad for her, and she needed to stay in perfect condition.

She was Diamond.

"Marisa, come inside," said Ivy, who was standing at the gate to the pool area.

She did as she was told. Dominic, the real Dominic, was waiting for her, and Nathan, the assistant, quickly left the room.

Dominic sat down on one of the couches. "Marisa, we need to talk."

Marisa's heart beat a little faster, but she decided not to let it bother her. "Sure," she replied.

Dominic never looked at her the way that the men and even a few of the women who fought for the organization did. He always seemed to be judging her, evaluating her, and it always seemed that she came up short no matter what she did. She didn't know why, but she longed for Dominic to be proud of her.

Ivy tapped her on the shoulder. "Sit down, Marisa," she said and Marisa heard a "don't be difficult" implied in her tone.

Marisa took the same chair that she had been in before. "What did I do wrong? Was it when I asked why we were trying to make him fight if he didn't want to?"

Neither Dominic nor Ivy said anything. They both just stared at her.

Marisa dropped her head. "I'm sorry. You both know what's best."

"Good," said Dominic softly. "But that's not all of it, Marisa. You've been having difficulties lately. Last night, I wanted to let you go celebrate, but you were too worked up. You weren't in control."

"You fell asleep without your pills or your headphones," said Ivy sadly. "You know that we are trying to recall your memories. We can't find your family without your help."

"I'm not sure that I want to find my family anymore," Marisa said, and she felt a sense of horror inside as if she had sinned in the worst possible way. She knew that she did want to find them, but she was tired of always wanting and waiting, of using her family as a reason to do things that she didn't want to do. She tried to tell Dominic and Ivy something that they'd want to hear, something truthful. "I love being Diamond."

Marisa looked up at Ivy. A surprising feeling of jealousy spurred her to say something more. "And I don't think you should be Scott's handler. You're my handler. I'm much better than he is. I saw him fight. I'd kill him."

Dominic raised an eyebrow, and Marisa thought he might have shifted slightly away from her on the couch.

Ivy smiled. "I have no doubt. It'd be gruesome."

There was something about Ivy's answer that Marisa didn't like. Normally praise about her fighting prowess made Marisa happy. Maybe she was feeling some effects from Armageddon.

Maybe she hadn't worn the headphones or taken her pills the night before.

"Why are you both so interested in him?" Marisa asked. "Lots of guys have won their first bouts. They don't get to come to the mansion until they've survived two or three. I don't remember us ever trying to convince someone to fight who didn't want to."

Marisa sat up. She had never asked so many questions, but it felt good. I am Diamond the Unbreakable, she thought. I'm the deadliest fighter they have. I defeated Armageddon. I deserve answers.

"Go back to your training. We'll handle Scott," said Dominic who sounded as if the conversation was over.

Without thinking, Marisa stood. She needed to go back to her training. She had been annoyed earlier when it had been interrupted.

However, she didn't have her answers, and today, she wanted answers.

She paused and said, "I'd rather wait until you both answer my questions." She forced herself to sit back down.

Ivy moved closer to her. "Marisa, I understand how you feel..." she started to say.

"Wait," said Dominic, raising a hand. "She's right. She deserves to know more. After all, she's Diamond."

Ivy glanced over at Dominic as she fell silent.

"First of all, Marisa, no one is more valuable or important to our organization than you are. You have worked so hard and fought so hard to prove yourself. We've been worried about you with your memory loss, and we've tried to protect you from as many problems as we could so you could concentrate on fighting. It's worked well so far. You've been able to focus, and at least for now, you are our champion. You know that, don't you?"

"Yes, Dominic, it has worked," she said, nodding, not really wanting to breathe. Was he pleased with her? Was he proud?

Why did she care so much about what he thought?

"I'm going to share some information with you, but I need you to get focused. It's time for us to find your family. It's time for us to restore your memories. We need to locate the doctors who did whatever they did to you. What happened to you could be happening to other children. Our organization needs to put an end to that. It's a cause that our sponsors agree with, a cause they've accepted because of you. So, I'll tell you about Scott, but you promise me that you will wear the headphones and take the pills tonight and do what you can to remember."

"Okay," she said, nodding until a pain in her skull made her stop. Moving the head too fast did hurt. "I promise."

"One of our sponsors is very interested in Scott. There's something about him that appeals to this sponsor. I'm not exactly sure what it is, but it's important to keep our sponsors happy, especially this one. He requested Ivy as the handler, but agreed that Ivy could stay with you as well. He feels that Scott can be our greatest fighter."

Marisa felt as if she had been punched in the chest. "No, he can't. I am." Her cheeks felt warm, and her stomach twisted. A sponsor couldn't really believe that. Could he?

Dominic smiled. "In any event, that's why Scott has the special treatment. I'm sure once he starts losing, the sponsor will grow less interested."

"And if he doesn't lose? What if he gets better?" she asked.

Dominic sat back. "Maybe you should get back to your training."

"Yes," agreed Marisa. She wouldn't let anyone defeat her. As she thought about Scott, another question came to mind. "One last thing. Am I allowed to go on a date?"

"I'll think about it. You've earned a reward," he said.

"Thank you, Dominic."

Marisa got up again and went to get changed. Scott wasn't a threat to her, but still, she needed to make sure she kept training.

She spent the rest of the day pushing herself, destroying concrete cylinders, putting a hole through the titanium wall and doing her full cycle of aerobics. After her nighttime shower, she was ready for bed.

Strange mixed-up thoughts about Scott still floated through her head. She took her pills and washed them down with a gulp of water. She picked up the headphones, just as she had promised Dominic.

Very gently, she pushed her thumbs through the speakers as she put them on. As soon as she felt the speaker pieces break, she stopped applying pressure. When they went over her ears, instead of hearing the relaxation sounds that Ivy told her helped her memories, the headphones were silent. She slipped into bed and turned off the lights. She whispered a soft prayer.

"I kept my promise," she said to herself as she drifted off.

Chapter 11 - Ivy

THREE DAYS AFTER HIS INTERVIEW, Scott was leaving his Latin American Culture and History class at Jefferson University and trying to decide if he wanted to get something to eat at one of the little places on campus or head back to his apartment.

In his broke days, it wouldn't have been a decision. He would have gone to the apartment and made a sandwich. Since he had money, he'd probably get some pizza or something, although he worried about breaking something accidentally.

The apartment situation was complicated. He wasn't talking much to Tyrell, though he wasn't really mad at him. An icy silence punctuated by "morning" and "hey" seemed to be where they were as roommates. He appreciated that Ty was trying to look out for him, but he didn't need his every move watched.

"I've got to stop worrying about all this stuff," he muttered. A pizza might do wonders for making things right again with Tyrell. He could order two or three and take them home with him.

One of the girls from class ran up beside him. "Hi, Scott, right?"

"It's Olivia, isn't it?" he said.

"Yeah," she said with a chuckle, "so, since we've both now confirmed that we know each other's names, I just wanted to tell you that I'm really impressed."

Olivia had bright eyes, straight blonde hair and liked dangly earrings. She skipped as much as walked alongside him, as she was nearly a foot shorter. Scott slowed down. He had been in a study group with Olivia once, but she had largely ignored him. He had a gift for being ignored.

"What did I do to impress you?" he asked, sounding more paranoid than he meant to. Scott didn't think he had said anything insightful in class.

"The working out. You have put on some serious muscles, and I think you've dropped some weight too since the start of the semester. You look good."

"Oh," said Scott, self-consciously rubbing his bicep. She was right. His arms were much larger. Every impact, even things like catching a ball or bumping into a table, seemed to be making him stronger. There was a surge at first, depending on the force of the impact. Usually it felt like he had tightened all of his muscles for a second, but after that feeling dropped off, his body changed. It was staying changed. He couldn't deny that he had never felt this fit in his life.

In his head he saw himself hosting an infomercial. "Burn off those unwanted pounds, shed those love handles and gain the body of your dreams. Forget diets and equipment. No more juicers or pills. Just fall down in a cyclotron a few hours before they turn it on. A few stupid bareknuckle brawls, amateur toughman contests and an underground super-powered street fight later and presto!"

"Hey, are you daydreaming?" asked Olivia, no longer looking as bouncy.

"No, I was… um…" said Scott.

"Waiting for me?"

Ivy stood on the quad sidewalk in front of him. She smiled at Olivia in a way that reminded Scott of a cartoon cat looking at a mouse. "I'm his personal trainer, and it's time for his workout."

"Oh," said Olivia, skipping sideways away from Scott.

"See you, Olivia," said Scott. "Thanks for the compliment."

Scott followed Ivy to the campus parking lot and over to a nice new-looking black SUV. "Get in," Ivy said as she clicked the doors unlocked and went to the driver's side. "Throw your backpack softly into the back seat."

He did as he was told. Once he was sitting in the front passenger's seat and Ivy was in the driver's seat, she turned to him. "Want to fight?" she asked excitedly with a gleam in her eye.

Scott coughed. "Um… what? With you?"

Ivy rolled her eyes and shook her head. "No. Don't be an idiot. Not with me. I'm your handler, and I don't have super-powers. That would be real exciting," she sarcastically emphasized the word real, "I'm asking you if you are ready for another fight? I have a special one lined up. You passed the medical tests and Dominic's ready to authorize that big payout."

"Uh... sure."

"Uh... great!" said Ivy, sounding annoyed. "We need to do some serious work. Let's take a drive. You don't have any more classes today, do you?"

"No."

"Good. Let's go."

"I was going to get a couple of pizzas."

"I'll buy you some later," Ivy said as she pulled out of the parking lot. She drove for a while, noticeably checking her rearview and side mirrors. Scott wondered where she was going, but he didn't ask. He was hoping they would arrive at the mansion.

They didn't. Instead, she parked in front of one of the many Megalopolis construction projects – a half-completed strip mall with 'For Lease' signs on the windows of each storefront. It wasn't what Scott had expected.

Ivy pulled her keys out of the ignition and dropped them in her lap. She turned slightly to face Scott. "So, what are your powers?"

"Super-strength and some resistance to injury," Scott said with a half shrug.

"How about the healing? Any ideas on the orange glow?" she asked.

"I haven't really thought about the healing, and I have no idea about the glowing. That happened for the first time during the fight with Night Howler. It made me a little crazy I think." Scott wasn't sure what to say. On one hand, he had committed to fighting and Ivy seemed to want to help him, but on the other hand, he had never discussed his powers with anyone.

"It was impressive. There's a lot about you that we need to figure out. Have you noticed that you are looking more..." she tilted her head, "... sculpted?"

"Yeah," he said. Scott was feeling uncomfortable. What did it all mean? What would happen when he couldn't become more sculpted? He thought about telling Ivy everything including how impacts kept making him stronger.

She reached out and rubbed his shoulder. "Scott," she said softly, "it's okay to be overwhelmed. It's obvious that you aren't used to any of this. We'll figure it all out together. Now, about your fight..."

Her phone rang. She held it up. "Sorry," Ivy said. "I need to take this."

"It's fine," said Scott.

"Not with me," Ivy said to him.

She answered the phone. "Yes? I'm with a client, and I can't talk. No, I really can't."

She sighed and ran her fingers through her hair. "Okay. We can't sell the jewelry. I don't care if someone wants to buy it. It has a flaw, and I think we can get it fixed." She paused and listened.

Ivy closed her eyes before responding. "No, it's still a valuable piece, and I'm not going to throw something with that much value away. It means far too much to me. Do we understand each other? Good. I need to go." She forcefully pressed disconnect.

"Who was that?" asked Scott. "Your boyfriend?"

"Something like that. It's complicated," she said.

"Are you okay?" asked Scott.

Ivy met his eyes, and hers started to glisten. She closed them. "Marisa's right. You are a nice person. Do you have a lot of people cry on your shoulders?"

"Yes," said Scott. "I'm the nice guy and good friend who gets cried on, usually when a boyfriend has broken up with someone." He felt disappointed.

"It's not a bad thing," she said, blinking. "But I need to remember to avoid you when I get upset. You aren't good for maintaining a façade."

Ivy took a deep breath, and then exhaled slowly. "I'm fine now. So, let's talk about you. We'll start with your name. Toughman is dead and gone."

"I like Valor," Scott said.

"Too superheroic," Ivy said, "People will start thinking your real name ends with –El or something. We need something tough or brutal. I got the inspiration from the theme for your next fight."

"Theme?" Scott asked.

"Halloween is coming up. So, you got to fight a werewolf and now you are going to fight..." she said with a smile.

"What?" Scott asked, not knowing what to think.

"A zombie. And we'll call you... the Survivor, the last man standing," she said.

"I don't know."

"Do you like Oblivion or Judgment better?"

"No."

"Okay. Those were some of the other finalists. Bloodbath too," she said with a chuckle. "We can change it after the fight if it doesn't play well. So, do you really want that pizza?"

Scott nodded.

"Well, we should go and get it, but you don't want to eat too much. The fight's scheduled for tonight."

"Tonight?"

"Yes, tonight. Remember, we don't give much notice. Keeps the bouts private. Don't worry, I'll be in your corner, so don't let your brain get eaten."

Chapter 12 - Zombie Survival 101

A FEW HOURS AFTER A FAILED PIZZA DELIVERY ATTEMPT, Scott was sitting beside Ivy in her SUV, which was parked on the street in a largely vacant industrial park. Like much of Megalopolis, the park was created to draw in future businesses, not to meet the demands of current business. One day, it would probably be full and bustling with trucks coming back and forth to loading docks. Of course, if that were the case, it wouldn't make a good place for a fight.

"Climb into the back. Your clothes are back there. Get changed. I'll help you with anything that you don't understand. If you embarrass easily, the windows are tinted, so don't worry."

"What about…?" he started to say.

She laughed. "I'm not going to watch you. Even if I did, I'm your handler and medically trained. Trust me, I'm more interested in getting the rest of your DNA test results back." She checked her phone.

"Okay," said Scott, clambering past the seats into the back of the vehicle. There were some bags and cases. What did she mean by something he didn't understand? He opened a case and found a ripped and apparently well-worn biker jacket. A pair of boots in his size sat in a bag and another bag contained a pair of black pants made out of a material that he didn't recognize. They seemed to have faint circuitry patterns on an inside layer that reminded him of extremely thick tights, though on the outside it looked like some kind of dark canvas cloth.

"The pants are weird."

"They have a neo-cloth with vital system monitors…," Ivy hesitated, "… basically, they have the type of tights that superheroes wear on the inside with a few tech things to let me keep an eye on your health. I want to see what happens to you when you get into combat. It'll help me train you, and if you get in real trouble, I'll know. Make sure you take your underwear off before you put them on."

Great, thought Scott feeling remarkably uncomfortable as he tried to stay as down while he changed. He noticed that the carpet in the cargo area of the SUV was very soft and clean. A new car smell clung to everything. It took longer than he wanted, but Scott managed to wriggle into the pants. They looked loose on the outside, but he could feel that inside layer.

Another bag had new and very normal-looking socks. "Socks too?"

"I thought you might want to avoid potentially messing up your old ones," said Ivy.

He put on the socks and boots without incident, something that he was thankful for. He took his shirt off and opened a final case, expecting to find a replacement shirt. Instead, it held a plastic bag like the kind hospitals used to keep a patient's garments and some plastic sheets with strange designs on them. "Okay, Ivy, there's no shirt, just some plastic sheets and a hospital bag."

"Put your street clothes in that bag. The sheets are temporary tattoos. Put one or two on your chest, but make sure they are visible. I'm partial to the ankh myself. You need to put on the ace of spades card as well. It's for one of our sponsors. There should be a mask in there too. It's black with eyeholes, triangle cuts. Hold it to your face for thirty seconds and it will self-adhere."

He saw the mask and picked it up. "Really?"

"Yes, really. It uses your sweat and body heat to activate. Comes off with some alcohol or enough force at the corners. Again, it's the sort of thing that supers wear."

"What about my shirt?"

"Scott, you don't need a shirt." He could hear her grin as she spoke.

He put on the temporary tattoos, placing a large black ankh over his heart and an American flag on the back of his right hand. He wasn't sure what to do with the ace of spades and finally decided on the side of his neck. He wondered if one of the sponsors was a casino. The mask went on easily and felt surprisingly good. He tossed his clothes in the hospital bag and put on the jacket which had seen better days.

"My new style is cutting-edge consignment," he said as he made his way back up front.

"Nice," said Ivy, glancing up from her phone.

Scott sat down and stared at the warehouse. A zombie was inside somewhere, waiting for him. He looked down at himself, at the ankh on his chest, at his musculature. What had happened to him? What was he about to do?

"Calm down. Remember to breathe," said Ivy.

"I've never fought a zombie. I'm not sure I even believe in zombies," said Scott. "And I've never worn a ripped biker jacket without a shirt."

"Don't worry, you carry it off well, Survivor." She winked at him.

One hundred thousand dollars, Scott reminded himself.

"So, what do I need to know?" he asked.

"They smell. I hope you didn't eat any of those pizzas when you dropped them off at your apartment."

"No, I left them in the fridge for Tyrell and wrote him a note. I only had that slice with you earlier. And I used the bathroom like you said, but when you told me to remember to go to the bathroom, it made me feel like I was a 5-year old," Scott could feel his heart race faster as he kept staring at the warehouse. It was an ordinary concrete building, but all Scott could think about was the zombie inside.

"Trust me, that was the best piece of advice that I could give you. Zombies are slow," said Ivy, matter-of-factly, "Usually, anyway. However, they can be fast in short bursts. They don't feel pain. They are strong, but they can also be decaying, so bones might break more quickly. The key to defeating them is to crush their skulls. They won't give up otherwise. Some varieties can be infectious, so don't get bitten. I suspect you won't have to worry about infection from these, but you should try to avoid it to be on the safe side."

"I have to kill it?"

Ivy put a hand on Scott's shoulder. In an exasperated tone, she said, "We are talking about a zombie. It's already dead. You can't kill it. You are getting to defend the city. Stay on the offense, don't slow down and get them. If things go badly, you can always run, but I doubt Dominic's going to want to pay you if you do."

Her phone beeped. "That's the alarm," she said. "The cameras should be in position. Once you are inside, remember to close the door. We don't want a zombie roaming through the city. This will be fun. It's an early Halloween special. Crush some skulls."

"Yes, ma'am."

Scott got out of the SUV and walked over to a side door of the warehouse. He tried the knob. It was unlocked. Taking a deep breath, he opened the door and went inside. He made a point of closing the door behind him.

The warehouse was dark although not pitch black. Moonlight shone faintly through some skylights high above the warehouse floor. A few small windows in the up near where the walls met the roof helped with the illumination as well. He took a few steps forward. A thought struck him.

Had Ivy said 'skulls' as in more than one?

Scott heard the sounds of propellers whirring. He looked up. This time he noticed that one of the skylights was open. Small drones with lights and cameras flew into the warehouse. Several beams shone down on Scott. A voice echoed from the drones.

"Unlimited Underground Fighting is proud to present a horror and gore fest for the ages! In our first ever Halloween special, we feature the return of the Survivor, formerly known as Toughman, who overcame all odds to defeat a werewolf in his premiere bout. This time, he's going to have to earn the name Survivor!"

Several harsh mechanical sounds came from large metal shipping containers around Scott. He was blinking, trying to adjust to the new lights only moments after trying to adjust to the darkness. The sound of moaning came from all around him.

"That's right! Tonight, the Survivor is not fighting one, two or even three opponents, but an absolute horde of undead. Your favorite theme in television and video games has come to life! It's a Zombie Apocalypse."

Thriller by Michael Jackson played from the whirring propeller light camera things. Scott's eyes had mostly adjusted. Zombies had filled the room in front of him. He heard moaning and shuffling noises behind him as well. He was surrounded.

They weren't people in costumes or makeup. The odor of death and decay was overpowering. Scott tried not to breathe. This whole situation was deeply disturbing, but he wasn't about to go down due to a smell. As his eyes watered, he at least hoped that the smell alone wouldn't defeat him. He lifted up his jacket to cover his nose and mouth.

All around him was a grisly scene of animated rotting corpses. Bones jutted from maggot-ridden flesh. Some of the bodies had eyes missing and visible gashes and wounds. A slurping wet sound came from one decaying woman whose entrails dragged along the ground. An armless man stumbled next to a woman wearing a wedding dress covered in mold stains. All of them came closer, and they reached for him.

The music stopped.

Scott nearly froze. He wasn't sure where to begin. There were so many and he wasn't ready. A zombie lunged and grabbed him. Teeth locked around his forearm. Another zombie thrust herself at him.

Pulling his arm free of his first attacker's jaws, he punched the lunging female zombie. He heard a crack as bone splintered.

The horde was suddenly on him. Nails scraped across his mask. He could feel teeth on his shoulder. The smell of rot and death was overwhelming.

Scott started swinging wildly. Bones broke as bile and blood sprayed with each punch. Scott made a primal scream as he pushed his way into the mass of dead bodies. After the scream, he nearly choked with his next breath. Hands entwined themselves into his hair. He reached up and snapped the dry wrists.

He slammed into a shipping container. The horde pressed against him. He held his breath and remembered what Ivy had told him. He needed to crush skulls. He backhanded one of the zombies in the temple and aimed a punch into the head of another.

He took a breath and got a lungful of formaldehyde and bleach as well as rot. Scott's eyes burned, but he kept swinging at the heads of the zombies. With each blow, a zombie fell, but it seemed that another replaced it.

Scott stopped worrying. Nothing mattered but smashing skulls. He wanted a weapon. He reached behind him to see if he could find something. His fingers crunched into something that felt like aluminum. He grabbed whatever it was, trying to bring it up to smash yet another zombie. Yellow dead eyes glared at him.

With a loud screech, Scott swung the shipping container across the floor. A terrible mix of splintering and wet noises replaced the moans and groans. Realizing that he had an advantage, Scott lifted the container over his head. He brought it down in front of him, crushing more zombies as if the container were a giant foot and the undead were ants caught beneath it.

There were several still close to him, grabbing and clinging to him. He felt a tooth tear at his ear. Scott grabbed at that one, catching it and ripping the head from the body.

He didn't remember the rest of the battle. All he knew was that at some point, he ran out of bodies to fight. Sweat steamed off his chest. An orange glow burned faintly over his flesh.

"The winner – the Survivor!" announced the propeller cameras.

Scott watched them fly up in the air and out of the skylight, leaving him alone in his own personal charnel house.

He suddenly realized that he had done it. He had won.

Chapter 13 - Another Party

AT THE MANSION, Marisa lounged on a couch in the sitting room that opened to the pool, while all around her Dominic's clientele celebrated Survivor's victory and praised the genius of the bout. The air was filled with a mix of perfume, alcohol, laughter and excitement.

She should have been happy. Dominic was pleased with her, and he had let her come down early to the viewing party. The assistants had brought her a beautiful red gown to wear. She even had a wrist corsage which partially covered the neutralizer bracelet she wore. Marisa actually liked the way the bracelet vibrated against her skin. Her hair had been styled and one of the makeup artists had done her face. She had nearly gasped earlier when she had seen herself in the mirror.

Although she was surrounded by people, she felt terribly alone.

A red-haired woman in an emerald gown stood close to Marisa's couch. She said, "I love zombies. That was one of the most violent things I've ever seen. What did you think?"

It took Marisa a moment to realize that the woman was talking to her. "Yes, it was violent," she said with the words coming out flatter than she had meant.

"Maybe we'll get to see Survivor tonight," the woman said to Marisa, before turning to a gentleman in a suit in hopes of finding better conversation.

"Maybe," whispered Marisa. She had watched the battle and saw when Scott froze. It was pathetic. He didn't know what he was doing, and he should have been killed. He just happened to be strong enough to find a way to survive. "That's why he's now… Survivor," she said.

Of course, everyone had loved the fight. The whole room was filled with people raving about the battle and wondering where the zombies came from. They thought that Survivor had been amazing.

She glanced around the room, searching in vain for Ivy, knowing full well that she was with Scott. Ivy was supposed to be here. They always watched fights together. Marisa enjoyed discussing the bouts with Ivy and analyzing them. Tonight, they should be talking about Survivor's strengths and weaknesses and how Diamond would deal with him.

Marisa shifted on the couch as a waitress walked by. She wasn't allowed to have any of the drinks or the food. Nothing here would be on the list. A somewhat dashing man winked at Marisa. She gave him a faint smile and looked down. She wasn't allowed to touch the men either.

Loneliness washed over her again. Thoughts of her family came unbidden into her head. She wanted to remember their names. Papa and mama were names she decided, but there had been brothers and sisters too. She wondered if she had any friends.

Marisa blinked. Her eyes were growing wet. It was time to think of something else.

So, what if Ivy were here? What would Ivy say about Survivor? First, he didn't know anything about fighting. He didn't strike properly. He was slow. He didn't defend himself well. Second, he was easily rattled and distracted. He didn't focus.

She sighed. This was making her feel both sorry for him and slightly disgusted that so many people were gushing over him. Didn't anyone here know how to analyze a fight?

She continued to think about Scott. On the plus side, he was strong enough to lift an empty metal shipping container over his head, which meant that he was more powerful than she had thought. Of course, it also meant that he hadn't used his strength very well against Night Howler, and it certainly didn't put him in her league. He seemed fairly resilient, but surviving corpses didn't make him unbreakable.

"He's not made for this," she said.

She thought about his eyes and the way he had asked her out for coffee. She imagined that same man on his knees in the middle of that pile of corpses, vomiting or perhaps crying from the horror of it all. A strange feeling of compassion welled up inside of her. Maybe it was for the best. She'd get Ivy back, and he'd go back to whatever life he had before he ended up crippled.

And where would she go? What would she do the day Diamond lost?

Just the thought made Marisa uncomfortable and scared. The world seemed very different now that her headphones were broken. She had become more aware of her compulsions to obey commands and was able to resist. She no longer desired to please Dominic so much. She had found herself thinking about trying to leave the mansion and wondering about the rooms that she wasn't allowed to visit. She had even realized that it was strange that she didn't know how to drive a car.

More importantly, she had given up the pills. The night after she had broken the headphones, she had held the yellowish pills in her palm and crushed them into powder as she pretended to put them in her mouth. She smiled at the thought of yellowish stains under her pillow where she had rubbed her hand clean on the mattress.

It had now been four days with no headphones and three out of four with no pills.

Marisa was doing her best to obey commands and act as subservient as she could. It wouldn't do to have anyone realize that she was able to make her own choices. It was only a matter of time until someone found out the headphones didn't work, but for now, Dominic seemed quite pleased with her. After all, he had let her come to the viewing party and watch the fight.

She stared across the room at Dominic.

Dominic looked the part of the wealthy host moving among his many admirers. Currently, he was listening to an older man tell a story as two beautiful women clung to the old man's arms. The women were young, and if Marisa didn't know better, she might have thought that they were the man's daughters or granddaughters. She should have ignored the scene, but today, there was something about the man with the young women that made her angry.

As Marisa considered getting up, a woman with long blonde hair in a gold dress interrupted Dominic's conversation. Marisa had seen her many times, but she had never spoken to her. That wasn't unusual with the assistants. They had orders to avoid Marisa, probably to avoid any accidents.

Another new feeling sprang up inside Marisa. Why should everyone need to avoid her? She could control her strength. Other than a handful of trainers and her opponents, she had never hurt anyone.

The older man walked away from Dominic with a sour expression while his arm ornaments smiled and giggled. The blonde leaned close to Dominic, whispering something to him. Marisa noticed that they clasped hands. Dominic nodded slightly, and he looked across the room.

Marisa followed Dominic's eyes to a thin white-haired man who wore a noticeably ill-fitting suit. As she noticed the man, a chill rippled down her spine. Her mouth went dry and she started trembling. Memories flashed through her head. The white-haired man was in her head, wearing a white coat.

"Does she understand a word of English yet?"

"Now, young lady, we'll undo the clamps once you're back in your special room."

"It would hurt less if you'd stop screaming."

"Take your pills. You are doing so much better than any of the other subjects."

Marisa snapped back to reality. She didn't want to breathe. She turned away from the white-haired man for a second and caught her breath. When she turned back, he was gone.

He had been standing by a door to the pool.

She carefully stood, not wanting to run, not wanting to draw any undue attention. Dominic wasn't looking at her. She made her way through the crowd, out to the pool. One of the assistants smiled at her.

"It's a lovely night," she commented.

She saw him at the gate to the pool, near the parked cars. He was staring wide-eyed at her. She took a few steps in his general direction, but tried to make it appear that she wasn't noticing him.

He bolted.

Marisa strode over to the gate. The man was already opening his car door. Throwing any semblance of pretense aside, she vaulted the gate and ran over to the car. He started pulling out, but she caught the vehicle. Digging her hands into the hood, she said, "Stop."

The man obeyed. He put the car in park. Marisa walked over to the driver's door. "Get out," she ordered.

He got out. His face was paler than his hair. "Please, don't."

"Don't what?" she said, placing her hand on his shoulder.

He noticed the neutralizer bracelet under her corsage. He blinked and hints of a smile tugged at his mouth. "They don't work on you, do they?"

"No, they don't. Who are you? How do I know you?"

"Perfect," he whispered. "I was one of your doctors."

Her hand tightened ever so slightly on his shoulder.

"Marisa." The voice belonged to Dominic. "Let him go."

Chapter 14 - Confrontation

SLOWLY, MARISA RELEASED THE WHITE-HAIRED MAN. She knew that if she didn't obey Dominic that he would know about the headphones and the pills. She wasn't ready to ruin her entire life, but she wanted answers.

Dominic firmly said, "Step away from him."

Marisa took a large step back.

"She works," said the white-haired man, "The bracers don't work on her system. The whole theory about stopping powers by disrupting the nervous system doesn't work on her. She's like the design."

"She's exactly what she should be," said Dominic. "Doctor, it's time for you to leave. You weren't supposed to be here." Marisa heard the threat in his voice.

"I know," said the doctor, a tear streaking down his cheek, "but I just wanted to see... it's so amazing to see her... our Marisa. Flawless and beautiful. I had to come and see. I also wanted to ask you about Mr. Miller. I don't understand how he can be so..."

"Goodbye," said Dominic, going over to the car and assisting the doctor in returning to his seat. The doctor glanced up, but he said nothing more. He started the car and pulled away, sparing her one last look.

Marisa stood still as he drove off. Dominic walked over to her side.

"Dominic?" she asked, trying hard to sound scared and confused and not angry and demanding.

"Yes, Marisa."

"He said he was one of my doctors."

"He was," Dominic said.

She reached over and grabbed Dominic's jacket with both hands. "Why was he here?" She almost shrieked the question.

Dominic put his hands on Marisa's arms, not that he could do anything to stop her. He cleared his throat. When he spoke, his voice was soft and slow. "Marisa, that man was delivering some information about the DNA of Survivor. Unfortunately, Survivor's DNA is not what the sponsors had hoped it was, unlike yours which is flawless."

"He was one of my doctors," she said. She wanted to shake Dominic, but she knew that would be wrong. Even though she thought she had overcome the compulsions, she still didn't want to hurt him.

Dominic nodded. "I know who he is. He's one of the connections that I've worked very hard to make. That man is one of my best links to find your family. I didn't tell you about him because I didn't want to get your hopes up only to dash them. You don't deserve that kind of pain. I think we are close to finding them, Marisa."

"Tell me, please. Tell me everything you know, Dominic. Please."

Dominic glanced down at his jacket. Marisa released him. She didn't really trust Dominic, but she wanted to believe him with all of her heart and soul. She wanted to believe that he would find her family. She wanted to see them. She wanted to remember everything about them and more than that, she wanted to create new memories.

"Marisa, as much as it pains me to say this, I'm not going to tell you what I know, because I'm not certain about anything. We've spent a long time searching for your family. There have been a number of leads over the years, some of which seemed very promising, but none of them took us to your home. At the current stage, we are close. The trail has led us to Colombia. We're at a very delicate point, and we need a gentle touch. Do you understand?"

She bit her lip. Could it be true? Was Dominic close? She dared to hope. "There's got to be some way that I can help."

"There is." Dominic gently touched her cheek. "Fight and win. The one thing that we need is money. You are very good for the off-shore gambling operations. The people who come to see you pay a fortune, and most of them bet against you. That's good for our finances. Keep fighting and keep winning, and I promise you, I'll have the resources to find your family. When I do, I'll send you to join them. You'll be reunited. You have my word, Marisa."

His voice was so strong and reassuring. She searched his eyes for signs of deception, but she saw only cold hard resolve. Confusion crept inside her head. She looked down.

Had she been wrong about the headphones and pills? Was Dominic on her side?

He touched her chin. "Is my Diamond ready to shine?" Dominic smiled. He didn't seem upset in the slightest, and for some reason, that made Marisa worry.

"Yes, I am. I'm ready," she said.

"Very good. Stand over at the side of the pool," he said, adjusting his jacket before heading back to the gate.

Marisa followed, trying to refocus. She took her position, just as she had during the rehearsal. So many thoughts whirled through her head. She was Marisa, the lost girl carried off by soldiers. She needed to be Diamond, the unbreakable.

People had started coming out of the mansion, milling around the well-lit pool. She recognized one in particular, Simon Monroe, an ex-Marine built like a linebacker, who went by the name Razorwire. She hadn't noticed him before, but he was wearing a tailored suit like all the other men. When she had seen him last, he had been wearing exercise pants with metal wire lashing out of his body. He tried to smile at several of the people, but it seemed to Marisa that all he did was sneer. Some of the assistants led him around to the side of the pool opposite where she was standing.

She closed her eyes and imagined the crowd chanting, trying to shut out thoughts of her family. It wasn't working very well. She reopened them and looked at her beautiful dress. She silently said goodbye to it.

Dominic was suddenly in the middle of the crowd, holding a microphone. "Ladies and gentlemen," he started, "I am so glad that all of you could join us for tonight's special viewing. This is just the beginning of what we have planned. Assuming that Survivor is in any shape to fight again, you'll see how his strength matches up against titanium-osmium alloys when he battles one of the Ultra Task Force's Bastion Robots! And the werewolf, Night Howler, will return to face the poisonous touch of Toxin! And that's not all… you'll see Bloodthorn, Steel Dragon and more."

The crowd cheered. Several glasses were raised.

"Hold on to that applause, because I have something special for each of you. You are each invited to purchase some of our exclusive seats to a special live bout. There is nothing like the experience of standing only a few feet from superpowered foes fighting to the finish. And tonight, two of the most powerful beings on the planet were among you. First, let me present the deadly… Razorwire!"

Razorwire flexed in a bodybuilder's pose as barbed metal strands ripped through his suit, shredding it. Loops of wire extended from his skin and slashed through the air all around him, whistling as they did. He screamed as he struck a new pose, showing off his chiseled musculature.

There were several excited shrieks and cheers. The audience began to clap. Dominic spoke into the microphone again. "So, who do we have to challenge Razorwire? Who would be willing to risk being flayed alive?"

One of the assistants came over to Marisa and made a point of removing her neutralizer bracelet. She wondered why Dominic was pretending that the bracelet affected her when he knew that it didn't. She hesitated a moment.

"Allow me to present…" said Dominic.

I am Diamond, thought Marisa, as she tore her dress apart to reveal a white bikini covered in sparkling gemstones.

"Diamond the Flawless. Diamond the Unbreakable. Diamond, the woman who destroyed Armageddon!"

There were gasps. No one seemed to know what to expect from her. Two of the assistants carefully carried a large barbell over to her. She grabbed it with a single hand and threw it dozens of feet into the air, catching it as it came down and twirling it like a baton.

"That's over a thousand pounds that she's tossing around. Please see my assistants and reserve your place at our special invitation-only fight, Razorwire against Diamond!" announced Dominic. He lowered the microphone.

Assistants surrounded Diamond, letting the audience come close enough to look, but not touch her. She performed some martial arts moves and bent the barbell for them. She even blew a kiss to one of the men who was staring at the diamond that had been placed over her bellybutton. If Dominic needed her to fight and win, that's what she would do.

The crowd lingered forever, but she finally had a chance to slip away. She decided to head down to the gym to take her shower. She didn't feel like getting glitter and gemstones all over her bedroom, and she certainly didn't want to encourage additional cleaning. She was worried that someone would find the remains of her pills or discover that the headphones were broken.

A few of the lights were on in the gym. As Marisa walked in, she heard the shower running in the locker room. Had one of the assistants decided to have a late night workout?

"What's going on?" asked Marisa, walking into the showers.

The water turned off. "I'm sorry. I still feel like I've got all that dead stuff on me," said Scott. "Just a minute."

Scott stepped out of the shower with only a towel wrapped around his waist. "Oops. Uh… Marisa?"

Chapter 15 - Decisions

SCOTT FELT HIS BREATH CATCH and his chest tighten. He had expected to see Ivy, and somehow, having Ivy around didn't bother him, but Marisa was another matter entirely. She was tall, gorgeous and wearing some kind of gemstone-encrusted bikini. Her skin literally sparkled and he tore his eyes away as he felt color rushing into his face.

At that moment, he didn't have any of his new super-powered confidence. Instead, he was a teenager in high school staring at a beautiful woman unable to speak. He hoped his mouth wasn't hanging open and placed a hand over the knot holding his towel on. He blinked

"Sorry," she said as he looked over at a bench where his pre-fight clothes lay. She looked back to him. He heard her laugh softly. "I'll wait outside so you can get changed."

"Thanks," he said, rubbing his right hand over his face while still clutching the towel with left. He waited a second and let the heat in his face subside as he fumbled to get his clothes on. Ivy had taken the 'Survivor' clothes when she had left and hopefully burned them.

"I saw your fight," said Marisa from outside the locker room.

Scott pulled on his underpants first beneath the towel and swiftly got his pants and shirt on. "Great. What did you think? Ivy said it went viral." Even as the words left his mouth, he winced. The smell, the gore, the bodies, the entire thing had been horrendous. He fought back a bit of vomit.

"Um… you survived. It looked rough," replied Marisa with some hesitancy from outside the showers.

"It was rough. Definitely. And it's my last fight. I can't do that again." He walked out of the locker room.

She was right there, all too close, leaning against the wall, gleaming and sparkling. Her dark eyes were mysterious and beautiful. "Good," she said, "You aren't right for it."

He shook his head and ran a hand through his hair. She didn't think he was right for it. "What do you mean? I'm not tough enough?"

"No," she said softly, "you are too kind for it. You're different from the other men. I mean, I can tell you don't know how to fight, but..."

Scott held up a hand. "It's okay. You're right. I got powers, and I decided to cash in. It's not what I want to do. It's not what I should do, and I knew that. Ivy and Dominic paid me enough to cover my bills for a while. It's time I did what's right."

"What do you mean?" she asked.

"I'm not sure. Live a normal life. Maybe try and become a superhero."

The two of them were silent. Marisa studied him and her lips moved, but she didn't say anything.

Scott sighed. "I know. I sound preposterous."

"Save me," she whispered.

Scott wasn't sure if he had really heard her say the words or not, when the door to the gym opened. Ivy walked in, along with two strong-looking men in suits. Despite his strength, Scott felt nervous. Marisa stepped back and away from him.

Ivy glanced at Marisa. "I hope you aren't trying to intimidate the competition, Marisa."

Marisa shook her head. "No, I wasn't. I didn't know he was here. It was an accident."

"Competition?" asked Scott. "You aren't a ring girl?"

Marisa shook her head again. "No, I'm Diamond. I'm unbreakable." Confidence filled her voice as she spoke, and she seemed to stand straighter.

"Wait," said Scott, "if that's true, why haven't I seen you in any of the internet fights?"

Ivy answered. "Marisa only fights in special invitation bouts. She's the very best."

"And she lives here?" asked Scott.

Ivy nodded. "Yes. She's very valuable, hence the name. So, are you feeling better? Have you reconsidered what you said earlier?"

"I can't go out," said Marisa.

Ivy gave Marisa an icy look and the confidence seemed to bleed out of the glittering fighter. "Marisa, you should go. We'll talk later."

"Of course, Ivy," Marisa responded, as she started to go. She looked back at Scott and their eyes met. He saw something desperate and angry and pleading all at once in her expression. And then, she was gone.

"I can't do this anymore," said Scott. "I'm sorry, but I don't want to be Survivor. My strength is some kind of accident. This isn't who I should be or what I should be doing."

Ivy crossed her arms over her chest, "Fine."

"Fine?"

She shrugged. "If you don't want to keep fighting, I can't force you. You've been paid. I'll drive you home. I'm just disappointed. You were magnificent tonight."

"That's it?"

"What else is there?" asked Ivy, raising an eyebrow. "Let's go. I'll drive you home."

Scott followed Ivy out of the gym, flanked by the men in suits. Thoughts of Marisa filled his head. He knew that she needed help, but what was he going to do? Smash up the place?

And what was more, she was a competitor? He couldn't imagine hitting a woman. He wondered if that made him some kind of chauvinist, a wimp or a decent guy.

"Um...," Scott started, "what's the deal with Marisa?"

"Diamond is the best. She's undefeated. Way out of your league. Unfortunately, she was involved in some political issues in her home country. She's a refugee, here illegally. If she was discovered, she'd be sent home to certain death."

"Wait, even though she's undefeated in superpowered combat?"

Ivy chuckled. "The stark truth is that no one's invincible. Listen, the less you know about her, the less you have to worry about death squads. Hopefully, we'll be able to get one of her asylum petitions accepted soon. If you change your mind about fighting, the good news is that with your potential, you'll get to see her again."

"No," said Scott, still trying to decide if he should do something drastic. "I'm done."

"Sleep on it, and if you want to call me back, there's no problem," said Ivy nonchalantly.

They had gone up a set of wide stairs to a hardwood-floored entry hall and the bodyguards moved past them to hold open double doors leading outside. Ivy's SUV was waiting.

"Thanks, guys," muttered Scott under his breath.

Twenty minutes of Ivy driving and next-to-no conversation later, they pulled into the parking lot of the Leonard Building. Scott undid his seat belt.

"Remember," said Ivy, breaking the silence. "Sleep on it. You may be upset and worn out now, but you are giving up millions. Retirement in your mid-20s doesn't sound so bad, does it?"

"No, I guess not. Thanks, Ivy. I'm sorry that I'm not able to do this."

"You are a nice guy, Scott. I think that you might be one who could prove the old adage wrong. I hope I see you later. If not, have a great life and invest some of those winnings in a retirement account now."

"Thanks, Ivy. Bye."

With that, Scott carefully shut the door of the SUV. As he walked up to the doors of the Leonard Building, he saw the reflections of Ivy's headlights as she pulled away.

He swiped his access card, the night desk guy stared at him, and he made his way to the creepy elevators.

"Welcome back to your regularly scheduled life," he said to himself as he stepped into the elevators.

Chapter 16 - No Escape

"I CAN'T GO OUT."

"Save me."

"I can't go out."

"Save me."

Marisa's voice kept echoing in Scott's head as the lights flickered in the elevator while it took an interminably long amount of time to reach the fifth floor and open its doors. Now that he was done, he felt relieved, but she was still there and trapped.

"Save me," she had said.

Scott didn't believe Ivy about Marisa's asylum petitions or the death squads.

As he headed for his apartment, he tried to convince himself that what Ivy said was plausible, especially for someone who dealt with super-powered warriors, but he didn't believe it. His stomach knotted up. Marisa needed help, but he wasn't sure how to help her. He wished that he'd find some inspiration, but he decided that he'd better settle for a pillow.

Inspiration threw open the door to his apartment before he could put the key in the lock.

"Get in here," said Tyrell. "Man, I can't believe you."

"What?" asked Scott. "What time is it anyway?"

Tyrell led him into the living room. The flatscreen was on and displaying an internet video. Scott froze.

"Yeah, that's right," said Tyrell with an irritated but self-satisfied flop on the couch. "It's Survivor versus the zombie horde. Want to watch with me?"

"Uh… no, not really. It's late, man."

"You've got to see this Survivor guy. He's amazing. Let me pause it for you, so you can get a good look at his face. Do you see who that is?"

The screen froze on Scott's face. He had the black facepaint on. For a second, he hoped that Tyrell might not know.

"That's right!" said Tyrell. "It's your long lost twin brother from the planet Argon who happens to have super-strength and doesn't want to tell his roommate how he's making extra money. Oh, wait... you don't have a twin brother, do you? That means..."

"Ty? Look..."

With mock astonishment, Tyrell leapt up from the couch and dropped the television controller in pretend shock. "Oh my god, Scott! You've got super-powers. This is incredible! That explains the broken toilet paper holder in your bathroom and the busted doorknobs and that time the refrigerator door was off and all that. It's probably some kind of experience where you black out and are overcome by the urge to bust up zombies."

"I didn't know how to tell you. I mean, you don't want to know."

"Semi-amateur fights? Remember when you told me that? Scott, I thought you were on drugs! I was worried. I'm still worried. What the hell? What if one of those zombies followed you home, like to here or something? I'm pretty fond of my brain."

"It's okay. I quit. I'm done."

Tyrell fell silent.

"You quit?" he asked uncertainly. "Seriously?"

"I quit. I can't do that stuff. I mean, fighting those zombies was awful. Putrid gore is not a smell I want to relive." Scott tried to smile, but he didn't feel like he was joking.

Tyrell sat back down on the couch. He asked suspiciously, "So, what now?"

Scott joined him. "I don't know. Try not to break things I guess. Live a gentle life. Mom always said my soul was like that."

"Uh huh. So, I'm not prying or anything, but besides strength what do you do? And when did you get these powers?"

"I heal fast and I'm a little invulnerable. I keep getting stronger the more I get hit. I'm not really stable. Remember that cyclotron thing where I felt sick? I'm sure that did it. I should go to a doctor, but if you could figure out who I am, well, they definitely will and I'll probably get arrested."

Tyrell folded his arms over his Chinese martial arts movie t-shirt. "For what? Fighting a super? Killing zombies? Man, if they arrest you for that, they'll have to arrest every hero who gets into an accidental fight with another hero and wrecks a few buildings. It happens all the time. You haven't killed anyone, right? No one's filing charges against you."

"I guess not."

"Okay, then you should go to a doctor. I want to make sure you don't mutate into something."

"You're right."

"Wait, are you actually listening to me?"

"Yeah, Ty, I am. And I should have told you."

"Nah, we both know heroes need secret identities. And before you ask, I'm not interested in being your sidekick if you go the superhero route. Maybe support staff. Do you think if I went into a cyclotron that I might get stronger?"

"No," said Scott, leaning his head back and closing his eyes.

Tyrell laughed. "I didn't figure, but it's a fun idea."

Scott found himself thinking about Marisa. Tyrell might have been right about the fights as to whether or not they were illegal, but whatever they were doing with Marisa was wrong. He didn't have any solid reasons, other than Ivy always seemed to say what he needed to hear, but he didn't believe that she or Dominic were trying to get asylum for Marisa.

He also didn't like the way her expression changed when they gave her orders.

Thoughts of modern slavery and human trafficking documentaries made him shudder. Was he sure that was happening? No. Could he imagine it? Yes. Was he willing to take the chance that everything was okay?

These were the same people who nearly fed him to zombies.

Scott cleared his throat and opened his eyes. "I need to do something."

"What? Get a drink?" asked Tyrell.

"No, I need to call that federal agent. Those guys are doing something wrong. There's this woman, nice, hot, but there's something wrong with her, really wrong. Human trafficking kind of wrong I think, or well, superhuman trafficking. I don't know. I just feel sick when I think about it. She needs help. I don't know what to do, but maybe they will."

"Call them. Do you still have that phone?"

"Yeah, I do," said Scott. He drew it out. For a second he wondered if Ivy had used it, but there wasn't any record of outgoing calls. The strange thing about the phone was that he had never charged it, but it still had power. It looked like the sort of thing government people investigating superhumans might use.

He called the number stored in the contacts. The phone rang once, and a woman answered.

"Is this Scott?" she asked.

"Yes, it's Scott. Look, you probably know what I've been doing I guess. The guys who paid me to fight, they have this woman at their house. I think she may be there against their will. She needs help and I think you should investigate. She asked me to save her."

"When are you going back?"

"I'm not. I quit."

"The only way we are going to obtain enough evidence to get warrants and stop them is if we have someone on the inside. If you want to stop them and help that woman, you need to be that person. Can you rejoin their operation?"

"Well, yes." Scott swallowed. This wasn't what he wanted.

"Get in touch with them tomorrow and see if you can get back on the inside. Call us back when you've rejoined them and we'll give you further instructions."

"Okay, I'll do that. Thanks."

The phone disconnected.

"You okay?" asked Tyrell.

"No, I don't think I am," answered Scott. "So much for my regularly scheduled life."

He didn't want to go back, but despite that, he felt like for once, he was certain that he was about to do the right thing.

Chapter 17 - The Nightmare Returns

THE BROOK SANG A SONG OF PLEASANT BURBLING WELCOME to the blue sky and the bright sun. A big blue butterfly raced along the path, pausing to land on bright green leaves. It was faster than Marisa, but she wasn't going to give up. She was going to follow it until she reached the magical place that butterflies and rainbows came from, or at least until she reached the tree that she wasn't allowed past.

There was a loud scary noise, followed by another and another and another. She froze and her heart pounded. "Mama?" she whispered.

She heard screaming coming from the village, coming from home. There were more scary noises. She didn't know what to do. She was scared, more scared than she had ever been, but her family was there.

"MAMA! PAPA!" she screamed and she ran, thinking about her brothers and sisters and everyone.

Suddenly, there was a big man, a soldier, and he grabbed her. He hurt her and wouldn't let go. There was fire and yelling.

And her papa lying on the ground in the scariest pool of red that she could imagine.

Thick burning smoke filled the air. She couldn't breathe, and she couldn't move because the solider wouldn't let her go.

"Papa?" she choked as she opened her eyes. She couldn't breathe. She wasn't a little girl anymore. She was in her room at the mansion, but there were men here, soldiers maybe, wearing gas masks. There was a fog in the room.

She couldn't move.

She heard a sound like the air conditioner but much louder.

A man touched her wrist, before he pulled off his mask. It was one of the doctors from the mansion. "It worked. She's paralyzed. You can all take your masks off now. It's dispersed enough for us. We can apply the anesthesia, and she won't remember a thing. Pity that we have to use all of it. It's expensive stuff. You aren't going to take it out of my part of the budget, are you?"

"No. It's the cost of business," said a man standing on the opposite side of her bed as he pulled off his mask. It was Dominic. He gazed disparagingly down at her. "Oh, Marisa. You've been such a disappointment. Breaking your headphones and not taking your pills. How long have you been out of control? I should have known. We all should have."

The others removed their masks. Marisa couldn't move her head to see all of them. She wanted to look directly at Dominic, but she couldn't even move her eyes.

"I know that you are frustrated right now," said Dominic, "and probably feeling pretty helpless, but I promise you that you aren't anywhere close my frustration level."

Marisa's heart gave a single hard pound in her chest. Fear whispered to her. Dominic was angry, and she never wanted to make him angry.

"Yes, I do," her thoughts contradicted her. Raw fury flooded through her mind.

She heard Ivy's voice. "I think her lips moved."

"Her lips didn't move, but get the anesthesia ready in case she does," said Dominic. "I want to have a few words with her first."

"This isn't necessary," said Ivy.

"Maybe not, but it's deserved and it will make me feel better," replied Dominic. "Marisa, do you have any idea how much we've invested in you? The only reason that you are alive is that we bought you. We paid for you and it just so happened that you had the right set of genetics for our scientists. You have no concept of how lucky you are and absolutely no appreciation of how good your life is. I'm sure you don't remember, but this is the third time you've tried something like this. Ivy convinced me that the first time was a fluke, but I see how you stare out the gates. You can't be satisfied with pools and good food and beauty and glory. No, you have to want freedom and keep dreaming about that family of yours."

Marisa felt her eyes start burning. Everything was getting blurry.

"Dominic, I wouldn't," said Ivy.

"I know you wouldn't, and that's part of the reason why I'm in charge. So, Marisa, Diamond, here's the truth. Most of your family was murdered by some kind of revolutionary army. Your child soldier brother sold you so whatever third world cause slaughtered your village could have some financing. We bought you. We saved you." Dominic pointed at his own chest when he said "we."

He paused and leaned close to her.

"Without us, you would have died in some whorehouse in a dirt poor country. Instead, we gave you physical perfection and luxury. All our sponsors want is your genetics and the pleasure of watching you fight. But instead, you keep trying to find freedom. If you had a better attitude and stopped resisting, you'd be working for our sponsors directly. Anything you wanted would be yours for the taking as long as they knew you'd be loyal. And they would have paid all of us handsomely. But you aren't loyal. You can't stop dreaming. You want to escape. Pitiful."

Marisa's mind whirled around tossed about in a maelstrom. She wasn't sure if anything was true. She prayed that it was all a dream, no, not a dream, a terrible nightmare. They couldn't be gone. None of this could be true.

"Want to know how we caught you? That naïve young man who has undergone some kind of quantum restructuring that he can't possibly comprehend decided to call us. You see, I thought he seemed too idealistic to trust, but I hoped that he might be a good genetic match for you. The trouble is that his tests are back and whatever has happened to him doesn't make any sense on the genetic level. What happened to him has to do more with atomic structure than chromosones. We can't duplicate that. He's useless for our designs. Still, he was popular on the videos. I guess it's that natural sincerity, but when it came to loyalty to us, he decided to call the federal government."

Dominic straightened up. "Unfortunately for you both, he decided to use the phone we gave his friend."

"Do we have to do this?" asked Ivy.

"Ivy, that's enough," said Dominic, taking a breath. "Ah, I feel much better. The air seems quite clear. Give her the anesthesia. I want Diamond back."

The doctor placed something black and rubbery over Marisa's nose and mouth. She heard a loud hiss and felt her tongue and nose go numb.

"I have the perfect solution to our problem," said Dominic.

It was the last thing Marisa heard before everything faded into oblivion.

Chapter 18 - Change of Plans

TWO NIGHTS AFTER CALLING THE FEDS, Scott pulled his car up beside a large warehouse inside one of the as-yet mostly empty industrial parks outside of Megalopolis. Several expensive luxury cars were parked in the dimly-lit lot. He had come to the right place.

"So, how long do you want me to stay under this blanket in the backseat?" asked Tyrell.

"Until I get back, federal agents surround this place, or you feel like calling 911 and seeing if the Megalopolis police department can get here," replied Scott, thinking that he sounded nervous. "Do you have my spare keys so you can drive out if something's wrong?"

"Man, you've only asked me that about fourteen times since we left the apartment."

"Ty, have I ever told you that you are the best friend in the world?"

"Damn, Scott, get yourself together. You are going to have another fight. You aren't going to die."

Scott took a deep breath. "If I do get killed or something, you know my parents' number?"

"Yes, and I know all your social media passwords too. But, you aren't going to die. You are the Survivor, remember? Focus on getting pumped up for your bout or whatever you do."

A couple of men in work clothes started walking toward Scott's car. "Stay down. I need to go."

"Good luck, man. And I hope you see that Marisa lady. The Feds didn't give you any idea when they might play cavalry, did they?" asked Tyrell.

"No, and I still don't know why they gave me a fight so soon after I rejoined. I keep hoping it's because of the zombies."

"You were in the millions of views. It's the zombies. Now go before someone notices the moving and talking blanket in your car."

Scott got out of the car, shut the door and walked over to the men. "I'm Survivor," he attempted to snarl in his toughest-sounding voice. Whatever intimidating effect he had hoped to create slipped a touch when he coughed immediately afterward.

"Mind if we check?" asked one of the men.

"Um... I have my driver's license in my wallet," said Scott, reaching into his pocket.

"Stop, kid. We don't need the wallet. Just don't retaliate if you are Survivor."

As Scott gave the speaker a questioning look, the other man hit him in the head.

"Ow!" said the man who punched Scott, grabbing his hand and rubbing his knuckles. "Goddamn it! He's like a brick wall."

"Sorry," said Scott.

The realization that he had super-strength and at least some amount of invulnerability suddenly struck him. It wasn't that he didn't know about his powers, but he spent his days hiding them, treating his abilities as an inconvenience except for his fights. To see his powers outside of the fight world was strange.

Scott realized that he didn't even know how strong he was.

He thought about making a smart comment like, "You should've let me get the wallet," but the guy seemed to have actually hurt himself. He reminded himself that he was here to observe all he could. After this was over, he'd call the federal agents on the phone and report.

And maybe they'd swoop in and save Marisa.

"Are you going to stand there or go inside?" asked the talkative guard.

"Oh," said Scott, realizing that he had started daydreaming. He kept thinking about Marisa and exactly how good she looked in that sparkling bikini, but that wasn't why he wanted to save her. There was something in her eyes, something hurt and suffering.

As he walked up to the door of the warehouse, where more guards stood wearing black suits instead of work clothes, he reminded himself that he'd probably never see Marisa again even if he did manage to get her out. She might go back to her home country or be put somewhere to keep her safe.

That was perfectly okay with Scott as long as she and anyone else held against their will were freed.

A second realization struck him as the guards asked who he was and checked him for weapons. He wasn't doing any of this for money or even himself anymore. Somehow, that made things better. Maybe he did have a bit of a superhero inside of him.

A man greeted him. "Ivy told me to show you to your locker room. Same costume as your last fight, including the face paint. There's some oil as well that you are to rub on your chest. It'll make your muscles gleam, good for the clientele."

"Okay," said Scott.

He caught a glimpse of men in tuxedos and women in expensive gowns. Waiters and waitresses wove in and out between them, carrying trays of goblets.

"We have an audience?" he asked.

"Yes. After your last performance, you've been promoted to the big time. Private spectacle for our sponsors, invitation only. Dominic pulled a lot of strings to make this one happen in a hurry. You are something special."

"Thanks. I guess he wanted to make sure I was still committed. Who's my opponent?"

"It's a mystery bout," the guide answered.

They reached a door, flanked by two more men in black suits. "Here's your locker room," said his guide. "It's not the best accommodations, but your clothes are inside. When you hear your name called, you will exit out the other side into the cage. You have about fifteen minutes to get ready."

"Cage?"

"It's to protect the audience."

"Makes sense, I guess."

Scott went inside and was greeted by dirty green and beige tiles, several sinks, a wooden bench with his fight clothes neatly folded. He decided to check the toilets first as he was rather nervous. They functioned just fine. He quickly got changed. The light wasn't great and he nearly got the oil and the face paint mixed up. Ivy had left a note, which he worked to read. It didn't say much, just offered him encouragement, congratulated him on the special fight and apologized for not being around to coach him.

About thirty seconds after he finished getting dressed, he read the note again. Butterflies swarmed inside him. He was back inside, but he had nothing to tell the Feds. He imagined himself saying that the bathrooms worked as he paced to the back door, hoping that he'd be able to hear his name.

He tried to take a few breaths to calm himself down. He had never had an audience. What if he got distracted? Would they cheer for him? Would they boo him?

Scott glanced around for Ivy. Her absence bothered him. Why wasn't she here talking to him? Who or what was he fighting? He had come back, so she should care if he won or lost.

"Okay, if it's a robot, try to find a power source. If it's more than one opponent, focus on dropping one and then the other. Whatever you do, don't panic and stay focused. Get through this," he told himself, "and try not to talk to yourself too much."

He managed to grin at his own joke.

At that moment, he heard the announcements begin. They were loud enough to be perfectly audible through the locker room door.

"Ladies and gentlemen, please direct your attention to the cage in the center of the chamber. This structure is made of Ultracite, the strongest material known to man. It will not bend, and it will not break even with superhuman force, and you will witness superhuman force tonight on a scale that borders on the unimaginable. Now, I will remind you that with super-powered combatants, you will experience shock waves. Of course, that's part of the thrill. Now, for this special unannounced feature bout, we have a true treat for you. For the first time in front of a live audience, let us present the man who single-handedly overcame the zombie apocalypse. You've watched him over the internet, now see him live! Presenting our first combatant, Survivor!"

Scott felt goosebumps rise on his arms as he heard the crowd roar. He opened the door to see a huge cage door open in front of him. He strode inside and waved to the crowd of people on all sides. He heard the cage clang shut behind him. A rush of adrenaline went through him. He gazed on the open cage door maybe thirty feet away from him and the door beyond it, waiting for whatever was about to come out. It was a large metal door, probably some kind of storage shed.

Something big could be behind it.

He closed his eyes and tried to relax and listen to the crowd. He had never had so many cheers in his life, and for a moment, he questioned whether any of these people had any idea that something was wrong with these fights.

"And now, his opponent, unbreakable and undefeated…"

The door opened, and Scott felt his blood turn to ice.

Dressed in a glittering leotard covered in gems, glistening from body oil, Marisa strode into the cage opposite Scott.

"Diamond!"

The cheers of the crowd drowned out the clang of the cage locking behind Diamond.

"A battle of the sexes, but what makes it more exciting, more thrilling, is that this is a fight to the death!"

The crowd stood and the roar became even louder.

Diamond approached him. He couldn't take his eyes off her. He thought his heart might explode.

Scott swallowed and forced down a breath. They would talk and find a way to fight their way out of this.

"Marisa…," he said.

She shifted into a combat stance. Her eyes were soft for a second. "I'm sorry."

"Wait," he said.

Her eyes hardened. "Survivor, the name's Diamond, and I'm the woman who is going to kill you."

Before Scott could say anything else, she kicked him in the head.

Chapter 19 - Hidden Strength

SURVIVOR FLEW INTO THE SIDE of the cage from the force of the kick. Diamond didn't hesitate. She charged over to him, smashed him once more into the cage and then flung him across the cage into the bars on the other side.

He hit hard. As Marisa watched, a sudden flash of light caught her in the eyes. Colors sparkled in her vision. She couldn't see anything. A feeling of rage welled up as she knew she had the advantage, and some idiot with flash photography had ruined it.

She felt Scott, no, not Scott, but Survivor grab her, wrapping his arms around her body. Even as she shifted her weight to wrestle free, she realized something was wrong. He wasn't grappling with her. He was hugging her, holding on to her. He wasn't squeezing or trying to hurt her. But, if he was trying to hold her, he was about to learn that he wasn't nearly strong enough.

There was pain in his voice. "Stop, please. I want to get you out of here. We don't have to fight."

She pushed his arms up, slipped under his grasp and slid around behind him, reversing his... hug. Her vision had cleared. This wasn't the way it should be. If they were going to fight, he needed to fight back. She was behind him now and she locked her arms around his shoulders and locked her fingers behind his neck, holding him in a full nelson. She knew that she should press and break his shoulders or his neck, but she didn't. She just held him.

"Fight back," she said, almost wondering why she was asking.

"No," he said.

She wanted to let him go, but this was a bout. This was what she trained for, and what she lived for. She wasn't Marisa; she was Diamond. She had to do this. She had to win.

However, if this was going to be a spectacle, there needed to be some excitement. She released him and spun him around to face her.

He swallowed as their eyes met. Scott, no… Survivor, she reminded herself, still had those kind eyes, but they were pained. Seeing his eyes made her angry, but whether it was the pain or the kindness that caused it, she didn't know. He didn't strike her or even raise his arms to defend himself.

She needed to end this match. She was going to win; there was no doubt. Survivor wasn't as strong as she was, and he didn't know how to fight. She felt sorry for him, and for some reason, that made her feel sick to her stomach.

The crowd roared as Diamond punched Survivor in the face and followed with a strike to the chest and the abdomen, before dropping him with a spin kick. Each blow made a crackling noise when it landed, and someone was shining lights on Scott when she hit him. He was glowing a yellow and then orange color it seemed as he fell to the floor landing face first.

She reached down and grabbed his jacket, tearing it off his body, lifting him slightly as she did. He fell solidly back down and lay there apparently gasping. She held his jacket up, showing it off to the crowd and then ripped it to shreds. The crowd began to stand and chant, "Diamond, Diamond, Diamond."

The cheering helped to make her not think of Survivor as Scott. She had tried to give him a chance, even though only one of them was going to live through this fight. She stepped on his back. She didn't want to see his face. All she needed to do was to step on the back of his neck, and it would all be over.

She raised her arms to salute the crowd, and her feet went out from under her. Suddenly, he was grabbing her and squeezing. She was still trying to figure out what had happened when she realized that she couldn't take a breath. He was stronger than she had thought or maybe he was growing stronger as they fought?

Scott had hoped that Marisa was going to stop when their eyes had met, but after she unleashed on him, he realized that she would only stop, really stop, when he was dead. As much as he liked her and wanted to help her, he wasn't ready to die.

Unfortunately, she was strong, far stronger than the werewolf had been. He couldn't believe that he had survived the pounding she had given him. However, after every blow, he knew that something was happening to him. He was changing, growing stronger and more powerful. His body was healing as well, and it felt like someone had literally started a fire inside of him. He could imagine a nuclear reaction surging in his chest.

Despite that, she was faster than he was, and she had combat training. When she had kicked him, he let it knock him off his feet. He had played dead until he thought he could grab her, and it had worked.

She was writhing in his embrace and slammed him in the face with an elbow. He thought she had shattered his skull, but immediately felt a rush of power. The world was changing colors, becoming harder to see.

Diamond managed to half-force Survivor's arms apart and half-slip away. She punched him again and again. She felt better. This was the way it was supposed to be... a fight.

He swung at her, but she blocked it and followed up with another strike to the face. He yelled in agony and she took her knee and smashed it between his legs.

"Stop!" Scott shouted, as he swung out at Marisa. She blocked yet again, but this time, it didn't matter as the force of his blow sent her flying across the cage.

Scott grabbed his temples. They were throbbing. He felt so much power churning inside him. He shivered from the sensation. Light started shining around his hands. He wasn't sure what was happening other than his body was becoming unstable. He couldn't let Diamond keep hitting him. He looked over at her as she slowly got to her feet.

Diamond shook her head. Her mind twisted and turned over thoughts, and she tasted blood in her mouth. How had he done that? She had out-wrestled him a moment ago. He was getting more powerful as the fight went on.

She knew that she needed to clear her head and start thinking about how to win, but thoughts of trying to tear Survivor's head off his body kept interrupting her. She didn't know where they were from at first, and then, she remembered being in her bed.

Dominic had said terrible things, but she couldn't remember what they were. All she really knew was that she had to win this fight. That's what she was – a fighter. She was Diamond.

Survivor came over to her and grabbed her arm, squeezing it tight enough to hurt. She tried to break free, but she couldn't. With her free hand, she punched him in the head, but he slammed her into the side of the cage. He pressed his body against hers, pinning her against the bars.

"I'm not going to kill you," whispered Scott, "but I can't save you if you kill me."

"I need to win. I'm supposed to win," she said. This close together, it seemed to her as if his skin was flickering and flashing. She blinked.

Images flashed through her mind of her family. She saw the soldiers. Marisa felt hot tears in her eyes. She shuddered.

Scott pulled back, releasing her from being crushed against the bars. She saw worry cross his face. She realized that the shuddering and the tears had made him step back.

Her mind seemed clear. Something had happened, and Survivor was stronger than when they started. She wasn't going to be able to beat him senseless.

She dove to the side and managed to step behind Survivor. He seemed to be having trouble concentrating as well. She slipped her left arm around his neck and used her right arm to lock a rear naked chokehold. She hoped that cutting off the blood to his brain would be enough to drop him.

He grabbed her arm and squeezed, threatening to break it. She yelled in pain, but she wasn't going to let go. He turned around, as she hung on and threw himself backwards against the bars. She yelled louder as she smashed against the cage.

"I'm Diamond. I'm unbreakable," she said, trying to remind herself.

Scott felt the world spin. Even as Diamond choked him, he could still feel his body shifting, trying to hold all the power inside him. He slammed her backwards again, but she wouldn't let go.

His world went dark.

Survivor collapsed, but Diamond kept the chokehold in place for a few extra seconds before releasing it. She had done it. She had won.

"Kill him! Kill him! Kill him!" chanted the crowd.

It was time to finish him.

She had destroyed robots before. She had shattered the demon-possessed Armageddon, but she had never killed a human being before. When Ivy had told her about the fight, she had been thrilled, unnaturally so now that she thought about it - a fight to the death, Survivor vs. Diamond, a bout for the ages. This was her chance to show everyone that she was the best.

Scott hadn't wanted this fight, and it was Scott who lay on the ground beside her. His body was still glowing, energy flowing underneath his skin. Gemstones from her leotard covered the floor around him. She had envisioned killing him, imagined a dozen ways to do it, most of which involved decapitation.

The thought made her want to vomit now.

She gave herself a hug and winced as she breathed. Her left arm hurt badly. She could feel Scott's hands as if they were still trying to tear it away. This was supposed to be an easy bout. She had been so excited.

Scott had wanted to help her.

Something about the faint flashing coming from the light Scott was emitting or maybe it had to do with her head smashing against the cage, but she remembered. Dominic had done all of this. Her family was dead.

"Diamond, finish him!" shouted Dominic over the announcement speakers.

She had to listen to Dominic. She wanted Dominic to be pleased with her.

All she could think about were Scott's kind eyes.

Fury burst from her heart. "No!" she nearly shrieked. "NO! I won't kill him like my family were killed. I won't."

The intensity of her outburst surprised her. She was shaking and tears streamed over her cheeks.

The crowd murmured with uncertainty.

"Don't worry, ladies and gentlemen, because we have one more special surprise bout for you tonight. Diamond may not kill Survivor tonight, but…"

The large door at the end of the cage opened. Marisa saw the flickering of flames and dark brass armor. Her eyes widened.

"… her next opponent, Armageddon, is back from his near destruction. And after he destroys Diamond, he'll make sure we all remember the end of Survivor. Diamond, you may be unbreakable, but demons regenerate. For your entertainment pleasure, the rematch that you've all wanted, Diamond versus Armageddon."

Armageddon was inside the cage, his horned helm tilted in Marisa's direction. His body went ablaze with fire.

"Armageddon, Armageddon, Armageddon," chanted the crowd.

Chapter 20 - Armageddon

BREATHING HURT. Marisa could barely move her left arm. Memories and emotions fought for her attention. She was distracted.

Armageddon wasn't.

Lowering his head, he charged at Marisa, flames erupting all around him. She dove to the side, but he still clipped her, sending her spinning to the floor.

Gritting her teeth, she pulled herself to her feet. She expected Armageddon to attack immediately. Unfortunately, she was right.

A metal hand grabbed her face, and Armageddon lifted her into the air. She used her right arm to latch onto the burning brass armor for leverage and did her best to kick him. She made contact, but only with enough force to make several ringing noises.

He flung her into the ground. She spat blood. Marisa coughed. She had never hurt like this before. Despite the pain, she rolled away from him as he tried to grab her again. She impressed herself by leaping back to her feet.

Armageddon hit her with a fiery punch as she retreated from him. She needed another second or two. She risked a quick glance at Scott. A rear naked choke cut off the blood to the brain after about ten seconds, but once the blood started to flow again, he would wake up about as quickly.

She ducked as Armagedoon tried to grab her and kicked him in the midsection with a satisfying clang. The monster took a step back, and his flames flared in response.

Images of her village burning filled her head. She gasped at the clarity of the memory. She was there, witnessing all of it, and the big soldier grabbed her.

But it wasn't the big soldier, it was Armageddon, crushing her. She wasn't high enough to headbutt him the way she had in their last bout, though she could smash her head against his shoulder. This time as the fire raced over her body, she couldn't breathe. Her ribs screamed, and she tasted more blood in her mouth. The audience exploded with screams, louder than ever.

Her heart nearly stopped. Armageddon's vise-like embrace loosened slightly.

The crowd was chanting, "Survivor... Survivor... Survivor."

"Let her go!" shouted Scott.

With a grinding metal noise, Armageddon's right arm released her. She fell as Armageddon dropped her with the left.

For a moment, she thought that Scott resembled nothing as much as an angel. A halo of light surrounded him and his skin glowed.

Armageddon raised his fists over his head and swung them down at Scott, who raised his own arms to block. Another loud clang echoed through the warehouse, and Scott glowed with an even brighter intensity, but he didn't budge.

Scott charged into Armageddon, seemingly ignoring the flames and knocked him back until they crashed against the cage. Scott locked his hands on cage bars on either side of Armageddon and drove his shoulder into the midsection of the monster.

Marisa stood up. Scott was pushing right where she had landed that solid kick. A groaning noise came from Armageddon's body as the brass became deformed, but the demon-fueled warrior wasn't giving him. Thunderous fists smashed down on Scott's back.

Scott cried out with each blow, and his skin shone even more brightly with each punch.

The audience had fallen silent. Many of them had left their chairs and started to back away from the cage. Some other figures were moving toward the cage, but Marisa had trouble making them out due to the light coming from Armageddon's flames and Scott's skin.

Armageddon's punches stopped. Scott let go of the cage and stepped back. His hair had been burned off, and he lost his balance and went down on all fours. Marisa could see spasms in his back, and she heard him moaning.

Cherry-red flames spurted out of a gaping rent in Armageddon's midsection. His upper body and legs were twisted in relation to each other, as if he was a child's action figure that had been nearly snapped in half. The flames on the outside of the armor started dying. Marissa thought she saw a ghostly skull form in the red fires.

She went over and launched a flurry of kicks into him. Each one sent pain running through her, but she didn't care. She didn't want to deal with demons any more.

Armageddon crashed to the floor with a hollow clang, and the fires went out all at once.

Marisa could see Dominic's men surrounding the Ultracite cage. They all wore gas masks.

"Once again, Armageddon falls," announced Dominic, "but who will be the ultimate champion of the cage, Diamond or Survivor?"

"I'm done, Dominic. I remember. No more lies," Marisa said.

The crowd murmured and booed. A few yelled, "Fight! Fight!"

"I'm sorry to disappoint you all, but it appears that we'll have to handle things in the tradition of the Romans when gladiators refused to fight. Next to your chairs or tables, you will all find gas masks. I'd advise all of you to please put them on, as it may get hard to breathe here in a moment, unless one of them decides to finish the fight."

Scott stood up. He had an angry, determined glare on his face and strode toward her. For the briefest of instants, she wondered if he intended to fight her again. Instead, he walked past her to the bars of the cage. He braced himself and gripped them.

"Diamond, I need you to hit me in the back whenever I nod my head. We are leaving."

"Survivor, those are Ultracite. Nothing can break them. I know. I've tried. That's what they use to contain super-villains like Defiance."

If Scott heard her, he didn't listen. Instead, he began to strain. She saw veins stand up in his skin and his muscles ripple with effort. The bars didn't move. A few of Dominic's soldiers stepped back and started to watch. They seemed to be amused.

"Survivor appears to want to entertain us with a feat of strength," announced Dominic.

Scott nodded his head. Marisa didn't want to hit him anymore, but she punched him in the back. He nodded his head again. "Harder!" he said.

She hit him again and again, increasing the intensity. Scott began screaming. At first, she thought it was because of the pain from her blows, but he kept screaming even louder when she stopped striking him.

A few members of the audience mockingly clapped.

"I think we've seen enough. Now, let's finish this. Which will be? Gas and disappointment or a thrilling end that leaves everyone pleased and one of you covered in glory?" announced Dominic.

Scott stopped screaming and a vibrating ringing sound could be heard echoing through the warehouse. He took a deep breath and his body blazed like a small star. He screamed.

And the Ultracite bars snapped apart.

"GAS!" shouted Dominic.

Scott staggered through the opening and collapsed into a fetal position.

Marisa wanted to check on him, but she knew that she had to stop Dominic's men from gassing them. She caught one and tore his mask off before throwing him across the warehouse. Several guards threw gas grenades, and the crowd of the rich and decadent shrieked and screamed as they ran for the exits.

Marisa stopped to grab another mask and ran over to Scott. He coughed and shook. She put the mask on him. She wanted to say something, apologize or thank him, but she hoped there would be time enough for that later. She picked up and started to carry him out.

One of Dominic's men stepped in front of her. He stared at her, and she glared back. She started to put Scott down, but before she did, his eyes indicated that he realized that he was a normal man facing Diamond the Unbreakable. He did the smart thing. He ran.

Instead of running for the exit, Marisa ran for the nearest wall. The memory of running down the path to her village went through her head, but she knew that she wasn't running toward death this time.

She was running to life.

She smashed through the side of the warehouse, making her own exit. As she reached the parking lot, she saw a scene of pure chaos. A few limos had crashed into some expensive sports cars as everyone tried to flee. She wasn't sure what she wanted to do, but she knew that she didn't want anyone to escape. A number of large shipping containers were stacked beside the warehouse, and she thought of Survivor fighting the zombies.

She put Scott down, wanting to explain, but not wanting to take off her mask. She ran over to the containers, enduring the pain in her ribs that she felt with each step. She dug her fingers into the corrugated metal to get a good grip and then flung them into the parking lot. Within a few seconds, she had blocked the escape routes.

A few cars had made it out, but she took some satisfaction in knowing that the well-dressed would have to flee on foot if they wanted to escape.

"Hey, don't kill me! I'm on your side. Marisa?"

A black man waving his hands, each one holding a cell phone ran up to her.

"Who are you?" she asked. When he didn't answer, she realized that she was muffled by the gas mask. She removed it and asked again. "Who are you?"

"I'm Tyrell, I'm Survivor's side… I mean, support guy."

"What?" she asked as she watched his eyes go to her chest.

He snapped his head up. "I'm his best friend. I called the Feds, but no one answered. So, I had my cell phone, but I wasn't getting reception, like it was blocked, so I ran that way and called 911. The cops are coming. I told them it was super-powered, so they may have the Renegade Program guys."

Marisa heard sirens. She didn't want to go to jail. She was illegal.

"No, don't panic," said Tyrell, putting a hand on her shoulder and then swiftly removing it. "I called these other guys too, called the Paladin Program. They help people with powers and stuff. I told them that Scott thought you were a victim of human trafficking. They are coming to help you. It's okay. Speaking of Scott, where is he?"

"He's over here," she said.

Tyrell looked at Scott, who was spasming and glowing. His hair had been burned off, and he had streaks of blood and ash and smeared temporary tattoos on him. The only one of Survivor's tattoos that Marisa could make out was an ace of spaces. "What happened to him?"

"He rescued me," she said.

Chapter 21 – The Beginning

SCOTT SAT ON HIS BED at the Paladin Program's mansion. Today was the day that he would finally be released. He glanced over at the monitors that had been his companions for the past couple of weeks. They were now off. It was a pleasant change.

He rubbed his hands on his jeans. It was good to wear jeans and a t-shirt again instead of a hospital gown, even if he had to wear a special bodysuit underneath them. He picked up the hand mirror on his nightstand. Bristly dark hair had started growing on his head, and thankfully, his eyebrows were growing back. He had read somewhere that they didn't always regrow.

There was a knock on the door. He looked at the clock on the wall and wondered yet again why it wasn't digital. It seemed early for his normal morning checkup. Besides, he was supposed to be free to come and go today. He shrugged. "Come in."

"Hey, man!" said Tyrell.

"Ty!"

Scott got off the bed and ran over to hug his friend, remembering to be gentle. He let go and Ty clapped him on the back. Scott gestured to his visitor chair and Tyrell sat down as if he owned it.

"Dude, you aren't glowing anymore! They came and got me and told me that I could visit. They also said you might want me to drive you back to Leonard so you can go through all your stuff. The guys said that you have some decisions to make. So, are you going to become a superhero?"

"Yes, no, I don't know, I guess not exactly if I don't want to, but maybe."

"Wait," asked Tyrell. He smiled. "So, I have to ask after an answer like that. Brain damage?"

Scott laughed. "No, thankfully. I'm very lucky. There's a genius here who saved my life."

"Dr. Kingsmythe?" asked Tyrell. "I'm allowed to know his name. They did lots of background checks, and Dr. Kingsmythe asked me about all of your personal habits. I even told him about how you leave toothpaste globs in the sink."

Scott shook his head. "I missed you. I'm sorry that I didn't tell you everything earlier."

"Whew," said Tyrell.

"What?" asked Scott.

"That apology totally sounds like the Scott I know."

There was another knock on the door. "Come in," Scott said.

"Good morning, Scott," said a tall, thin, blonde man in a British accent. Under his white lab coat, he wore blue jeans and a t-shirt with the periodic table and a joke. He had a full beard and moustache, and his eyes seemed ablaze with a thousand ideas at once. He looked over at Tyrell. "Good to see you, Tyrell. Did we get Scott back in good order?"

"Yes, sir, Dr. Kingsmythe," said Tyrell, standing up.

"Do you feel ready to stop the treatments?" he asked Scott.

"Yes. I think I'm okay."

"Pity in some ways. The quantum energy fluctuations that you generate are quite fascinating. I think I'll find several applications for them. Just remember that you absorb kinetic energy. Your body holds on to a certain amount of it and if you absorb too much too fast, well... it would make for an interesting event." Dr. Kingsmythe said.

"Event?" asked Scott.

Kingsmythe shrugged. "Not exactly sure what would happen. Quantum fluctuations. Anyway, never mind that, I wanted to tell you that I have a special visitor for you."

"Doc, I'm already in the room," said Tyrell.

Kingsmythe laughed. "I'm not quite that absent-minded. Well, not usually," he admitted. He held open the door.

Marisa stepped inside. She was wearing an "I love Megalopolis" t-shirt and a pair of blue jeans. She beamed as she walked over to Scott.

"I have a special visa. I get to stay," she said.

"I... ah... have to ask Tyrell a few more questions. We'll be back in a few minutes," said Dr. Kingsmythe.

"What questions?" asked Tyrell, as Kingsmythe ushered him out of the room. "I can answer in front of Scott."

"Now, who's being absent-minded?" muttered Kingsmythe as they exited.

Scott stared at Marisa, and she stared back. They both smiled.

"Are you okay?"

"Yes."

"Well, Dominic's still out there, but he doesn't control me anymore. So, I'd like to go out for coffee," she said, "but you have to drive."

Scott smiled.

"I can't think of anything I'd rather do."

THE END

About the Authors

Wayland Smith

Wayland Smith is the pen name for a native Texan who has lived in Massachusetts, New York, Washington DC, and presently makes his home in Virginia. His rather unlikely list of jobs includes private investigator, comic book shop owner, ring crew for a circus (then he ran away from the circus and joined home), deputy sheriff, and freelance stagehand. Wayland is a four time participant in, and survivor of, NaNoWriMo, having made the 50,000 word goal each time. A black belt in shao lin kung fu, he is also a fan of comic books, reading, writing, and various computer games (I'll shut Civ down in one more turn. Really). He lives with a beautiful woman who was crazy enough to marry him, and a goofy dog with a fondness for peanut butter and white wine. He has previously published *In My Brother's Name* with Blue Oranda Publishing.

Dara Hannon

Dara Hannon lives in the US with her two cats. When relaxing, she enjoys reading, doing crafts and MMORPGs. She admits to being a coffee addict who can't stand the taste of espresso. She is also the author of *Broken Faith*, published by Blue Oranda Publishing.

Harry Heckel

Harry Heckel has published roleplaying games and fiction for over two decades, including several books for White Wolf Game Studio. He co-authored two novels for Black Library under the pen name "Lee Lightner," *Sons of Fenris* and *Wolf's Honour*, now collected in the *Space Wolf Omnibus, Vol.2*. His previous work for Blue Oranda Publishing includes *The Krueger Chronicles: Souls of the Everwood (Book 1)* and *Balefire and Brimstone (Book 2)* and Book 1 of *The Crimson Hawks Adventures: In the Service of the King*.

Also by
Blue Oranda Publishing

Wayland Smith
In My Brother's Name

Dara Hannon
Broken Faith

Harry Heckel
The Crimson Hawks Adventures
In the Service of the King (Book 1)

The Krueger Chronicles
Souls of the Everwood (Book 1)
Balefire and Brimstone (Book 2)

Brad White
Jake Conrad Mythological Mysteries
Servant of the Muses (Book 1)
A Pearl for Her Eyes (Book 2)
A Jake Conrad Omnibus (Coming Soon)

www.ingramcontent.com/pod-product-compliance
Lightning Source LLC
Chambersburg PA
CBHW060801120626
46557CB00001B/58